It Takes Two to Tangle

The Brothers of Chi-Town, Book 5

CHERYL BARTON

Cheryl Barton Publishing, LLC
P.O. Box 962
Reisterstown, Maryland 21136
www.crbarton.com

Ordering Information:
Quantity sales.
Special discounts of this novel are available on quantity purchases by corporations, associations, and others. For details, contact the publisher at the address above. For orders by U.S. trade bookstores and wholesalers, please contact prez@crbarton.com

ISBN 13: 978-1-948950-35-0

ALSO BY CHERYL BARTON
WWW.CHERYLBARTON.NET
Upcoming Release

Bachelor Series
Bachelor Not for Sale
A Designed Affair
A Perfect Combination
Love at Last
Twelve Bachelors for Sale

Amorous Occupations Series
The Artist
The Bookkeeper
The Chef
The Dancer
The Electrician

A Lovers' Heart Series
Heartthrob
Heartbeat
Heartbreaker

Brothers of Chi-Town Series
I Can't Let Go, Book 1
Swagger and Baggage, Book 2
Claiming His Child, Book 3
Always Bet on Black, Book 4
Crashing Into Love, Book 6

Malibu Hearts Series
And Then There Was You

Divas of High Hill
Secrets, Book 1

Dear Reader,

Back together again! Here we are with another brother who puts his lady first! These fellas in Chicago are setting the days and nights on fire all for the women they love and in book 5, *It Takes Two to Tangle,* Tucker Glass is no different. He made no bones about his love and affection for Nichelle Michaels from the first time he laid eyes on her. From page one until the very last page, he fights to make sure he will always have that love in his life. Let's take a trip through the first four books to let you see how all this fiery love out of Chicago started. We still have three more books to go, so sit back, relax and indulge in, *The Brothers of Chi-Town,* the series.

First there was Carter Garrison in, *I Can't Let Go.* He'd only known unconditional love with Sienna and when he woke up and realized his life would never be the same without her in it despite his indiscretion, he fought with all that was in him to prove to her that their love was worth trusting him again.

Then there is Torrence Allen in, *Swagger and Baggage,* book 2 in the series. He assumed Reese Michaels was the same woman he'd dated back in college who didn't want to commit to one man and so he didn't think of the impact their newfound love would suffer from his baggage which showed up and showed out to claim him as hers. He wasn't ready for Reese's reaction, nor did he plan to give up on her. He was in it to win her heart back by any means necessary.

In the third installment, Claiming His Child. Dexter Patterson spent a lifetime never feeling loved, when as a child, he bounced from one unloving foster care home to another. It wasn't until he was faced with becoming a father, unexpectedly, that he realized he needed to open up his heart, not just to being a father without knowing what that meant, but also to being a man who was sorry for breaking the heart of the woman he found himself in love with but not yet ready to deal with it. To him, falling in love with Alyssa Kincaid wasn't easy, but he wouldn't change it for anything – not even when they both suffered

In book 4, *Always Bet on Black,* Delvin "DJ" "Black" Michaels finds that he can't escape the woman who stole his heart and without realizing it, at the same time, she drew him into her world of crime and trickery causing him to lose his job as a New York City police officer. The loss wasn't because of anything he did, but for what he witnessed that could take down an entire police force. To escape the wrath of his choice of a bed-mate, "DJ" returns to Chicago where he thought he could start his life over again as head of security at a casino owned by his future brother-in-law. Before he gets his feet wet in his new position, he comes face to face with a woman he knew as Justice Cooper, whose real name is Avalon Hart. If he thought he found her irresistible in New York, he's doomed now that she's in Chicago, enticing him with a mere look from her hazel eyes while reminding him with her sexy body of the nights they ravaged each other, forgetting the outside world existed. He knows of her history, but he still can't let go of the steamy nights they shared and he realizes that she wasn't done with him yet – not with his body nor with his heart.

Thanks again for how you support my work. I hope you enjoy this next brother from Chicago. Trust that politicians got game too!

Happy Reading!

Cheryl

Introduction
The ending of *Always Bet on Black*, book 4 of *The Brothers of Chi-Town* Series is your pathway into book 5, *It Takes Two to Tangle.*

As they made their way around the outside of the crowd, DJ led the way through the curtains since he knew where the door in the back was located. As they walked down a long narrow hallway, they came upon the sounds of two people giggling behind a door that DJ knew should be locked. He took out his keys which opened every door in the casino and when the door swung open, he almost forgot who the man was who held Nichelle in his arms, kissing her wildly. Pulling them apart, DJ reared his arm back in what he knew was going to be one of the hardest punches he'd ever landed until a strong arm behind him grabbed him before he could put his force behind the punch.

"What the hell!" DJ shouted and turned around where he came face to face with Gary.

"Calm down," Gary told him.

"Really? Your guy has his lips all over my sister and you want me to calm down? You need to tell Councilman Glass to cool off and get the hell away from my sister!" DJ shouted.

Reese stepped up.

"Nichelle? What's going on here and why are you in some closet with Tucker?" she asked.

"Okay, both of you calm down and DJ, don't you dare throw a punch. We are not in the hood anymore!" Nichelle yelled.

"Then, somebody better start explaining or we're all

going to the hospital. I know I can't take Gary, but I'm going to rip Tucker here a second one if he doesn't back up from you. He's like, fifteen years older than you!" DJ shouted.

"DJ, stop it and I know how old he is and how old I am. If you calm down long enough, I can explain," Nichelle tried to persuade.

DJ looked to Reese who was nervously tapping her foot and he looked to Tucker who looked like a cat had his tongue. A minute ago, that tongue was all over his sister. He really wanted to knock him out!

"Let me explain," Tucker finally said.

DJ started to jump in when Nichelle raised her hand and stopped them both.

"No, let me," she said to Tucker and then turned around. "I've been seeing Tucker now for about six months. We were going to go public with our relationship after the campaign started and then we found out that we can't go public, but we are still seeing each other. I've been secretly meeting up with him and Gary has been helping us keep it quiet," she explained.

DJ looked around and then his eyes filled with anger landed on Gary.

"Gary? Gary! You've been helping me with Avalon's stuff and you knew about this and didn't say anything? What the hell?" he asked.

"Look, man, this wasn't my story to tell. I'm good at what I do because I keep secrets where I'm supposed to," Gary explained.

"I can't fault that," DJ said, "but I can fault this guy and my sister. Somebody explain all this secrecy," he said.

"My turn," Tucker interjected. "This isn't all on Nichelle to explain. I'm in love with your sister, but I recently found out that I'm officially still married. My divorce was never final, which I didn't know and now my ex-wife won't sign the divorce papers," he explained.

"That's right because it takes two to tangle and the two that will be tangling to the Mayor's mansion is Tucker Glass and me, his wife, Antonia Glass," said a voice behind them all.

All heads turned and all eyes landed on reality television start, Antonia "Roxie" Johnson or Glass depending on who's asking. She was the latest overnight sensation on a locally filmed show called, "One Sister to Another". Everyone knew about the unreal, reality show and the fake drama that's drummed up with each episode. Looks like the drama was about to enter all of their lives.

"Antonia? What are you doing here?" Tucker asked. He wasn't expecting to see her at the event, hoping to put off any further interaction with her until he'd had a chance to figure out the new drama in his life; unexpected drama.

"Okay, this has officially become a circus," Reese joked.

"I'm here because I heard from a reputable source on your staff that you were seeing someone and I'm here to claim my spot as first lady of Chicago. I helped you get here and I intend to reap the benefits or your campaign is dead. Like I said, the two who are tangling will be me and you. Who's ready to toast to that? Tucker, you know where to find me and don't make me wait too long. I don't like to be kept waiting," Antonia shouted and after gulping down the last of the drink she held in her hand, she threw the expensive crystal wine glass to the floor and walked away.

Tucker looked where it broke into a million little pieces and then looked around at everyone, unsure of what to say or do next.

"What in the world is going on?" DJ asked, turning to Reese, hoping she would at least know what to say.

"You're still married to her?" Reese asked Tucker. "I thought that was dead and buried. Have you all seen that show? That chick is crazy. Tuck, you better check around for cameras because that dramatic entrance and exit Ms. Roxie just made was not for our sake. She's up to something and I'm sure it's not pretty," Reese said and laughed.

DJ wasn't finding any of this funny and was pissed that Reese did. Nichelle looked shocked, Tucker looked pissed off and here Reese was laughing like a crazed woman herself.

"If you're married, your hands or any other body part shouldn't be touching my sister, so back up, bro. Seriously, I know you're a councilman and all that, but this is my sister and she doesn't need this kind of drama in her life," DJ said and moved toward Nichelle. When she stepped back from him, he stopped moving.

"Listen, I can't explain it all right now, but I will. Don't ask me to stay away from Nichelle because I can't. I'm in love with her and yes, I may still be married to Antonia, but there has to be a way that I can fix this without dragging Nichelle into anything."

Tucker then turned to Gary.

"What do you need, Councilman?" Gary asked.

"Check to be sure Antonia's show isn't here recording. I don't need that right now," Tucker exclaimed.

"You don't need this right now? You think this is about you and that psycho wife of yours? I've seen the show and

fake or real, she likes to keep mess going and they'll be hell to pay if my sister gets hurt," DJ said.

"I can speak for myself!" Nichelle interrupted. "Stop speaking as if I'm not here. Tucker explained everything to me and I'm okay with it. He'll get a divorce and everything will be fine," Nichelle said, leaning over to take Tucker's hand, holding it tight.

This time DJ did laugh, but not as loud as Reese had done.

"Nichelle, that shows your immaturity. Did you not see Antonia just fly through here? I think she's made it clear that nothing is about to be easy and you're going to get caught in the middle. Are you ready for your business to be out in the public, getting scrutinized and made fun of? That's what will happen and if I'm correct, Antonia will spin everything in her favor. Back away, sis. I'm telling you to back away," DJ pleaded. "Reese, help me here. Tell her this isn't going to end well," he added.

"I don't know what's going on or what will happen, but I have been where Nichelle is, wanting a man that may not be hers, but look at her – she's not backing away from Tucker and right now isn't the time to deal with this. There are a lot of people here tonight and we need to get back out there. This Antonia chick? I remember her and she's always been about a bunch of mess and I'm sure we haven't seen the last of her. I have to say, I already like her spunk, though. She came in here and stole the entire scene. I guess being on a reality show has taught her a lot about garnering her audience," Reese said.

"Look, I'll take care of this. Thanks, Reese, for being on our side," Tucker said.

Reese sucked her teeth and turned to him.

"Oh, do not mistake what is going on here. I love my sister and she has no business with you. Stay away from her, Tucker, until you are no longer a married man and from the looks of things, this tangle just got interesting!" Reese exclaimed and walked in the same direction as Antonia had.

DJ was left standing with his mouth wide open trying to find the right words.

"That's it, Reese? That's all you're going to say and where are you going? We need to talk some sense into Nichelle," he said and hoped that Reese' pause before finally leaving meant that he would have her to depend on with this. He still wanted to hurt Tucker, but he didn't want to make a bigger scene than Antonia had.

"I have learned to let adults live their lives their way and Tucker knows me. He's known me a long time. I'm surprised he's hooked up with our sister, but Nichelle knows to reach out if she needs us. Right now, I want to see if there are cameras recording her show. I secretly watch every episode, but not one of them is as wild and crazy as the mess that goes on with the brothers in this town. It's non-stop craziness. I just love all the drama in Chicago! You brothers in Chi-Town are fire!" she added before disappearing behind the black curtain.

DJ wasn't intrigued. He didn't want his sister tangled up with some married man and his outlandish wife. He'd just gotten out of dealing with his own brand of drama and knew he didn't want the same for his sister. He started to say something when Tucker pulled Nichelle to the side and they began to whisper. She may not understand it, but the web she was now tangled up in with Tucker and Antonia was only the beginning.

1

"My life is crashing and burning and all you can say is, it's not that bad!"

Tucker Glass could feel his anger boiling over and with every bit of restraint he could muster up, he kept his distance from his attorney, Martin Sutherland, whose mere presence was irritating. The smugness he found when he looked into Martin's face pissed him off. Tucker was already second-guessing asking the man to stop by his home this early on a Monday morning following what he saw as a devasting weekend, not just to his career as a politician, but also to his personal life with a woman he had no idea he'd fall in love with as fast as he had. The heart wanted what it wanted and his wanted, and still wants Nichelle Michaels. She brought a zest to his life that he didn't realize had been missing. As the City Council President, also making him Vice Mayor for the City of Chicago, he spent most of his time focused on work and not his personal life, but he'd found a way to live a little more because of her while still following his political dreams. Now, both were tinkering on the edge of collapse.

Turning away from Martin, Tucker stormed across the dark brown hardwood floor that covered his living room and into his dining room, in his brown Magnanni Men's Single-Monk leather shoes, his favorite brand. His frustrated steps caused an echo against the interior light brown brick walls of the two rooms, a customization that he could admit was one of the best decisions he'd made after buying the brownstone and having it completely remodeled on the inside. Why he was thinking about walls at this very moment, he didn't know, but for a brief second, he was distracted from the plight of how his life had taken a downturn in one day.

Passing through the dining room and into the kitchen, he could still hear Martin mumbling about something and whatever it was, he didn't care. Ignoring him, he grabbed an ice-cold bottle of water from the refrigerator and paused at the beige and brown six-seat island, gripping the edge with his free hand. If his skin were lighter than the mocha tone, he would be able to see his knuckles turning red from the force behind how tight he was holding on, the way he was holding on to as much of his sanity as possible. It was definitely a struggle.

Inhaling, he walked back into the living room to find Martin leaning back on the brown leather sofa with one leg crossed over the other at the knee where his hands linked as his usual silver wire-framed glasses hung low on his nose. He still wondered why Martin even bothered to wear glasses since he never looked through them.

Going over to lean against the brick encased fireplace, Tucker placed his free hand in his pocket and took a huge gulp of the cold liquid, feeling it as it passed down his throat. He was thankful for the coolness that also helped to tamper down his anger, at least briefly.

"Tucker, what I'm saying is that we can fix this and you can move on with your life. It's too early in the morning to be this wired up. I would say have a drink to calm your nerves, but it's only seven in the morning on a Monday."

Tucker glared at Martin while looking from his face to the glass that sat in front of his guest on the cocktail table; a glass filled with gin and coke. Pointing to it, he watched Martin's eyes follow the direction of his finger.

"Clearly, that's not an issue for you. You walked in the door and immediately requested a drink and your exact words were, a strong drink. So that this conversation doesn't turn from my dilemma to your drinking this early in the morning, let's focus on the issue at hand. What the hell happened? How can I *still* be married to Antonia or Roxie or whatever she's calling herself these days or is she spitting drama? She actually demanded that she become first lady of Chicago when I win the election, which I will, you know. Well, at least I thought so before she showed up. Can you imagine what the people of Chicago will think finding out that I'm still married and also seeing Nichelle? I can already see my ex-wife spinning all of this in her favor, drumming up sympathy from those who support that dreadful reality show she's on," Tucker said. "How could you have missed this? I expected you to be on top of this when I hired you as my attorney. If what she's saying is true, your work is *sloppy*," he added.

What he wanted to do was be as calm and collect as Martin was about it all, but he had barely gotten a wink of sleep since the night of the fundraiser a few days ago at the largest casino in Chicago, the *Montiel Avage*, owned by Torrence Allen, a good friend.

"Tuck, listen, I know you're frustrated and I promise I'm going to fix this. I can't explain to you *exactly* how this happened..."

Tucker moved from the fireplace and stood directly in front of the cocktail table which kept him from leaning over and grabbing the sixty-five-year-old by the suit collar and tossing him to the floor. He leered at the old man.

"Wait, really it's true? I'm still married to her?" he screamed.

When Martin's hands came up in defense, Tucker saw fire. He'd hired who he thought was a lawyer on top of his game.

Martin had been his lawyer for years, representing his interest in the non-profit he started on his thirty-fifth birthday, where partnered up with the boys and girls club of Chicago to bring mentors in to help inspire and educate Chicago's youth. He trusted Martin to look over every contract along with looking out for his interest in several gyms he was part owner of around Chicago. When he decided that his marriage to Antonia Hall was over, realizing they were on two different paths in life, he trusted the man to work on his behalf so that he could focus on his political career. How could an attorney who has been practicing for almost forty years miss something as simple as making sure a divorce was final and clear?

When Martin stood and exhaled loudly, Tucker waited to hear his explanation.

"Tuck, listen, it's me, Marty," Martin said.

Hearing Martin call him by his nickname sickened him. This was not the time to use friendly banter and to call on their years of friendship and mutual respect, something that was out the door and he wasn't sure any explanation would do at this point.

"Don't call me that. Let's stick with Tucker and Martin. I want you to be as business-like as you can possibly be and tell me what happened. You found out it's true?"

Tucker began feeling the need to sit down as his pulse quickened and he could feel small beads of sweat forming on his brow.

Tugging on his crisp white shirt, he could feel the collar tightening around his neck. Dressed for heading into the office, even his dark brown, custom made suit by Tom Ford started to feel weighty. Removing the jack and loosening the beige paisley tie, he threw the jacket on the single brown leather seat across from his sofa and he wondered if bad news was what he'd continue hearing for the rest of the week. The week had just begun and it wasn't looking too promising.

"Let me apologize for the oversight and yes, it's true, you are still legally married to Antonia Hall-Glass. Since the divorce isn't final yet, that's still her legal name. With the divorce, she was going back to Antonia Hall and wanted to be known by the name she prefers going by as an actress which is, Roxie Hall. That's where the issue is. When she signed the original divorce papers, she signed as Roxie Hall, not as Antonia Hall-Glass. After I got your call in the middle of the night, I reached out to her attorney yesterday, who wasn't too happy to hear from me on a Sunday and I asked her about the situation. She stated, she reached out to me several times about this and I swear, I don't remember her office doing that. I'll check with my team later today when I get to the office, but yeah, it appears she is still your wife and if you win the election – *when* you win the election, she will be first lady of Chicago unless we work on getting the papers signed immediately," Martin explained.

"How could you let this happen?" Tucker asked, finally taking a seat, trying to still his rattled brain.

"I've been thinking about this all morning and based on the time frame of when her attorney says she reached out to my office and sent me new papers, I believe it was when I was working on that big embezzlement case and when I also found out my wife was having an affair with a much younger guy, something she called an "entanglement", but truth is, it's basically an affair. This guy was in his thirties. Can you imagine that? My wife who is sixty with some young thirty-year-old!" Martin exclaimed.

"I don't give two shakes about your wife and her young lover. This moment right now is about me and how my life is screwed up because you were going through something! We all go through things, but I expected you to be on top of this. If it wasn't for the fact that I had a prenuptial agreement because of my business ventures, I guess I would be paying alimony without being legally divorced. Following this through to the end was your responsibility. The amount of money I pay you to look after my legal matters is enough for you to know how to deal with your personal issues and other cases while also taking care of my legal issues. Do you know how this could ruin me professionally and personally? Well, personally, I think I'm done. I can't even get Nichelle to answer my calls."

"Listen, I know I screwed up here and when I get to the office, I'll have my team on this right away. We'll get those papers over to you to sign and get this over with, well except for one small, small issue," Martin lamented.

Tucker was not impressed when Martin tried to use hand gestures to minimize the size and importance of any issue associated with a divorce that didn't happen.

"What now?" he asked, exasperated at this point.

"Your wife's attorney..."

"Ex-wife," Tucker cleared up.

"Right. Your ex-wife's attorney did mention to me that because the documents are outdated now, we can't use those originals. I asked her to refile them and send me new ones and I'd get your signature expeditiously and she just happened to mention that she won't be doing that. Because you never signed the updated documents with her correct signature on them, they plan to protest the divorce. She wants to work on your marriage," Martin explained.

Tucker stood up so fast when his anger finally did boil over, that the chair behind him toppled over backwards with a loud bang, but it wasn't as loud as the pounding in his head.

"Are you kidding me right now?" he shouted. "Tell me that's not true and that I am not back in the midst of a divorce with Antonia for the whole world to now have a front seat to. You and I both know that this will be a part of her television show even if I don't sign an agreement to be a part of it. That won't prevent her from talking about it from her perspective," Tucker said.

"Well, wait now. We can get an injunction to keep her from discussing anything about this," Martin tried to explain.

Tucker was done. He expected more from Martin and now his confidence in him was slipping quickly.

"I have a law degree Martin, so I know how this works. I also know that she can talk about her own personal business without mentioning me or any situation involving me directly and with the internet and social media, she won't have to tell more. She would only need to let something slip to the right person and our business will shoot across the country like lightning. What will happen is, people will do their own digging and in the midst of it all, Nichelle will be the one to get hurt. They'll find out who she is and follow her to the school where she's a counselor. They'll stalk her and sit outside of her apartment questioning her every time they see her. Everyone loves a juicy story and this will definitely be one. People live off of drama and to have a candidate for Mayor out here with this kind of three-way drama will overshadow the needs of the people of Chicago and what they expect from their Mayor. She will spin this to increase her dollar flow and her value on that show she's on called, *The Next Big Queen of Hearts*. Have you seen that trash? I don't want my life displayed on that show when I'm sure most of what will come out will be untruths. This will devastate Nichelle's life and she's not a public figure," Tucker said, pacing back and forth.

"Well, she should have expected her life to become public if she was going to date a politician. That's how things work. I understand your need to protect her and maybe now is the time for you to think more about your career and less about your personal life. You can quiet that part of your life, focus on your campaign and when you're Mayor, you can have any woman you want. I saw that article in *Essence* magazine that applauded you for being one of forty African-American politicians under forty who are doing great things, let alone being named one of the hottest bachelors in the country. You can have your pick of women and perhaps one more on your level. Do you really have a lot in common with a twenty-six-year-old? She just finished college, right? I mean, before her, you were seen with quite a few extremely beautiful women; one was an actress and I even remember a sexy runway model," Martin asserted.

Tucker took a few moments before he responded to what he now deemed, blatant disrespect of the woman he loved. He didn't care that Nichelle was twenty-six to him being thirty-nine. He didn't expect that the moment he saw her one day six-months ago that she would be the woman who he felt completed him. What they did or did not have in common was no one's business and definitely not his lawyer who couldn't even keep his own wife happy.

Rubbing his hand down his face to give himself time to pick his words carefully, he turned to face Martin head-on and from the look on his face, he could see the man knew the moment he'd crossed the line and now, there was no turning back.

"Let me make something very clear to you. I don't care how many articles are written about me, applauding my work or the state of my singleness – which I am not, and I don't care how many women I've dated or even bedded, that's not the issue here. I am in love with Nichelle and that's not fake, phony or temporary and what we have in common is a mutual respect for the love that has blossomed. I screwed that up the other night and hurt her, not because of Antonia's announcement, but because of how I handled it after the fact. For that, I am deeply sorry that she's crushed right now, but let me be very plain when I say this – don't you *ever* disrespect her again! She's an incredible woman and I've never been happier than I've been since I met her. I'm not looking to replace her, I'm not looking to appease Antonia and I'll be *damned* if I let my career be judged by how I live my personal life. I'm not hurting or killing anyone and I have a right to live my life my way," he explained.

"Oh, true, true, but also not so true. You may think you have a right to live your life your way, but not if you plan to be Mayor. The people will expect much more from you and, especially from the person you plan to have on your arm. I like Nichelle and I think she's a beautiful young woman, but is she First Lady of Chicago material? Will she be the kind of woman needed when you one day run for Governor, which I'm sure that's in your plans, or perhaps a Senate seat? I'm not trying to disrespect her – I'm trying to help you see the bigger picture. Maybe your ex-wife isn't the most restrained in her approach to life, but she does have an audience that could potentially be your audience and could help with your career. Yes, I screwed up and I can fix that, but you need to think with the right head and rethink your approach. You've been able to keep your relationship with Nichelle pretty quiet, so letting it quietly slip away won't be an issue. I just think you could benefit from a partnership with Antonia. It can't hurt your career and the family values edge of being a married politician could take your numbers over the edge with those who don't want a handsome, single man in the Mayor's office, going from woman to woman. They want the family values you speak of in your platform and all your speeches. Think of the how your platform will explode with adding to your base of supporters," Martin said.

"So, what you're trying to do is take the spotlight off of how you messed this up and now want to help me fix it by seeing the positive side of not having final divorce papers? You're really trying to sell me here? Okay, I've had *and* heard enough. This conversation is over. I need to get to the office and you need to leave. I expected you to come with a more plausible explanation than you were going through something and your wife had a boy-toy and so you didn't do that job that my checks were covering," Tucker said, walking toward the front door, hoping Martin would follow. He was through talking. He was ready to throw him out the door. If Martin only knew the level of restraint he was using right now.

"Tucker, listen – I know this conversation turned left, but once you have had a chance to calm down, you'll see that you can spin this in your own favor," Martin pleaded.

Tucker turned when he opened the door and gestured for the man to keep walking, but that's not what happened. He had to add some finality to the visit.

"This conversation is over and not only that, you're fired. I expect to have originals of every file you have regarding me and the work you've done for me over the years. Our working relationship is over because your lack of respect for what I want when it comes to my life as opposed to what you think I should be doing solely for my career is disturbing to me. I didn't ask for your advice and I don't need it. What I need is an attorney who will do the work I pay him to do and to make sure he's not the cause of stress. Thanks for coming by so early in the morning and just to reiterate, you're fired."

Tucker moved back when Martin, who was clearly upset hearing that he'd just been fired, tried to move closer to him in a friendly manner, with the nerve to have a slight smile on his face.

"Tuck, come on. I think you're blowing this out of proportion. You're firing me over that one slip-up?"

"I'm firing you because I need an attorney who will look after my legal interests and follow my instructions. For the first time in all these years, I realize that's not you – at least, not anymore. I'll expect files to be delivered to my office by the end of the week."

Just when he thought Martin was about to continue talking, he watched the old man go through the door and head down the first of the eight red-brick steps that led to the street. When Martin turned in his direction, he slammed the door and turned around.

Alone with his thoughts, he had a lot of fixing of his life that needed to be done. First, he needed to get Nichelle to respond to him. He'd messed up when after Antonia made her revelation at his fundraiser and Nichelle ran off, he didn't go after her. Instead, he was needed on stage for the speech he'd prepared. He didn't choose Nichelle; he chose his career and he gave his speech, leaving her alone in her embarrassment.

Perhaps, she wasn't embarrassed since those who knew were all family and friends to her. The look on her face told him that she wasn't happy and that she was certainly confused. As he watched her run off in her beautiful navy-blue gown which fit to her curves perfectly, he noticed the way her hair bounced as she moved, remembering how he loved running his hands through her long, soft tresses when they kissed. He wanted nothing more than to have Nichelle in his arms right now, but her lack of response to his many calls and text had gone unanswered for the rest of the weekend. He didn't want to pop up at the school where she worked, though he was tempted to. He needed to know that she was alright.

Checking the time, he was running late for his first meeting of the day. Sending a text to Tellis, his best friend and the man who drove him everywhere he wanted and needed to be, he grabbed his suit jacket, straightened his tie and picked up his briefcase. Tellis responded back that he was pulling up to the door. Tucker knew he needed to get his head back on business, at least for now, with the heavy day of council meetings on this schedule. Not far from his thoughts was Nichelle. He had to prove to her that he was still all-in with her and he would find a way to finally get his divorce from Antonia despite the plan she has of staying married to him. That's wasn't going to happen on his watch.

2

Roxie danced around her hotel room, still pumped from her performance at Tucker's fundraiser at the casino. Her only point of discontent was that she didn't have a camera crew following her to get footage to use on her reality show. The Next Big Queen of Hearts, was going to be her bridge to a career as a serious, major actress in Hollywood. That night she was in rare form. She was still over-the-top with excitement over how good she played that role. The look on everyone's face when she took center stage in front of them will be something that she'll take with her for the rest of her career. She loved being a master at her craft.

Calming down, she now had to deal with an issue she hoped she would be able to put off for some time. She had to return her roommates phone call.

She and Shadow Mason had been roommates since she made the move from Chicago to Los Angeles after what she thought was a major career choice. She was hoping to get big roles based on her beauty and acting acumen, but so far, her biggest role had been the reality television series.

She had joined the show after three episodes and she had been turning things up ever since. No one was time enough for Roxie Hall. Her beauty, brains and the way she could snap-back at everyone made her a show favorite throughout the first season. With plans underway for a second season, starting in a few months, she needed a bigger storyline that focused on her for more than just being the 'around the way girl' who had attitude and didn't mind being in the middle of a brawl or two.

People called her boisterous, rowdy, loud, uncouth, foul-mouthed and brassy, but she called it being herself.

She didn't know when she'd become more of the character she played and less of the person she was before she'd set her eyes on being a Hollywood starlet. Growing up, she had to make a lane for herself if she was going to be noticed. She didn't have much family to speak of, at least family that wanted to be associated with her. She didn't make friends easily, but she always had her looks at that usually got her what she wanted; it got her Tucker.

When she met him, he was fresh out of law school and in his first term as a City Council member in Chicago. He was fine and every woman who saw them together was jealous. He'd made a name for himself with the ladies, but she was the one who was able to get him down the aisle and it wasn't because she was a great cook or took care of the home. She worked her sexual magic on him and it turned her into a wife!

After they got married, she moved into his brownstone and her ideal life wasn't that of a politician, but she started thinking about being an actress. She was always told that she had the look and what she needed was a way in. She started looking closely at herself and found things that she would love to fix like her nose, her breast and definitely get rid of the fat around her thighs and stomach. She needed that look. Tucker loved her just as she was, but that wasn't enough. Even her own mother told her that she wasn't all that attractive and that she was lucky to get a man like Tucker. Those words bounced right off of her, since the relationship between mother and daughter had never been a good one. They never got along and she blamed her mother for the estrangement from their family.

Growing up, she never understood why she had family in Chicago that when they saw her, they would run the other way or cross the street to not have any interactions with her. She was told by her mother that it was all because of jealousy, but she knew it was something else, just not what.

She had cousins who turned their noses up at her from a young age. Family whispered about her and her mother and they were never invited to family events.

As she grew older, she didn't care about them, but she did care that her own mother had turned against her right after high school.

Before becoming Roxie, and as Antonia, she had graduated high school by the skin of her teeth. If it wasn't for a few teachers who found themselves in uncompromising positions with her, she would have failed. When she thought that there would be some kind of graduation celebration for her, she found out that her mother was moving in with some man she'd met months ago and they were moving to Atlanta, leave her in Chicago to fend for herself.

At eighteen, life was rough for her. The day her mother left, the only advice she gave her was to use what she had to get what she wanted. When her mother told her that she knew about the teachers she'd been messing around with, her only opinion was that she'd been stupid to not reap a financial benefit from all that laying on her back and dropping to her knees. Roxie was hurt and disappointed that her mother thought so low of her. Rather than be disgusted that men took advantage of her daughter, she was more pissed that she was unable to get anything out of it.

The day her mother drove away, leaving her at the house of a friend, she cried for hours. Later that night when the husband of that 'friend' approached her about the things he heard she'd done for her teachers and how he wanted a piece of that, she packed the few things she had and talked her way into the apartment of a girl she worked with at a local fast-food joint. She lived with her for about a year until she was able to rent a room from a woman who became a grandmother figure in her life. That woman, Ms. Sally, helped her enroll in college and taught her to save her money. After graduation, she was finally getting somewhere in life. Ms. Sally died right before her college graduation and though the house they lived in wasn't much, it had been left to her in Ms. Sally's will since she didn't have any children of her own. That helped her get up on her feet and a few years later, she met Tucker. That started her real come-up, but now that come-up was on a downward spiral. Life in Hollywood wasn't what she thought it would be.

Once she made the move to Los Angeles after getting some minor roles, she thought she was on her way to the top. Roles picked up and she was able to make enough money to have several surgeries to fix the things she saw that she hated about herself. She was also a hustler. She had so many jobs to make ends meet that there were days when she barely slept, but a lot of people with dreams like hers were doing the same thing. The day she landed the role on the reality series, her life really changed. She'd gotten her first check and thought that she was rich. She was able to trade in the old Honda she drove from Chicago to California in. She found a better place to live than in a two-bedroom apartment with three other aspiring actresses. She had met Shadow Mason, another actress who was at the same audition for a movie role, small, but still a movie. They weren't up for the same part, but for the same movie. Shadow was cast in the movie and Roxie was thanked for her time. She and Shadow had hit it off at the audition and within a week of becoming friends, she moved into Shadow's Malibu rental. The difference between them was that Shadow had come from money because both of her parents were in the entertainment business. They were helping her get to her dream by supplementing her with the money to live the Hollywood lifestyle, something Roxie loved. She got to live it though she didn't have much money. She still had to pay some rent and now that she was behind on that and had jetted off to Chicago without paying it, Shadow had been calling her non-stop for days.

Picking up her cellphone, she apprehensively dialed Shadow's number.

"Hey, Shadow."

"Roxie! Where are you? I thought you were only going to be gone a few days to deal with a personal matter. You've been gone a week and you owe me three months back rent on your room. I can't keep carrying you. I'm here to make money too."

"I know, I know. Look, I'm waiting on my last check from the season on the show and as soon as I get that, I'll send you your money immediately. Can you give me a few more days?" she begged.

What Roxie didn't admit was that she'd already gotten her check and had already spent most of it. Shadow didn't need to know that. She'd been able to play on Shadow's kindness for a while and was hoping to continue until she got her life on track.

"Come on, Roxie. You have to help me out here. I don't mind you staying here, but just because you were living at that house most of the time for the show, you were still living here too and that means you still have to pay rent. I told you what my parents cover and we agreed to split the balance and your half is way past due. How much longer until you get your check? Did you ask Nancy, your agent about it?"

"I was just about to call her and decided to call you back first. My cellphone has been acting crazy. I haven't been getting any calls or texts and when I called the phone company, they told me to turn it off and turn it back on and then all of your messages came through along with a bunch of others. Sorry it's taken me this long to call you back. After I talk to Nancy, I will call you."

Roxie bit her bottom lip, waiting and praying that Shadow would believe her as she always had.

"Okay, but as soon as you get your check, call me. Some guy came by here looking for you. He said something about a missing watch and asked me to tell you to call him. He said he's been calling you."

"I will. Listen, I need to call Nancy and get this money thing cleared up. Thanks for being patient with me. I'll call you back."

Roxie hit the end button and threw her phone on the bed.

She walked over to the large, bay window that overlooked downtown Chicago and wondered how she'd gotten herself in such a mess. Not only was her roommate out for her for money, but now, so was Wallace, a rich man she'd met and had a few romps with. She never thought he'd miss one expensive watch when he had dozens of them. She'd taken that watch one night after spending the night with him. She'd also slipped a few hundred dollars from a metal lockbox he kept in the top of his walk-in closet, something she discovered on one of the occasions when he'd left her in his house alone. She had already sold the watch and pocketed the fifteen thousand she'd received. That was her cushion money while she figured out a way to get back into Tucker's life. Swindling Wallace wasn't the first man she'd gotten over on. She shuddered at the thought of the things she'd done to make ends meet. She was hoping for a cleaner slate a game on the up-and-up without resorting to sleazy behavior, something she actually learned from her mother. She wondered if her mother would be open to a visit while she was closer to Atlanta than she was when she was in Los Angeles. They spoke by phone maybe once a month, but she hadn't seen her in a long time.

Having no family or real friends, maybe with her slight stardom, her mother would finally welcome her with open arms. If not, she hoped to soon have Tucker and his arms, she would love being in on any given day. Speaking of Tucker, there was someone close to him that she needed to see. With the moves she was hoping to make, she was going to need some help from an old, young friend and she knew just how to persuade him.

3

After the mostly quiet ride to City Hall, Tucker exited the black Navigator truck after letting Tellis know that he'd be at in the office all day and wouldn't be ready to leave until later that evening. He knew Tellis would head straight for the gym, one of the locations where they were two of the three owners. Their friendship went back to their days of playing high school baseball together, and coming from the same southside of Chicago neighborhood, they had been through a lot as kids and as friends. He was glad that Tellis knew him well enough to not ask why they rode in silence, except for the casual references to how busy of a day he was approaching at City Hall.

Neither brought up the events of the night of the fundraiser and only a best friend would know when the time was right to address the elephant in the truck. Tellis knew to wait and he was thankful for that.

After his meeting with Martin, he wasn't in the mood to talk about the situation at hand. He needed his mind clear to handle the business of the day and his day was about to get started the minute he walked into his office.

After going through security, Tucker was happy for the elevator ride to his office where he served as President pro tempore of the Council and also as Vice Mayor of Chicago, presiding over council proceedings in the absence of the Mayor, something he'd been doing a lot more lately than he had in the three and a half years since being elected into the position by the City Council. Some people called him Councilman or City Council President, while others called him Vice Mayor. He answered to either.

The current Mayor, Roderick Alston, was planning on retiring and not seeking reelection. Tucker didn't have plans to run for the Mayor's office until Roderick shared with him that he was hoping he would want the job.

Roderick had been Mayor for twelve years and was looking forward to retiring to spend more time with his wife, four children and nine-grandchildren. He'd spent his entire life as a public servant, missing out on a lot of activities with his family and he now wanted to do nothing except spend all of his time with them, as well as moving to his cabin on the water to enjoy retirement.

Tucker spent weeks thinking about the possibility of running for Mayor and knew that those who had always supported his career would expect him too. He'd checked with his own parents, who lived in Palm Beach, Florida where they had retired to after his father sold his interest in the financial investment firm he'd helped start forty years ago. Charlotte and Randall Glass were ecstatic that he was thinking of running for Mayor, though his mother once again brought up her desire for him to settle down and find his forever wife and finally give her more grandchildren.

His youngest sister, Bailee, who at twenty-seven was looking forward to taking the bar after recently finishing law school and still lived in Chicago in a townhome her parents bought for her once their father retired and she decided to stay in Chicago.

His other sister, Amanda, who was three years younger than him and married with two children, was happy being a stay-at-home mother, raising his niece Maya and his nephew Austin, Jr. with her husband, Austin, who was the Vice President of corporate finance at the firm that her father once owned and where she'd actually met him one day while visiting their father at the office.

His mother hated that he was still single, since she didn't know that he and Antonia were still married. Charlotte Glass never cared for how loud and abrasive she was, but when he'd met and fallen in love with her, he was into having a good time and they could party until the sun came up. He thought they were a good match until her dreams of stardom and his desire to rise in politics took their agendas in two different directions. They had only been married five years with no children and as quickly as they'd fallen for each other, they'd fallen out of love.

His relationship with Antonia, when they first met, was hot and heavy. It was nothing for them to pull their car over onto a secluded street and have wild, untamed sex until the windows were sweating as hard as they were. What drew him to her was her beauty and how uninhibited she was sexually. He equated that to love and forever and asked her to marry him because he felt that was the next step in the plan for his life. He didn't regret their time together, but he could see years later, that what they had was purely physical and didn't do much for stimulating him mentally or emotionally.

She was always the loudest in the room, but people didn't mind because she was also always the most beautiful.

Antonia knew how to work a room with her gorgeous long legs and magnetic personality. Back then, she had a natural beauty that had since been enhanced with breast surgery, liposuction and other enhancements. He didn't think she needed any of that, but he understood that she wanted to do what she felt she needed to do in order to augment her beauty.

After they split, she moved to Los Angeles when started getting small roles in low-budget films. She then got the call for a role on a reality television show around eight women all vying for parts in blockbuster movies. The show was over the top dramatic with catfighting, hair pulling, glass throwing and lots of man-stealing.

The current temperature of Hollywood was that people loved those kinds of shows and she definitely had the personality to bring the drama. He avoided watching it, hating to see her behavior, but if that's what she wanted, he was happy that she'd found it. The issue now was that she was bringing her brand of drama back to his life and he wasn't having it. He wasn't sure of what he could do about it, but there had to be an answer that gave him back the freedom from their marriage that he thought he was already living.

As the elevator stopped on his floor, Tucker made his way through the throngs of people moving about in the long hallway as he headed straight for his office. His assistant, Adrienne, was on the phone when he walked into the outer office and he waved to her and others who were also on their phones conducting city business. He was happy for the reprieve from having to interact with anyone in conversation. He just wanted to get into his office, close the door and get his thoughts together.

Dropping his briefcase on the top of his desk, he removed his suit jacket, hung it up and looked at the stack of phone messages on his desk. Alongside those were a stack of folders with a printed copy of his calendar for the day sitting on top. Adrienne was a master at helping him stay on track with his day. Before he got down to work, he sat in his office chair and turned it around to look out over the Chicago skyline. Leaning back, he let his thoughts turn to the woman his mind never wanted to be absent of; Nichelle Michaels.

She, on the other hand, was the complete opposite of his ex-wife. Though there was no doubt that Nichelle had outer beauty and he could admit that it was that beauty that first drew his attention, it was their first conversation at the elementary school where she worked as the school counselor that sealed the deal for him. He knew within five minutes of talking to her that he wanted to ask her out.

At that time, Nichelle was twenty-five, fresh out of graduate school the year before and was loving her job working with kids. He'd gotten a call that the school wanted a representative from the Mayor's office to come and speak to the kids on career day and he volunteered to go. The minute he walked into the main office at the school and saw Nichelle walk in to greet him, he saw her big, beautiful smile and was immediately smitten. He could tell that she was much younger than he was, but she was an adult and that was all that mattered when it came to how his heart skipped a beat when he saw her.

That day, she had been wearing a navy-blue suit with a white buttoned-down shirt and on her feet, were a pair of high-heeled, navy shoes that played a peek-a-boo game with her bright red painted toes, which matched the polish on her fingers. He immediately checked for a wedding ring and not seeing one, he relaxed.

When she greeted him with a handshake, he didn't want to let go. Her hands were soft and the shake was inviting and confident. He loved a confident woman. When she spoke, there was a shyness and a self-assurance mixture that appealed to him.

Though he was close to six feet tall, her height was enhanced by the high stature of her shoes, bringing her close to his chin. Her hair was naturally long and curly and that day, it was swept to one side and tucked behind her ear, giving her a sexy allure that had him thinking of a way to ask her out after the handshake. He held back and dealt with the business at hand first because he was there for the kids.

Nichelle had the responsibility of bringing him up to speed on the purpose for his visit and how to interact with the kids. When she asked him to follow her into her office, he couldn't resist watching her walk and when he looked down at her legs, his favorite feature on a woman, his mind had turned to mush. Nichelle was gorgeous.

He smiled bright when he entered her office and sat in the chair opposite her desk, after she'd taken her seat. Before he lost his nerve, he did tell her that she was beautiful and hoped that he hadn't been out of line. When she tilted her head to the side, smiled and thanked him, he was glad he'd complimented her. They spoke for about fifteen minutes before he headed off to the first of four classrooms he was visiting for the day.

As they walked the hallway together, they passed by other prominent Chicago dignitaries, including Carter Garrison, one of his good friends and the man who would also become his campaign manager. He was happy that when he called Carter about career day, he was more than happy to spend the day talking about the importance of education and following dreams.

After greeting each other, Carter gave him a weird look where days later, he explained that he saw something that made him smile. When Tucker asked what it was, Carter commented that he felt a vibe between him and Nichelle as they walked together in the brief few minutes he interacted with them and wondered what would be next. Little did either know that months later, he and Nichelle would be involved in a relationship.

Carter knew Nichelle because he was friends with Reese, Nichelle's sister and Tucker himself had known Reese through her connections with Carter, his wife Sienna, who was also Reese's best friend and through Reese's fiancé, Torrence, who he also knew through his acquaintance with Carter. Torrence had welcomed the idea to host one of his biggest fundraisers for his campaign.

After speaking to the kids in each of the classrooms assigned to him that day, he walked back to the office with Nichelle and just before leaving her office after she thanked him for his time, he turned back around and asked her out to dinner. She declined, to his dismay, and being the persistent guy that he was, he asked her why. He didn't think she was expecting him to ask because he caught her off-guard when she couldn't immediately come up with a reason for declining. She asked if she could just decline without a reason and he said yes and thanked her for her time.

Two weeks later, he was still thinking about her and as he

sat in his favorite deli in downtown Chicago, he was about to call Carter and ask about her to see if he knew if she was seeing anyone, when he looked up and she walked into the deli. She wasn't dressed in work attire, but was still just as gorgeous and sexy in the lavender sweat suit which hugged her in all the right places. His body jumped to attention at the sight of her, not just taken in by her outward appearance, but remembering the desirous feeling he felt the first time he'd met her. He put his cell phone away, happy that he hadn't called Carter and then stood and walked over to her as she stood in line to order food. That day was still as clear in his mind as if it had happened the day before.

"Hello," Tucker said the moment he walked up to her in line. When she turned around and recognized him, she didn't look at him as if he was creeping her out or as if he was some kind of stalker. Instead, she beamed and greeted him with a handshake. He once again took her hand and like before, he didn't want to let it go. When she looked down at where their hands were joined, he realized he was on the verge of finally creeping her out.

"Hi, Vice Mayor Glass or do you prefer City Council President Glass?"

"Tucker. Please call me Tucker. Those titles sound so official," he said and laughed.

When she laughed with him, he finally let go of her hand.

"Sorry about that. I guess I didn't have to be that formal, but I didn't want to call you by your first name, so I went with what was safe."

"If you're good with Tucker, let's go with that. Is it okay if I call you Nichelle or would you prefer Ms. Michaels?"

"If you're Tucker, then I'm Nichelle."

"It's interesting running into you here. I see great minds think alike when it comes to the food here," he said.

"They make the best buffalo chicken wraps in the entire city. That and the fresh baked apple pie. You come here often?"

He didn't want to say that he would come everyday from this point on if he had the chance to keep running into her.

"I usually order and pick it up at the take-out window. Today, I decided to slow down, grab a book and enjoy a little break and grab a sandwich to eat in."

"You get breaks?" she quipped.

Tucker already loved their banter.

"Not often, but when I do, I take advantage of it. It's a beautiful Saturday and every once in a while, I try to squeeze in time for myself. Are you getting take out or can you join me at my table where I'm sitting all alone?" he said, trying to make a sad face, but lost it when she smiled at him.

"You said you wanted time to yourself and I see you have a book over there on the table."

When she pointed, he looked too and then turned back to her.

"I will throw that book away and never think of it again if you will agree to join me. After all, you did turn me down when I asked you out to dinner and since we are both here where fate has intervened, you can't possibly turn me down again especially after all this witty conversing we're doing. Please join me?"

He waited while the idea of what he was asking ran through her mind. He saw her struggle, yet he didn't want to let her off the hook by changing her mind. He really *wanted to get to know her and running into her this way, he already knew they were meant to meet today.*

His original plan was to hit the gym and spend the day at home catching up on ball games he'd been recording for the past week. He knew the scores and who had won each game, but he still enjoyed watching the games from the start.

"Um, sure. Let me get my food and I'll join you," Nichelle said.

Tucker felt his back straighten and wondered if this is what it felt like to win! He was excited. He started to walk back to his table and then turned back around.

"Okay, now, do I need to wait here with you to be sure you don't try and sneak out the door? I promise I'm a good guy and if you want, I can get my mother on the phone to confirm that," he joked.

"No, that's okay and I promise I won't ghost you, at least not yet. I'll see how the conversation goes."

Laughing with her, he turned and walked back to his table, placed his book on one of the other three chairs and waited. As he did, he kept his eyes on her and took in everything about her. Had he ever met a woman as beautiful as her? He wasn't sure he had. What he was sure of was that today was about to be the first day of many dates for them, and whatever amount of time they were going to have over lunch, he was going to make sure he walked away with a second date.

"Vice Mayor Glass?"

Tucker turned around, startled by Adrienne's sudden appearance in his office, pulling his mind away from the day he'd met Nichelle and back to present day.

"Sorry about that," he said. "Good morning."

He cleared his throat and sat straight up in his attempt to focus.

"Good morning, sir. Do you want some coffee and are you okay? You looked like you were a million miles away staring out that window."

Tucker shook his head yes.

"I'm good for a Monday morning."

"That's good to hear. You'll be happy to know that your schedule isn't as heavy as was planned. Several meetings have been moved to other days and your afternoon has freed up. You had a few other meetings that I moved from today and if you want me to put them back, I can do that, unless you'd like the free time."

Tucker picked up his calendar and looked it over.

"I'll let you know. For now, you can leave it open while I take some time to look over what's on the agenda for today. Yes, I'd like a cup of coffee, today, just black with a little sugar, no cream."

"Uh, sir, about this past weekend. I want to say that I heard about what happened. If I didn't have my sister's baby shower to go to, I would have been there. Omar mentioned it to me this morning and I'm sorry that Mrs. Glass showed up. Oops, I'm sorry. Should I call her that? I remember she hated any reference to calling her by her first name, but insisted on being called Mrs. Glass at all times. I guess that just stuck with me," Adrienne said, bemused.

"No worries. I guess calling her that would be a factual truth since I am still legally married to her. Are there a lot of people whispering about it?"

"No, sir. Omar swore that he only told me in confidence in

order to help you through the day. He said he was standing not far away when it all went down. He asked that I let him know when you arrive so that he could step in here to see if you needed any help with anything. He had me pull your lawyer's information in case you wanted him to reach to Mr. Sullivan for you in order to get him in here as soon as possible."

Tucker smiled. He liked how his team was always ready to jump in and think ahead of him.

"I've already met with Martin this morning before coming into the office. You should be hearing from someone at his office, if not today, then in a day or so."

"Oh? So, you won't need me to set up a call or a meeting or have Omar come in?"

"No, that won't be necessary. I fired Martin this morning. He is why my divorce is not final from Antonia and after my meeting with him, I think it's time I sought out new representation. It's actually beyond time, but I've been with him so long that I let his slip-ups over the past year or so go by, but not anymore. This latest screw up could cost me the election if it becomes drama that's blown out of proportion and takes the place of the real work of running for office. I do need you to set something up with Carter Garrison. Can you see if he's free for a call this morning? If he's available, I could meet him at one of his dealerships, depending on which one he's at today. He'll be a master at how to fix this image wise, especially if Antonia unleashes Roxie on me here in Chicago."

He laughed at his assistant's sudden feigned look of horror.

"No, not Roxie. That would be more than we could all

handle."

"You've seen the show?"

"I have and it's pure entertainment. She's quick with the comeback and her facial expressions and hand gestures are lethal. And that tongue – oh my, she is something."

"Yeah, and I've lived it and don't plan on going back," he said.

"You're going to get the divorce done quickly?"

"I doubt if that's Antonia's plan, but it is mine. We'll have to wait and see. First, I need to speak with Carter and then I need to get an attorney. I will have my work cut out for me when it comes to my ex-wife."

"Sir, what about Ms. Michaels? How is she holding up with all of this?"

Other than her and Omar, his executive officer, not many others knew about his relationship and he wanted to keep it that way.

"I haven't spoken to her yet. She's not returning my calls or texts and that's understandable. Antonia can be an overwhelming presence and Nichelle does not like the spotlight."

"I'm sure after a few days, she'll reach out and everything will be fine. She'll understand that whatever happened wasn't your fault and I'm sorry you had to fire Martin, but not really sorry. I could tell that he was slipping a little, forgetting paperwork, appointments and follow-ups. Maybe Mr. Garrison can recommend someone."

"I'm sure he can and I'll be sure to ask him."

"Great. I'll give him a call to see if he has some time to speak with you today. Do you need anything else besides your coffee?"

"Yeah, some knee pads for all the begging and pleading I may have to do in order to get Nichelle to hang in here with me through all of what Antonia thinks is in her plans."

Tucker was joking and serious at the same time.

"I'll check Amazon," Adrienne laughed and left his office, shutting the door behind her.

Tucker laughed knowing the image of him on his knees pleading with Nichelle was a sight to see. At this point, he would do almost anything to clear things up and get them back on track. His plans to have her in his arms, making love to her all night after the fundraiser had already been a bust. He needed every chance to have that again.

4

Reese made her way through the crazy traffic yelling at her car again and again to dial her sister Nichelle's phone number and each time the call went straight to voicemail, she became angrier and angrier. It wasn't like her baby sister to ignore her phone calls or to have her phone turned off.

She'd given her a few days to gather herself after crazy Roxie Hall showed up at Tucker's political fundraiser stirring up drama and trouble, something she's good at based on the character she'd come to know and hate on the reality show she was on.

Reese knew of Tucker, but wasn't close enough to him to know a lot other than what she'd heard from Sienna whose husband Carter was Tucker's friend and campaign manager. Carter had hired her marketing and promotion firm to work on Tucker's campaign, but she wasn't directly involved. She had assigned that task to her best team and had let them do the work while keeping her updated on how things were going. She knew that Torrence, her fiancé, knew him as well, but not as well as Carter.

Tucker had been invited to a few of Sienna and Carter's parties and other events, but he either didn't show up or she left before he arrived and they never really interacted. Finding out that he'd been dating her sister for months was a total shock to her system and she needed answers. She'd let Nichelle stew long enough.

She had cleared her calendar of meetings for the entire day and as she drove through traffic, she didn't care what Nichelle's plans were for continuing to shut out the world, she was breaking through that barrier today.

"Alexa, call Nikki," Reese said again.

This time she was planning on leaving a message. When the voicemail message came on, she waited for the beep.

"Nikki, I'm serious when I say you better stop ignoring me. If you don't turn on your phone and answer my calls, and I know you're probably screening them hoping and not hoping to hear from Tucker, you better pick up and stop playing with me. I gave you a few days and now it's Monday and enough is enough. Answer this phone!" she screamed and disconnected the line.

As her favorite song, "Long Way Home" by Tamar Braxton blared through the car, she weaved in and out of traffic, determined to get where she was going. The lyrics to the song were definitely about her, especially right now. She, herself, was speeding down the road with her head all out of control. What she didn't need was another speeding ticket when she saw how fast she was going. Pressing the break, she slowed down, needing to get to her destination in one piece. Besides, Torrence would kill her if she got another ticket. He was always warning her to slow down.

Finding her exit, she pulled off and at the next light, she made a right into the parking lot. Finding a place to park her 2019 BMW M8 Convertible, a birthday gift months ago from the love of her life. She remembered checking out the car at the last Chicago car show and to her delight, Torrence paid attention to everything about her and went to one of Carter's luxury car dealerships in and purchased the car. She still beamed bright when she remembered coming home to their new house several months ago and seeing the white beauty in the driveway with a big yellow bow tied around it.

Turning the car off, she once again dialed Nichelle's number as she exited and again, waited for the voicemail to come on.

"This is your last warning, Nikki. Answer the *damn* phone and stop making me angry and now my anger is turning to worry. If I find that I should be worrying less and angry more, you're going to regret not taking my call," she shouted and hung up as she walked across the parking lot to the apartment building in front of her.

This was her fourth or fifth time at the new apartment building where Nichelle had moved into two months ago, a place she loved after hearing about Alyssa Kincaid's apartment here and how nice it was before she moved in with Dexter, another friend of theirs.

Nichelle was happy when an apartment became available and she could finally move out of the studio apartment close to the University of Chicago campus where she studied Sociology in undergraduate and then obtained her graduate degree in Social Work. As a graduation gift, Reese was happy to be able to help her sister get a new car and to also pay her rent for an entire year, allowing her to save up to buy a house of her own. There was nothing she wouldn't do for Nikki or their brother, DJ, especially when it came to helping them financially.

DJ, who was head of security at Torrence's *Montiel Avage* casino, was doing pretty good for himself, so he didn't need help from her, but Nikki had made the decision to further her studies and she didn't want her struggling to pay student loans like she had done. With Torrence's help, she was able to help her sister achieve one dream after another.

She was still angry that Nikki had kept her relationship with Tucker a secret. The man was thirteen years older than her. Though her sister was an adult, she thought that Nikki would end up falling in love with someone closer to her age, be it man or woman, knowing that for a year or so, a while back, Nikki had considered herself as fluid, being open to a relationship with a man or woman. She wanted to love based on her heart and not on gender. She was happy that she had found someone, but she was cautious about Tucker. She thought about him as she waited for the elevator to take her to the fifth floor.

One thing she knew about Tucker was his reputation with the ladies. Except for the time when he was married to Antonia, he was known to be the premiere bachelor and more than one time, she'd heard about his prowess when it came to women and how he never left a woman unsatisfied. From what she'd heard about him, he served up multiple orgasms as easily as a bartender handed out drinks and not a single woman could be found who had a bad word to say about him when it came to his expertise in the sack. Tucker, in plain English, was a playboy and he made it clear to women that he wasn't looking for anything long-term. His focus was on his political career and he didn't want anything getting in his way. Then he'd met Antonia and she changed all of that; how, she didn't know because the woman was vile and not someone she would peg as being Tucker's equal. After they split up, he went back to his old ways and no one cared because he was once again on the market as single. After the fundraiser, his single status was now in question and her baby sister was probably hurting.

Nikki wasn't the most experienced and though they'd had conversations about men and sex during their girl chats, she knew the Nikki had gone from no experience with men to being a woman who enjoyed sex, and not just her experimenting with women.

When she found out she was no longer a virgin, Reese didn't get too deep into her business about who she'd given her virginity to at twenty-five. She only wanted to know that she was practicing safe sex and had gotten on some type of birth control. A conversation like that should have been between their mother and Nikki, but her sister had always been closer to her when it came to heart-to-heart talks. Though they both had a much better relationship with their mother now than they had in the past, she and Nikki were still pretty close. Clearly, not as close as she thought because she had kept an entire relationship with a sexy politician all to herself. Determined to get answers, Reese wasn't planning to leave the apartment until she found out why there was so much secrecy.

When the elevator door opened, she marched up to Nikki's door and practically leaned on the bell. She'd already called the school and found out that she hadn't gone to work, but had called out sick, so she had to be at home.

Dialing her cell phone again, Reese waited for the voicemail to kick in, but instead, this time, the phone rang and her sister answered.

"Is that you ringing the bell like a crazy woman or someone from the fire department?" Nikki asked her.

"Damn right, so open the door or I'll break it down and I won't need an axe!"

Putting her cell phone away, she was not going to have a conversation with her sister on the phone when she stood directly on the other side of the door. She could hear the locks being turned and then the door opened. Not waiting to be invited in, she pushed her way in and turned with her hands on her hips and opened her mouth to speak and was interrupted.

"Nice suit. Is that Dolce and Gabbana? Deep pink is definitely your color and it looks amazing with those pink and black Christian Louboutin red sole pumps. You have to let me borrow them sometime," Nikki said, locking the door and walking over to the sofa.

Reese stood mystified at the casualness of her sister's demeanor, as if nothing was wrong with her not answering calls for days.

"Are you out of your mind? That's the first thing that comes to mind is for you to compliment my suit? Okay, I'll play along. Of course, my suit is Dolce and Gabbana, my favorite designer and the shoes are absolutely Christian Louboutin and no you can't *ever* borrow them after your behavior these past few days. Stop playing with me, girl!" she shouted, dropping her bag that matched her shoes on the love seat then sitting on the opposite end of the beige, plush sectional in the living room. When she watched Nikki reached for the remote to the television to change the channel, she grabbed it and threw it across the room.

"What's the matter with you? You're picking that up!"

Nikki demanded.

"Really? I wouldn't hold my breath on that. In fact, hold your breath as long as it's been since you've last answered one of my calls!"

"As you can see, I'm fine."

The nerve, Reese thought as she watched her reaching for a bowl of fruit that sat on the cloth sectional centerpiece.

She tried to snatch that away from her, but Nikki moved it out of her reach.

"Have you been in this apartment looking like this for the past few days? Since the fundraiser? You look a mess? Where did you get that granny robe from? Ugh, we need to work on your attire with a quickness," Reese asserted.

"I was trying to up my attire when I asked to borrow those shoes and you shot me down. I can't afford what you can afford, so don't be stingy with your stuff," Nikki said flippantly.

"Stingy is not a word you can ever associate with me. This sectional fit in here nicely and I see you finally got that television off the floor and on the wall."

"Torrence put it up about two weeks ago. I called him like you told me to."

"Oh, your man didn't offer to put it up on the wall for you?" Reese questioned glibly.

When Nikki turned her way and rolled her eyes, Reese laughed. At least she could see that she wasn't too far down in the dumps. When they had banter back and forth like this, it meant she was in some state of happiness.

"He did, but we didn't spend a lot of time in this room," she said and gestured toward the bedroom.

"Eww, I do not want to hear about your sex life with

Tucker Glass. What I want to know is why did you keep it from me and DJ? After the fundraiser, we got nothing from you and we were worried."

"I know and I'm sorry. Did you see Roxie Hall and her entrance? Ugh, I hate her on that show and I dislike her even more now, strutting in and making demands of Tucker. They're *divorced*!

"No, I don't think they are, but then again, I wouldn't know and clearly you don't know either unless Tucker has countered her claims."

When Nikki got up and walked away abruptly, Reese knew that she'd hit a nerve.

"You didn't say anything about the new art on the walls? Mom bought those for me as a gift. You like them?" Nikki asked walking back into the room with a bottle of strawberry kiwi in her hands and thrusting it Reese's way.

"Thanks, and yes, they're nice. You're beginning to be an expert at diverting and distracting and I don't like it. You've been taking too many tips from me and my behavior. Sit down and answer my question. What did Tucker say about all of this?"

When Nikki exhaled loudly, she knew what was coming even before she heard the words.

"I haven't talked to him. Ugh, I should have picked up the remote you threw across the room. I don't like this show that's on."

"If you don't stop, I'm going to toss this place! I don't care about a remote or about a show you currently don't like. I want to know why you and I can talk about any and everything, including the type of birth control you should get, but you couldn't tell me you were kicking it with the

Councilman Tucker Glass who is thirty-nine years old. Thirty-nine, Nikki!"

"Stop screaming at me and I know how old he is and trust me, we are not just kicking it. I'm in love with him and he's in love with me."

"Yet, here you sit alone, not going to work and looking like you haven't bathed all weekend. I think I can smell you and it's foul!"

"Liar! I never smell bad and I always shower. I knew you would judge my relationship with him, which is why I didn't say anything. You and DJ still see me as this little girl and I'm not. I'm a woman and I fell in love with a man who is older than me. He treats me like a queen and he makes me feel like I'm the most beautiful woman in the world and his age isn't an issue for me and it shouldn't be for you."

"Well, you didn't give me a chance for it to be an issue or not because you have said nothing about him. How long have you been seeing him?"

"About six months."

"Wait! He's the reason we had the birth control talk? You lost your virginity to Tucker Glass? Wow! You definitely went to the top of the class your first time out of the gate! He's a master with women. You didn't even start off slow with some inexperienced guy who is only out to chase his own orgasm. You went for the top of the class with this one."

"What are you talking about?"

"Don't tell me you have not heard about what an experienced lover Tucker is? I'm not saying he's a ho, but he has ho capabilities and I hear he's a master at it too," Reese explained.

"Heard it from where?"

"I know a woman he once dated or better yet, bedded and to this day, she still claims Tucker was the best lover she's ever had."

"And of course, you would prefer I date someone my age who would be less experienced than him? Should I have had a few experiences where I don't get any enjoyment out of it because, as you stated, some other guy would be out for his and not caring about what I got out of it?"

Reese waited before responding. She could see from the look on her sister's face that the conversation should be more serious and she was making light of it.

"Okay, let me start over. I'm happy that you fell in love and that you are having a great sex life. That should happen for all women. Would I have been pleased if it were someone closer to your own age? Of course, but if you didn't come across that person at your age who makes you feel the way Tucker does, then no, I'm not wishing that you'd dated someone your age and less worldly with the opposite sex. I know Tucker is a nice guy because Carter wouldn't be friends with someone who wasn't. You know the caliber of his friends and he takes character very seriously. Tucker is so experienced and I don't want you to get hurt, like what happened over the weekend. That's drama you don't need."

"I know and it wasn't his fault. Roxie barged into the fundraiser and tried to steal Tucker's spotlight. I'm just glad all that didn't occur on the main floor."

Reese shook her head in agreement.

"I know. After I left you when you ran to your car, you said you were fine and just tired. I didn't think you'd ignore me like I did something to you. You should know that I was going to worry."

"I'm sorry, sis. I just needed to think and I thought Tucker would come out, but he didn't. He left things up in the air and went to make his speech."

Reese started to respond, but first she watched her sister lower her head as if she were defeated. She reached across and lifted Nikki's head back up.

"Don't you dare look down on yourself about this. I never want to see you with your head held down because of the outlandish antics of a psycho like that woman. Tucker needs to fix his life and get a handle on Roxie before I do. From one loud-mouth to another, I know how toxic her behavior and her words can be. I have those same qualities, though I know how to control mine a little better."

Nikki snickered at her and she leaned back, surprised.

"Oh, really? You didn't control that she-devil when you caught Torrence cheating on you with that vile woman from Dubai. You really let Torrence have it. He told me about the tongue lashing you gave him!"

"Okay, true, but he deserved that. That woman he was screwing, Amari Lootah, with the rich daddy was a menace and she was definitely certifiable. I poured my heart out to the man and told him I loved him and then I found out he was giving that good loving to other women and not just Amari either, but that's all in our past. Our love was stronger than his discretions and to tell you the truth, we were not exclusive when he did his dirt, so I had to forgive him. He still deserved every word I said to him when I was pissed off and trust me, if Roxie doesn't control that wayward tongue of hers, I will set her straight as well. She better not come for my sister, is all I'm saying. How did you meet Tucker?"

"He was a speaker at my school for career day. I was

assigned to him and he asked me out. I said no and then two weeks later, I went to this deli downtown and he there was eating. He came up to me, invited me to share his table and before I knew it, we had been sitting for over two hours. I didn't think we would have much in common because he's older, but I loved talking to him. He's so intelligent and of course, easy on the eyes. I was a little pissed that I wasn't the only one in the deli who noticed how sexy he is. Women kept eyeing him the whole time. He gets that a lot, but his attention never strayed from me. A few days after that lunch at the deli, he sent me flowers at work and asked me out again. That time, I said yes. I've been seeing him since then and I promise you, he did not know he was still married, if he actually is. He couldn't have known and been with me. He's not that kind of man. One of the first things he told me was that he had been married and that his divorce was final. He had dated before meeting me, but nothing serious until he met me. Do you think he was lying to me?"

"Absolutely not. I don't think Tucker would do that. I talked to Sienna and she gave me a little insight into him since I couldn't reach you yesterday. She said that there isn't a deceitful bone in Tucker's body and if he's in love with you, he is in love with you. She also believes that if he is still married to Roxie or Antonia or whatever, there has to be a good explanation and she doesn't believe he would let it go all this time without making sure it was final. You need to talk to him and figure out what's going on. He hasn't called you?"

"He has. I haven't answered."

"Oh, so you weren't just ignoring me, but even him? Talk to him. I don't like all this secrecy you've living under, but I understand why. Sienna calmed me down from being angry at you. She said that with the spotlight Tucker would be under with his election campaign, she knew that he wouldn't want to expose you to any part of his public life until you were ready and knowing you the way I do, I'm sure all the secrecy was your idea and not his."

"Ugh, you know me too well. Yeah, it was me. He was going to introduce me the night of the fundraiser and with you and DJ being there, I knew the cat would be out of the bag at that time. Once Roxie showed up, that all ceased, which is why I left and went home. What is that woman's name? Is she Antonia or is she Roxie?"

Reese quivered with laughter.

"I don't know. I asked Sienna the same thing and she said both. She believes Antonia is more tamed than Roxie."

"Whatever. I was thinking about him and his career when I left. I know it's crazy to hear, but I was. Tucker doesn't need a scandal and the people of Chicago need his leadership. He's done so many amazing things for Chicago and he would do even more as Mayor. He's the top candidate and being involved with me and the people finding out he's still married, even it if was an error, could be detrimental to his aspirations. I don't want that. Tucker left me a message saying he wanted to talk to me and clear things up and how sorry he was for what could potentially drag me into this mess with him and that woman. I love him, Reese. I really love him. I don't want to be the cause of him losing what he has been fighting for."

Reese reached over and took hers two hands into hers and held them tight.

"Don't you dare let that woman come in and steal your

joy. Remember when I broke up with Torrence? I was willing to kick him to the curb and send him right into her arms without even fighting for the love I had with him and that would have been the biggest mistake of my life. I love him so much that it hurt me to be without him when we broke up and then I realized that I needed him as much as he continually proclaimed he needed me. I thought Torrence had so much baggage and I didn't want any part of that, but that swagger haunted me at nights when I was in bed alone. I wanted his arms around me, I wanted to make love to him and fix our love and my stubbornness almost left me without him. Don't do that to yourself. I'm not going to treat you like the little girl you claim that DJ and I treat you like. Instead, I'm going to say stop ignoring his calls and listen to what he has to say. If you find it's not too much of a burden for you to work through this with him, then tell him that. If you feel like your love can overcome anything, including Roxie Hall also known as Antonia Glass, then you fight for your man. Let there be no secrets between you. He's ready to tell it all to you and you should listen. That's the real grown up thing to do."

Reese stood to leave and Nikki stood up with her.

"You're leaving? I can make us something to eat."

"Oh, now you want my company. Girl, you need to get a shower, do something with your hair and get out of that granny robe, preferably tossing it in the garbage. I hope you don't let Tucker see you in that thing! I have to get to the office, but I may get a chance to swing by later if you cook me some dinner."

"Oh, I have some really sexy stuff for him and one is even crotchless! Yes, I will cook something later."

Reese doubled over with laughter as she opened the door to leave.

"That is too much information. No more keeping secrets from me. You can come to me with anything and I will listen."

"Without being opinionated?" Nikki questioned.

Reese whipped her head around and placed her hand on her hip right after snapping her fingers in Nikki's face.

"Oh, don't ask too much of your dear sister! I'm *always* going to be opinionated, but I'll also *always* be in your corner. Call that man and stop making him suffer. Don't send him back into the arms of that woman he was married to. That would be a tragedy when he can continue loving a rare diamond like you!"

Accepting the tight hug Nikki offered, Reese hugged her back even tighter and then turned to leave. When she reached the elevator door and heard Nikki's door close and lock, she pulled out her cell phone and called Torrence. She needed to hear his sexy voice and now that she had extra time before she had to go to her office, she was already thinking about going back to her house where she had left Torrence naked in bed. All that talk about sexy men and prowess had her thinking about how her own man continually rocked her world.

It wasn't often he got a chance to sleep in when he owned two casinos, one in Chicago and one in Las Vegas, and was currently in the midst of building his second one in Chicago. She smiled when he answered on the first ring.

"Hey, baby!" Torrence said in that deep baritone voice that she loved. Even through the phone, his voice made her legs shudder.

"You up?" she asked, as sexy as she knew how.

"After hearing your voice, I'm now up in more ways than just one. You should be here to see just how *UP* I am!"

"I'm on my way. Keep it up and hard for me!" she said as the elevator doors closed.

"You know how I do, sweetness," he swooned and she thought back to the night before and was ready for a repeat of that hot, sexy action.

Ending the call, she pushed the button for the first floor over and over again as if doing so would make the elevator car move faster. She was already dreading the possibility of the speeding ticket she may get trying to get back home to her man. With what she knew was waiting for her there, it would be well worth it.

Also, on her mind was what could be ahead for her sister when it came to tangling with Roxie. She would let Nikki work through it, but if Roxie tried it, she had her sister's back and Roxie wasn't ready for her. She wasn't as docile as her Nikki was. Somebody better tell Roxie or Antonia, whichever name she preferred, that Reese Michaels, soon to be Reese Michaels-Allen, comes with the fire!

5

Antonia walked into her hotel room after grabbing a quick breakfast sandwich a few blocks from where she was staying. She wasn't sure how many more nights she'd be able to stay at the expensive hotel, but she had an image to uphold. Already, she'd run into quite a few fans of her reality show who recognized her and if they had caught her slipping, that kind of drama, the unwanted kind, would be all over the social media blogs and sites and she couldn't have that.

Walking up to the mirror on the bedroom wall, she checked her reflection to see that everything was in place. She worked to adjust her false eyelashes, wishing she could have afforded to bring her makeup artist with her from Los Angeles or at the least, find one in Chicago who could keep her looking her best and freshest. She did her best on her own, but soon, she would need reserves.

Her money situation wasn't the best right now, spending most of it on the luxury house in the Hollywood hills she shared with a roommate and the rest on her new, fancy car that she was barely able to afford. She was glad that the reality show was recorded in a lavish twelve-bedroom, Malibu beachfront house and that she got to experience that kind of living eight months out of the year, but she wished it was every day during that time. Her contract had her at the house four days a week, which meant for the other days, she still had to maintain her spot with Shadow. That kind of living is how she always wanted to live and she was hoping her stint on the show would be her suffrage before the big life, a far cry from the okay life she lived with Tucker in Chicago.

Walking over to her closet, she looked through to find something else flashy to wear later when she dropped in on Tucker at the house they once shared. She needed something really hot and tempting. She had to find a way to get her clutches back into him and the only real good spot of their marriage was their time in bed. The sex was crazy and wild and she hadn't had any loving that good since him – not even the few jump offs here and there that she'd had since they split up. Besides the good sex, she needed his clout, his status and his connections if she was going to improve her position in Hollywood. She would *really* be the focus of attention being the wife of the Mayor of a city as powerful as Chicago. She would work up some drama with that angle, knowing the other women would be jealous of her fine ass husband!

Tucker was gorgeous and always had been from the moment she'd first laid her eyes on him. It wasn't lost on her that the same night they'd met at a club, that she'd let him take her in the back seat of his car. She had been just as hot for him as he was for her. That was her first experience of understanding when women say they had their back blown out! Tucker did that and their loving had gone up hill after that. He never disappointed. They would still be married if he'd been more supportive of her desire to be a major Hollywood actress. She thought she could settle for being on the arm of a sexy politician going to the hottest events and getting VIP treatment wherever she went, but that wasn't enough for her. She wasn't a public servant like him, but she did miss him.

He was six feet of lusciousness and there wasn't a woman who didn't want him as much as she still did. They were good together when it came to sex and she was always able to win him over with her body. Though she knew that he loved her natural beauty, she'd done well with her breast enhancement going from a sexy C cup to an amazing DD cup. She'd had other work done and knew that to keep up with the Hollywood status quo, especially at the age of thirty-six, she had to have a regular plastic surgeon on speed dial, which was quite costly.

The money she'd walked away from when she and Tucker split up was money she'd saved up during their marriage when he had covered all of their expenses. She'd done some work as a model and walk-on for various Chicago produced shows and full-time, she'd made her work as the owner of a hair salon. She'd sold it to have money for her move. She was ready for her next level and the key to that, was Tucker.

She'd known for a long time that they were still married and now that she needed him, she decided to bring that information into the fold and find out how she could use it to her benefit. When she heard that he was running for Mayor, she wanted to be a part of that. She could live in Chicago for the months of when she wasn't recording her show and play first lady of Chicago and get all the perks that came along with that until she no longer needed him and then she'd offer to finally sign the divorce papers and move back to Los Angeles full-time. First, she needed to get back into his life and sex was her golden ticket. The thought of being with him again made her body quiver with bliss. Tucker was a master at sex and she really needed it hot and spicy like only he could bring.

Second, she needed to find out more about this woman Tucker was involved with. According to her source at his office, he'd been seeing her for about six months and she was happy that she got her first glimpse of the woman at the fundraiser.

Nichelle was indeed much younger and a bombshell from what she could see; just the kind of woman Tucker enjoyed. What she didn't plan on was finding out that he was in love with her. That was obvious in the way he looked at her that night. She'd been watching from afar since the moment she had arrived and having her pointed out. Her beauty was flawless and she was young, much younger than she had hoped. Nichelle made her look like an old maid and she didn't like that at all. She would have to figure out how to come up with money to have a little more work done on her body. She had to stay competitive and not let a young twenty-six-year-old show her up.

Unzipping the red one-piece jumpsuit she had on, she stepped out of it and admired her body in the mirror, turning left and right to get an idea of places she didn't like that would need a doctor's attention. She was still hot and sexy and could definitely compete for Tucker's attention. Was he really in love or just lust? She would soon find out and that would allow her to see the angle she needed to come at him. In her thong and bra, she ran to the living room of the hotel suite when she heard her cellphone ring from where she'd left it on the counter when she came in. Grabbing it and answering it before it stopped ringing, she exhaled when her agent's name appeared on the screen.

"Nancy!" she shouted while adding a fake smile as if she could be seen.

"Roxie! How is Chicago and did you get Tucker to agree to staying married to you and letting us get some footage of the two of you getting back together? We also need to add in a drama angle. What about mad drama with that girlfriend you told me about? We could play up the three-way triangle love affair thing. Some people say it takes two to tangle, but I believe that the real entertainment comes when it's a three-way entanglement. Lots of celebrity couples play that way. That would look good on the show next season. So, tell me what have you been able to get done so far?"

Antonia looked around her hotel room, decorated in shades of gray and white and though there was a touch of luxury, getting the room was the only progress she'd made since coming back to Chicago a week ago. She wouldn't dare tell Nancy that and she wished the woman would call her Antonia when she wasn't actually working.

"Well, not much and no progress yet with Tucker. I haven't met with him, but I plan to do that tonight. I'm in my hotel right now finding the right outfit to really have his head spinning when he sees me. He won't be able to resist all this," she said, plopping down on the gray paisley antique looking couch.

"Okay, so you're going to woo him with sex. Okay, I can see that. Men don't turn down free sex and I wonder if once the two of you hook up again, if that makes the divorce decree null and void. We can look into that later. Right now, you have your work cut out for you. I got a call from the producer and he's looking at who they plan to cut before the next season and your name came up."

Antonia opened her mouth in total shock. After what she done for Larry, the show's producer, behind closed doors, she wasn't expecting to hear her name come up as a possibility of not returning for the next season.

"Really? That's shocking," she bewailed.

"You were good with throwing shade and causing drama on the show, which is what they want, but they need more. They need you to be even more over-the-top and you need an angle that they could focus on all season, something like finding out you weren't divorced from your husband and he's been sleeping with several women since you split while trying to advance his political career. It would be great to get some of these women on camera, you know with you confronting them for sleeping with your husband. The possibilities are endless," Nancy dragged on.

Bored with the conversation, she knew her spot on the show was up in the air and she also knew what she had to do to stay relevant and Tucker was the key.

"Do you think this could ever spin into me having my own show? Maybe something recorded here in Chicago? I mean, you and I know that I can bring the drama and there could be plenty of it right here. Imagine cameras following around the Mayor and his wife and thrown in would be enough drama to keep people tuning in each week just to see me."

"Oooh, yes and that sexy-ass husband of yours! I saw a spread of him in a magazine and all I could say is wow! If I was twenty-years younger – whew!"

Antonia held the phone away and glared at it.

"Really, Nancy? That's my husband you're ogling over and yes, I'm used to that. I have never met a woman, black or white, young or old that didn't fawn over him, ready to drop their panties at the notion that he wants to get in them. With you though? A fifty-year-old married white woman? I don't think so," she laughed.

"Child, just like a lot of other women, it's nice to dream. Now, what are you going to do? Tell me what's been going on."

Sitting and placing her crossed legs up on the brass and glass table top, she decided to over-dramatize her entrance at the fundraiser. She had to give Nancy something.

"I stormed into Tucker's political campaign and announced that we were still married while he was lock-lipped with his girlfriend and their friends were standing there. It was mad drama! He was in the arms of his lover, a much younger version of me – I see he has a type and I give them Roxie on a whole new level! I set it off up in there."

"That's what I mean! Get it, Roxie!" Nancy chimed in.

"After making my declaration, I waltzed off, leaving everyone with their mouths hung open. His little girlfriend ran off, but I still couldn't get closer to him at the end of the night. I'm going to pop up on him this evening to lay all of this sexiness on him. He is not ready for what I'm about to do to him. That will lead me back into his life, back into his bed and back on his arms as Antonia Hall-Glass, the soon to be wife of the Mayor of Chicago," Roxie explained.

"I've been meaning to ask you why your last name is Hall and not Glass right now. You also go by Roxie and not Antonia. You never took his last name?"

"I did. My name, as it is on my contract with your firm is Antonia Hall-Glass, but I use Hall for my stage name and you know why I use Roxie. I created that name thinking it had a ring to it back when I was in college. It kind of stuck when I started looking at a stage name. That's the name I've been using since I moved to Los Angeles. I'll gladly go back to Glass once I work out some kind of deal with him. I have someone on the inside that works for him who feeds me all the information I need. In fact, I need to get off the phone. I'm expecting him in a few minutes. I'll give you a call in a few days with a better update. I just got here, so not much has happened so far."

"Get it done, Roxie. Your career depends on this."

"I got this and call me Antonia when I'm not working," she shouted and hung up.

As she stood to go back into the bedroom, there was a soft knock on the door. She smiled knowing who it was. She started to cover her almost naked body, but also knew that this state of undress could work to her benefit; as it had in the past. Choosing to let her guest in, she ran her fingers through her long brown and blond streaked wig and headed to the door.

Opening it, she stood behind it until her guest was inside. When she closed and locked the door and turned to find him staring at her large breasts, which were barely contained in the hot pink demi-bra she had on, she smiled at the impact her sexiness had on him. Her eyes traveled down to where his zipper covered what she could see was an emerging hard-on and she smiled even brighter and sexier.

"Antonia," he said and she licked her lips in response.

For him, she wasn't Antonia.

"Roxie. Call me Roxie," she said.

"I see you remember our history together or at least some part of you remembers," she said walking closer to him. When he licked his lips in response to seeing her, she knew what that meant and knowing she had time, she was ready. Thinking about Tucker had her all hot and bothered and since her guest was here and clearly ready from what she could see, there was no reason to not indulge and use him as a substitute. He wasn't as good of a lover as Tucker, but when you don't have an option and one walks in, you use it.

"Oh, yeah, I remember."

"You were an intern back then, working for my husband. I think you were like nineteen or twenty. You certainly have grown, and, in more ways than just one," Roxie said, running her extra-long polished finger nail from his chest down to the top of the zipper of his pants where something hard and ready was ready to make an appearance.

"I was glad to get your call today, but next time call my cellphone. Tucker's assistant answers my line when I'm not in my office and I had just walked back in when you called and luckily, I was able to grab it before she answered."

"Well, if she had answered, I would have hung up and called back until you answered. Have you missed me? Have you missed these?" Roxie asked, making reference to the new expanse of her breasts.

"I see you've grown a lot since we last hooked up before you moved to Hollywood. You know, you were my first older woman and those I've had since you, have not compared. You put something on a brother!"

Roxie leaned her head back and laughed heartily. She loved watching men foam at the mouth at the thought of getting between her creamy thighs.

"Omar, I'm all for the fun you know we can have, but there is work to be done. You need to get me some information on Tucker and especially on that tart he's screwing. I have to come up with a plan to make sure he never looks her way again."

Moving closer to him, she made sure her body was flush against his, sending his desire for her into the atmosphere.

"I..I..can try, but that won't be easy. He's pretty private about his personal life. I mean, I know he's seeing her, but once he leaves the office, he pretty much keeps his personal life to himself. I don't know how helpful I can be. Adrienne knows much more about his life than I do," Omar said.

Roxie smiled when she watched him lick his lips again. She knew exactly what she needed to do to persuade him.

"Well, I think you can do anything you set your mind to."

Turning around with her back to him, she reached behind her and undid the snap that held the bra cups together. The moment the bra fell into her hands, she released it and allowed it to slide slowly to the floor behind her and between. Turning back slowly, calling on her moves as an actress, she moved her hands slowly up her body, cupping her own large globes and when Omar's hands reached for her, she swatted him away.

"What?" he questioned.

"Not until you tell me something juicy about Tucker and this woman. Tell me something you haven't already told me. I need an in to get close to him again. I'm going over to his house tonight and I need to know how to work him," she said.

"Wait? Are you going over there to, you know?"

Roxie smiled and walked away from him as she headed toward the bedroom. With her back to him she turned only her head in his direction.

"Why do you need to know? Are you jealous? You don't have to be. You and I have had this kind of fun for many years and Tucker never found out. You've been feeding me information for years and this should be no different. I want you to dig around his office, check his calendar, his computer, check Adrienne's stuff, I mean check everything! I need dirt and I need it now!"

To add more enticement, she reached down and slid her matching pink thong down her legs and wiggled her behind in his direction. When Omar began to cough, almost uncontrollably, she knew she had him.

"I will certainly do everything I can to get you what you want," he said.

"What about pleasing me and getting me what I want?" she slurred out, in a purring like manner.

"I will do anything you want."

"Drop the pants," she demanded. "I need some attention." Before she could get the next word out, she watched Omar stumble over himself to get his shoes off in order to get his black dress pants down his legs. To her amazement, when she turned to look at him again, he had removed his pants and whatever type of underwear he had on which had been hiding his, stiffer than a pole, penis.

"Done," he said and moved toward her.

"First, let's get something established. This is a freebie. Anymore after today and it will cost you some information and that information had better be worth me letting you back in between these thighs. Second, we wouldn't want Tucker to find out that you've been screwing his wife for years. You could lose your job and any connections he could have to your successful career in politics. Don't disappoint me when I need you the most and I'm not talking about what you're about to do for me in between the sheets. You know what I need, right? Say it!" she demanded. She loved the control she had over men, especially those foaming at the mouth with lust for her as Omar was doing right now.

"Information on Tucker and Nichelle and you need good stuff," he acknowledged.

"That's a good boy. Now, come on into this bedroom because Roxie needs it bad and from the looks of you, I'm not the only one!" she shouted and with the sexiest walk she could come up with on bare feet, she walked into the bedroom with Omar close behind her and ready to do anything she wanted and needed. To get Tucker back, she needed that kind of loyalty, even if it came with some time on her back. Like Nancy said, her career depended on it. For that, she was willing to do just about anything.

6

"Carter Garrison is on the line for you," Adrienne said sticking her head in his office door.

Tucker was glad he was finally getting a chance to talk to Carter. His morning had been busy with meetings and so had Carter's, so getting his call around lunch time was perfect.

"Got it. Thanks, Adrienne. Can you hold all other calls and no visitors?"

"Will do."

When the office door closed behind her, Tucker turned to his call.

"Bro!" Tucker exclaimed the moment he was alone.

"Hey, bro! What's going on? Sorry I'm just getting back to you. I've had a hell of a day," Carter said.

"Making big money moves at the dealerships?"

"Always, but that's not what had me tied up. Sienna had a doctor's appointment today and we made the mistake of taking Symone with us when I should have left her with Sienna's parents. I love my baby girl, but she cut up in that doctor's office. She didn't want to sit still. I tried to hold her on my lap when she wouldn't sit in the stroller and she didn't like that either. I put her down and she started throwing magazines on the floor, thinking it was funny. I told Sienna that allowing Symone to turn her playroom at home upside down was a mistake because when she isn't at home, she would think that was still okay. During Sienna's exam, Symone cried and screamed like someone was killing her. The crazy part was once the exam was over and we were leaving, she was as quiet as a mouse. That was exhausting. I dropped them back at home and headed to the office. I'm now trying to focus on work."

"Wow! That's a lot but well worth it I'm sure. I hope to have those problems one day."

"Man, I was sure you would have kids before me, especially after you and Antonia got together, I thought that the two of you would be popping out babies."

"Her ambition got in the way and so did mine. I assumed that time would come, especially since I waited until my thirties to get married. I'm glad we didn't because no child should be in the midst of a divorce. I want to be in the same house with my kids, raising them and seeing them every single day, not only on weekends. Being an attorney, I know how the courts lean to the mother when it comes to custody, not that Antonia would have jumped at the chance to have sole custody," he joked.

"Yeah, I hear you. So, she's back, huh? Is it true? Are the two of you still married?"

Tucker got up from his desk and walked over to sat down on the brown plush sofa in his office, taking the cordless phone with him. He was settling in for a deep conversation.

"Looks like my lawyer, Martin, screwed this one up. I signed the papers first and then they were sent to Antonia to sign. She signed with her stage name, Roxie Hall and not Antonia Hall-Glass. New papers were drawn up and sent to me from her attorney through Martin. He never did anything with the papers. In fact, he says he doesn't remember getting them, but I'm sure he did. He was going through some stuff, but that's no excuse. That's why he has a staff to handle those things, but only when he gives the right directions. He failed and now he's fired. I need to find a new lawyer to take care of this and my other affairs, personal and business. I should have changed attorneys a long time ago."

"Yeah, you should have. I told you that when you first asked me to run your campaign. I checked him out and he wasn't doing you justice. Say, my attorney is at the top of her game and I can send her your way. She's thorough and I have not complaints. She recently started her own firm with all the business I've been throwing her way. She represents all my business ventures and she's my personal attorney. She also represents Torrence and get this, she just took Jermony on as a client and you know how big he is as a professional basketball player. He just signed a new contract, one of the biggest ever. He's also sent a few guys her way too. With all that new business, she realized she was spending her time and effort in someone else's firm making them rich and it was time she made all that big paper for herself. Her name is Leslie Ward and I'm sure with a word from me, she'll take you on immediately and handle this Antonia drama. She'll even send someone over to Martin's office to get all of your files, paper and electronic. Pass me over to Adrienne at the end of the call and I'll give her all the information to contact Leslie. I'll shoot Leslie a text to let her know you'll be in touch and do it today."

"Thanks, man. I appreciate you and I appreciate you looking out for me with the referral. It's good to see a sister out here doing her thing like this. I met her at the fundraiser and I understand her firm made a big donation. I saw the list of donors on my desk this morning and I remember seeing Leslie Ward and Associates on the list of donors who contributed the maximum amount. I can thank her for her donation to the campaign and work out the details to get her on retainer when I call he later. This is a huge relief. Now, if I can just work things out with Nichelle, I can get back to feeling like myself," he said.

"Have you talked to her about all this yet?"

"Nah, she isn't taking my calls. I'm assuming it's because after Antonia dropped that information on us, I headed to the stage to give my speech without running to make sure she was okay."

His plan was to give Nichelle a few more days and then he was going to show up at her apartment and hoped that she'd let him in.

"Bruh, I've been meaning to catch up with you on all this. How could you not tell me you were seeing Reese's sister? I remember that day I saw you with her at the school for career day. Remember, I told you that I caught a vibe happening between you. I can't believe you haven't told me that you've been seeing her, especially as close as we have been working together on your campaign. This is huge! Have you talked to Reese yet?"

"No. Why would I talk to Reese?"

"Well, not that you would want to, but well, Reese is just that kind of overprotective sister. She had no idea you were seeing her sister and from what Sienna told me, Reese was pissed and ready to hang you up by your balls. She was able to talk her back from the ledge, making her understand that though Nichelle is her baby sister, she is still a grown woman and Sienna knows the kind of guy you are and that you would never play with her heart. You told me you were seeing a woman and you had fallen in love, but you were cautious about revealing it yet, to keep the spotlight off of her and because it was so new, you wanted time to enjoy it without the media being huddled around your every move. I had no idea it was Nichelle."

"Carter, I know everyone is shocked, but I'm being truthful when I tell you that I am in love with her and I want to be with her and only her. I didn't set out to fall in love with Reese's sister and for the first month, I didn't know that's who her sister was. I mean, she told me she had a sister and even told me her name, but I was so busy and so caught up in her that I didn't make the connect until you hired her firm to do the marketing and promotion. When I asked Nichelle, she said she thought I knew, but it just went by me. She also wanted to keep our relationship a secret even from her family so that she could just enjoy the moment. Nichelle asked for the secrecy, the privacy and I obliged because I was that smitten with her. Can you believe I just said smitten?" he joked.

"No, and I heard it for myself. This is serious for you. I didn't hear you say a word like that when you were with Antonia. I mean, I know you loved her back then, but listening to you make reference to Nichelle by saying smitten, yeah that's new."

"Man, you have no idea. I know I'm known for being a lady's man and I accepted that title for what it was when I was living like that, but not since I've met Nichelle. From the moment I met her, everything in my world changed. I had lunch with her at a deli a few weeks after I first saw her and for two hours, nothing else in the world mattered other than the time I was spending with her. Hearing her voice, seeing her smile and taking in her laugh was intoxicating. She has such a huge love for life and all things positive. She loves where she is in life and she loves what she does. To her, every day is a gift and that's how I see life. She thinks of others before she thinks of herself and you know that's me. That's why I chose a life of public service. I know she's younger by quite a bit, but when I'm with her, that doesn't matter. That never mattered to either one of us. We fell in love and now Antonia shows back up at this pivotal time in my life, when I'm finally living the life I wanted politically and personally and now both are in jeopardy. I need to fix things with Nichelle, but first, I need to deal with my ex-wife or she'll keep coming back bringing her brand of drama and that could potentially push Nichelle further away from me."

Tucker let the silence after his last words live in the air. He wasn't as concerned about his career as he was about losing Nichelle. To him, that was unacceptable unless she never wanted to see him again. She couldn't possibly hold him responsible for something he didn't know was true. If she could just answer his calls, he could explain. The minute he let himself feel again, he was close to losing the woman he loved. He wasn't going to let Antonia destroy something that meant everything to him.

"Don't let it happen. I can hear and feel your love for Nichelle, so don't give up on it. You know the state I was in when I didn't fight for Sienna when she divorced me. I had an error in judgement in a hotel room with a woman I had no business being with and that error tore my perfect life with my wife apart. I didn't fight. I gave in to her need to be away from me, something I understood. I let her go and then one day I realized, I shouldn't have given up like that. I knew she was hurt and I wanted to ease that hurt. I figured staying away and giving her the divorce was what was best for her even though it wasn't what I thought was best for me. I look back now and I realize that if I had let go for good, I wouldn't have her in my life while I'm living my best life. I wouldn't have Symone or my son that Sienna is carrying. My business was always on point, but I would give up every ounce of it to have my life with Sienna and my kids. They are all that matter. If Nichelle gives you the kind of joy you have always wanted in your life and I'm not talking about what you expect when in love; I'm talking about when everything is unconditional and you breathe new life every day you wake up to that life, then yeah, you fight for it. I chose to not let go and that was the best choice I've ever made. Don't let go of Nichelle if she is who you want. Leslie can help you with your ex-wife even if she now wants to come back because of a paperwork glitch. Have the life you want personally and professionally. Nichelle may just need a few days, but at the end of that, be there when she's ready to listen. Have the answers she needs and you can only get them from Antonia. Have you spoken to her?"

Tucker stood and paced around his office. It was this kind of encouragement that he needed. That's why he appreciated friends like Carter.

"I haven't. Antonia called here this morning and asked to speak with me, but I was in a meeting. She's staying at a hotel here in the city and I'm sure I'll get the chance to talk to her. I need to connect with Leslie first, get her on retainer and then find out if she thinks it's a good idea to meet with

Antonia without legal representation present for both of us."

"Do you still have feelings for Antonia?"

"No. Nothing like what I had back when we were married and nothing like what I feel for Nichelle. I care about Antonia, but I'm not in love with her."

"She's going to play games because she's scheming. Be ready for that and make sure you are on guard. Protect Nichelle from her because if you don't, Reese will show up and snatch Antonia's wig off with her head still in it. She does not play with it comes to her brother and sister," Carter said and laughed.

"I hear you and I know of Reese's reputation."

"Let me tell you about that reputation. You know, her firm has been doing the marketing and promotion for the campaign and that part of her you know, but when anyone pricks that web she has encased around her family and close friends, they'll never recover from her wrath. I'm meeting with her and your publicity team later this week. I also recommend we add on an additional image consultant. She can help with any clean-up we may end up having to do if Antonia brings more trouble. When I say protect Nichelle, I'm not speaking of protecting her from the spotlight of being involved with you. I'm talking about protecting her from whatever Antonia has planned because if it gets out of control, Reese is going to pound and things will get really ugly."

"I hear you and I understand. Look, I appreciate the talk. I know we didn't dive into anything business related and I don't want to tie up your entire day. What I really needed was this talk and this boost to get my personal life in gear."

"Hey, that's what our friendship is all about. You were

there for me when I was going through and I'll always be here for you. We need to get together for a game of pool or just hang out and get some drinks. I'm thinking of having a few guys over soon, get the grill fired up and playing a few hands of poker. You in?"

"I'm am there. Downtime is a necessity when it comes to dealing with Antonia. I've learned that from our past and I have a feeling, the worse is yet to come."

"I agree and I hope you're ready. I'll call you in a few days to follow-up on next steps with the campaign. There are some scheduled appearances I want to talk to you about and some that I'm not sure you should accept right now, but we don't have to deal with that today. I also added two new speech writers to the campaign. Both worked for Barack Obama when he was running for office. They'll be great additions."

"Great! How did you get them?"

"The former President, who is also my forever President is a big fan of Jermony. He made a call on my behalf."

"Man, it pays off to know people, especially Jermony."

"That's for sure."

"I look forward to meeting them. Kiss Sienna and Symone for me and thanks again for listening and for the advice."

"Anytime. Pass me to Adrienne so that I can give her Leslie's contact information. Don't forget to call her today. I'm about to shoot her a text that you're going to reach out to her because you need her help immediately."

"On it!" Tucker shouted.

Putting Carter on hold, he walked over to the door to let Adrienne know to pick up the line. When he looked up, he saw Omar coming down the hall. Was he just returning from lunch? He remembered seeing him leave two hours ago after getting a phone call.

"Omar, can you step in here for a minute?"

Besides his extra hour for lunch, he had another issue to raise with him.

"Uh, sure," Omar said and looked to Adrienne who cut her eyes away from him and picked up the line that Carter was waiting on.

As soon as Omar was in his office, Tucker sat behind his desk while his executive officer stood in front of it. He took a few minutes to flip through some papers on this desk, giving himself time to choose his words. He wasn't happy with the job Omar had been doing lately and he seem to have a habit of disappearing when there was work to do. He looked up when Omar didn't move to sit down; his choice.

"Are you just getting back from lunch?"

"Um, well, yeah. I forgot I had a doctor's appointment and I remembered it when I left to grab a sandwich. The office was about forty minutes away, so I'm a bit late coming back."

"You look a little disheveled. Did you roll around on the exam table? Your clothes are more wrinkled than they were this morning. I need you to make sure you look better than this because you represent me. Adrienne needs some extra help today with a lot of calls she needs to make about the new citizen's patrol league who will be meeting with top police officials to talk about crime in the city. She's overwhelmed and I'm not getting from you what you're paid to do. You've worked for me a lot of years, so you know what to expect. I hope the extended lunch served you well on the constituent's dime. Find an hour to give back tomorrow. Now, I need you to get me the numbers for the toy donation drive for this year and make sure we have a bigger location for the senior's luncheon that I host every year. I'd like more vendors to share information on finances and health for seniors. I also want to make sure there is someone taking down concerns from them on the things that they struggle with the most like water bills, light bills and basic needs like food and prescriptions. You also need to look over the resumes of the applicants for interns for this year. Last year we had five high school seniors and five college students. With the additional funding we have available this year, I'd like to add two more high school students and three more college students. There is a lot that they can help with and I need you to work up a plan for where they are needed the most and base the selections on how incoming interns would fit according to background, skill and their future plans. Lean toward those who are interested in a future as public servants. They will glean the most from the experience. Remember, when you're out longer than you usually are for lunch and it's not a scheduled meeting or appearance, let Adrienne know so that she can plan for your absence. I hope you enjoyed your lunch."

When Omar fake coughed into his closed fist, Tucker didn't know what to make of it, especially when Omar wouldn't look him in the eye. He was hiding something. He would need to keep an eye on him, especially in a year when his campaign was taking off. He couldn't afford to have any loose ends or misplaced loyalties. Omar's lack of interest in his work and in politics in general lately could be a sign that his time working for the city was coming to an end. He didn't want anyone working for him who didn't want to be there.

"I did enjoy it, very much. I'll get right on those things you need and my apologies for getting back so late. I don't usually do that. I've had some things on my mind lately and I guess I'm letting it get the best of me. I'm working it out. Again, sorry."

Tucker nodded his head and Omar turned to leave. As he did, Tucker realized he forgot to question Omar about telling Adrienne about what happened at the fundraiser. He knew his assistant would find out, but he didn't like the idea that it appeared Omar was gossiping. He needed those closest to him to know how to keep his business to themselves. He trusted Omar, but something was rubbing him the wrong way since the night of the fundraiser. Omar had been acting strange all night that night, watching the door as if he was waiting on someone to show up. Whatever it was or whatever was going on with him, Tucker knew he'd keep it on his radar. He had a lot at stake.

**

Antonia woke from an afternoon nap that she hadn't planned on taking and realized it was pitch black outside. She didn't know how long she'd been asleep. Looking for her phone, she checked the time and sat straight up in bed. No longer naked, after Omar left, she'd taken a hot shower to wash the scent of him from her body and put on a long t-shirt. She crawled back into bed after changing the sheets and started checking social media sites for posts about the last season of her show, especially the first of three reunion shows with the cast. There were still two more that needed to air. She saw that the show was trending, but there wasn't much talk about her other than how mean and nasty she was and how she should never be trusted as anyone's friend. She smiled knowing that this was the kind of talk she needed to happen about her. Now, all she needed to do was create some mess with Tucker and his tart and she could even be trending soon. It was every star's desire to be trending on social media. Even bad press was great press and most drummed up their own drama to keep their names on the social media sites. She may have to do the same thing.

Before long, she had nodded off and now found herself much too late to pay a visit to Tucker. She'd try another day. Tomorrow, she was going to meet up with some old friends in town for drinks and dinner and hoped that some of them would have some good gossip about Tucker that she could use. She was tossing in everything including the kitchen sink if it meant getting rid of Nichelle and having getting her husband back. She didn't care what she needed to do to make it happen.

Since she had no place to go at this hour, she got back into bed, logged out of her personal social media accounts and logged into a few of her fake accounts in order to post some negative drama on a few of her legit posts. She learned that trick from some of the biggest celebrities who found that no one paid them any attention unless there were negative, scathing posts to counter everything they say. She would spend the rest of the night pretty much fighting with herself and hoped that others would chime in. It's all about staying in the public eye, especially when the competition was thick with other reality show personalities. The ones in Atlanta and Potomac, Maryland were huge as well as the Basketball Wives series. She didn't want anyone to be as big as she was planning to be. She knew that these days, fake news was just as popular as real news and if fake news and posts was what she needed to drum up interest in her and her show, she was all about that life.

That life was going to secure her place with a better life and that's all she's ever dreamed of. She'd seen so much wealth after moving to Los Angeles and living in an expensive Malibu house for the show and with Shadow. She wanted her own. She didn't want to share a space with anyone, unless it was by choice. She didn't want to worry about money and looked to the day when she could set up automatic payments for her bills and not even think about them each month. Her time was now and if Tucker knew what was good for him, he would help her or suffer the consequences to his personal and political life. She didn't care which part of him she had to take down to get what she needed.

7

"It's been a week," Tucker said from the back seat of his state government-issued truck. He looked up from his iPad where he'd been working on pointers for an upcoming event where he would be the keynote speaker. This was the first speech he'd received from Carter that was written by his new writers and he was already impressed. They not only hit on all the important issues, but the wording matched the way he talked.

After a long week, he was happy to be leaving City Hall at a decent hour. He couldn't remember the last time he was heading away from the office before his staff, but at seven in the evening, that's exactly what he was doing. His plan for the evening consisted of a visit from his sister, Bailee, who he had not talked to since the fundraiser. Thankfully, she and his sister, Amanda, who had also come out that night to support him, had no idea of the drama that happened behind the scenes and literally, behind the curtain at the casino. He hadn't shared anything with them about the woman he'd fallen madly in love with, keeping it even from them because he wanted to respect Nichelle's request for privacy. He thought again about it being an entire week since he'd last heard Nichelle's voice or seen her and the space he's given her along with the privacy she wanted was weighing on him. He was glad when Bailee called and brightened his day with a suggestion of a visit to catch up along with her treat of Chinese food from his favorite spot, Lao Sze Chuan on Michigan Ave.

"Still nothing?" Tellis asked from the driver's seat.

"Nothing at all. No return call, text message, not even a smoke signal. No communication at all. I know I'm going crazy missing her and I can't believe she's not missing me as much. I mean, that may seem vain, but really? She doesn't even want to hear from me? I've never had that kind of non-response from a woman before. Whew! If I didn't love her so much, I wouldn't care and would have moved on by now. She got me man; she got me."

Tucker shut his iPad off. He was no longer interested in anything work related.

"At least you've been busy as ever this week. Tia was asking me about you last night. She's still having that couple's night out at the house this weekend and wondered if you were still coming and bringing your plus-one. I told her I would check. She's been complaining about not seeing her brother from another mother in a while and was happy to hear you would be coming and bringing someone. You don't usually bring jump-offs to public functions and she was curious about who the mystery woman was."

"Man, don't call women jump-offs and I'm only letting it slide when you're referencing Nichelle because Tia doesn't know who my plus-one was going to be. You know I hate that kind of term describing our beautiful black women, anyway. True, they are friends-with-benefits, but even women friends like that I hold up with the utmost respect."

"I know and you know I don't mean Nichelle. Tia just assumed you were bringing a friend-with-benefit. I'm just saying it that way because it's just you and me. I would never speak that to anyone else but you. What should I tell Tia now that I know things are not going well with Nichelle? By now, your relationship was supposed to be public the night of the fundraiser, so bringing her to the party would be a natural thing. Tia would really love Nichelle, especially from the makeup artist perspective. You know it's been hard keeping information about your relationship from her. You know she did everything to get information out of me about the mysterious woman coming to our house. Dude, she even tried to withhold that good stuff from me."

They laughed together. Tucker looked out of the closed, tinted window of the truck as they drove through downtown traffic. He knew that the happiest day of Tellis' life was the day Tia agreed to marry him and rescue him from his bachelorhood.

He knew that talk around town about his own personal life that had floated around about him before and after being married to Antonia was about his prowess when it came to his sex life, something he never tried to hide from anyone. He believed that as long as both parties knew what was up, there was no harm in indulging in some hot, sexy adult fun and he was never without that.

Tellis, at one time, had been right out there with him and when Tia came along, his buddy was ready, willing and did let that life go. He understood the love they had and thought he had finally found that with Nichelle.

"Not Tia! She didn't really try to hold out on you, did she?

But then again, she does carry your balls around in her bag!"

"Bruh, don't even try that with me. I'm not the one in the backseat sulking and on the verge of tears because my heart is broken. I was about to tell you to man-up, but then I am one of a few who know what Nichelle means to you."

"You're the *ONLY* one who knows that. A few more people know since the night of the fundraiser, like Carter and his wife, but for the most part, their knowledge of what Nichelle and I have is surface. Only you know the real details. Only you have seen me with her."

"Yeah. I have to admit that I miss having her in the backseat with you and seeing how happy she makes you. I've known you since, what, elementary school and I have never, ever seen you look at any woman the way you look at her, not even Antonia. Speaking of her, what's the latest on her? Have you talked to her?"

Tucker didn't want to think about her and least of all, he didn't want to talk to her. He was still trying to figure out how to handle her. For the most part, he was now able to exhale a little more than he had earlier in the week because he had finally connected with his new attorney, Leslie and she promised him she was on top of the situation. She also told him that there was no reason that he couldn't have a civil chat with Antonia as long as they didn't talk about any side deals to get her to sign the new papers. He was not to negotiate anything with her, but if he could get a look into her angle for why she's trying to get back with him other than her claim that she wants to be first lady of Chicago, she would love to get that information. What he would not do was compromise any of who he was or put his relationship with Nichelle at risk trying to catch onto what Antonia has planned.

"I haven't, but I plan to. She's been calling the office and my personal cell phone, but I've been holding off on anymore encounters with her. I've been focused on work and on Nichelle. My ex-wife is not on my list of priorities right now."

"Do you watch her television show?" Tellis asked.

Tucker looked at him through the rear-view mirror with a look that said he was being ridiculous.

"Have you *EVER* known me to watch *ANY* reality show? Come on, man. You didn't meet me yesterday. You know that's not my cup of tea."

"I'm just saying – you were married to her and I didn't know if Nichelle liked that sort of thing when it comes to those shows. She's got you all wrapped up and I was sure that if she watched it, you were all cuddled up somewhere with her being drawn in!"

"Ah, okay. I'm only taking these kinds of jokes from you and no one else. Nah, Nichelle never watches that stuff. She hates to see women, especially black women, go at each other like that, tearing each other down for a few dollars considering the fortune the networks and producers are making off of them tearing each other apart. Nichelle is more of an action, drama, science-fiction kind of woman, something I discovered that first day when we ran into each other at my favorite deli. It wasn't until I went to her place for the first time that I realized how much we really had in common. The woman must have over two hundred movies in her possession and most are films with black leads, action movies and most of all, sci-fi stuff. I mean, she has my favorite series, The Matrix, including the animated, Animatrix. She has all of the Planet of the Apes DVDs, the original series of movies that starred Charlton Heston. She has all the Star Wars movie, all the Star Trek motion pictures and even the Serenity movie and the Firefly series. I thought she would be into romance, you know, stuff like that. She loves romance novels, but as far as movies, she loves action and adventure."

"Seriously? That is you all the way!"

Tucker nodded.

"Exactly. I told her I practically had a mirror image of all the movies she had. She discovered I wasn't lying the first time she came to my house. When I tell you we love a lot of the same things when it comes to what entertains us, to what we love to eat, it's not a joke. She is my spirit equal, man," Tucker admitted.

"I hope this all means you're not giving up on her. I really like her. I was a little hesitant when you told me how old she was, but I can see how that wouldn't matter because seeing the two of you together was like watching my own road to love and marriage. You and Nichelle have that thing between you that could be forever and I know you want that. I never thought you had that with Antonia. I know you loved her and I know at one point she loved you, but that deep connection and that drive on the path together to building your future as a couple was missing."

"Bruh, have you heard me pouring my heart out here? Of course, I'm not giving up on her. I'm going to marry her; she just doesn't know it yet. I knew that from the moment I met her. I don't know how to explain that exactly, but I know that she's the one for me."

Tucker heard himself say the words and that didn't scare him. After his marriage to Antonia ended, he declared he'd remain single and focused only on his career in politics, never allowing a woman to get close to him again, but fate had a few tricks for him that he was unaware of and now, he was more than happy to say he was on board for a life with Nichelle if she would just talk to him.

"It's the weekend. What are your plans? Are you going to try and connect with Nichelle, since I'm pretty sure you're not coming to our gig, and that's fine? I understand. You know Tia; she will have another one soon."

Tucker sat up straight in the backseat and thought about his weekend plans. He didn't have much planned other than hanging with his sister tonight and, tomorrow, he was meeting Carter and a few other guys to play pool and hit a few cigars at their favorite place on the south side. His plans were all good, but they weren't what he would choose for himself. Without answering Tellis, he pulled out his cellphone and like all week long, he was going to leave Nichelle another voicemail message. He would cancel all plans if he could reach her. He had to find a way to turn his life and his love around. He couldn't go another week wondering how much she was hurting and he didn't want he going through her feelings without him. They needed to be together to solidify what they had against every force that was coming to destroy them – especially in the form of his ex-wife.

He looked at his phone and secretly hoped that the fate that was with him the day he'd met her was also with him as he was prepared to hope beyond hope that she was ready to hear from him. All he had at this point was hope.

8

Tucker dialed the familiar number, breathing heavily with each number he pushed. Her number was programmed into his speed dialing, but he wanted to dial the actual number. His silent prayer was to hear it ring.

After hitting the last number, he expected it to roll right into voicemail, but this time – it didn't. The phone actually rang.

"Hello."

Tucker almost leaped out of his seat when he heard the sweet sound of her voice. It wasn't enough for him that he could call and hear her voice on the recorded message. He needed to talk to her and he was now, finally getting his chance.

"Baby. Wow, you actually answered. I've been calling you all week. I miss you. I'm glad you turned your phone back on or were you just sending my calls directly to voicemail?" he asked. "Are you okay?"

"I'm doing fine and I'm sorry about ignoring you for a week. I just needed a little time," Nichelle said.

Tucker exhaled loudly and when he looked up, he smiled at Tellis who gave him a thumbs up over his shoulder. He was already feeling rejuvenated as if he hadn't spent the entire day in City Council meetings talking until his throat was dry.

"I understand that. Have you been listening to my messages? We need to talk about all of this and I swear, I had no idea I was still married to Antonia. I also had no clue she was in Chicago. We haven't been in contact in over a year. She just showed up out of nowhere."

"So, it is true that you're still married? That's been confirmed?" she asked.

"Yes. My old attorney let the ball drop on that. I have a new attorney who is working to make sure that situation gets rectified immediately."

"Still, this could work against you running for Mayor and all. What if you had introduced me at the fundraiser and then word got out that you are still legally married? I don't want anything to keep you from fulfilling your dream of becoming Mayor. You've come too far and your ex-wife is off the chain. Did you hear she's all over social media giving hints of something she'll be revealing that will rock the world of her fans? She's trying to allude to her marriage to you, saying she's going to reveal a true side-piece who's trying to ruin her life. Is she talking about me? This could get really bad, really fast."

Tucker could hear the worry in her voice and he knew the kind of antics Antonia could deliver, but he wasn't going to get caught up in that and he didn't want Nichelle to be worried about that either.

"Stop reading the blogs and social media posts. You now know what she's about and it's best to stay far away from it. I'm getting my lawyer all over this, but don't let her drama keep us apart. I promise you that this will all get worked out. We are in this together. It's just you and me – three's a crowd. I prefer how the two of us tangle. I miss you, baby. Have you missed me?" he asked.

At this point, Tucker didn't care how his words made him sound. He knew some men never spoke from their heart thinking it made them sound soft, but he never wanted Nichelle to think that she had to pull, beg or plead for his love and affection. He gave it easily because that's how much he loved and adored her.

"I miss you, too. I'm sorry about this week. My sister came by on Monday and really let me have it because I was ignoring her calls, too. I see how wrong and hurtful that is and I didn't want to do that to you. I know this isn't your fault. You wouldn't mislead me into thinking you weren't still married and besides, all the secrecy was my idea and not yours," she admitted.

"Baby, you know that if I could scream my love for you from the highest mountain, I would do it in a heartbeat and damned the repercussions from anyone who thinks I'm not entitled to live my life because of a paperwork error. Can I see you? I love hearing your voice over the phone and I'm glad you answered, but what I need is to see you and hold you in my arms. What are you doing tonight?"

"Nothing. I just got in from work. I did have a client who needed her makeup done for a television show, but her appointment was postponed until tomorrow evening. I was planning to relax at home, do some laundry and catch up on my reading. What are you up to?"

"At the moment, I'm in the truck with Tellis."

"Hey, Nichelle!" Tellis yelled over his shoulder.

Tucker smiled when he heard Nichelle laugh on the other end.

"Tell him I said hello."

"Nichelle said hello," he relayed.

Tellis gave him another thumbs-up.

"Where are you headed, to a meeting or other event?" she asked.

"No. For a change, I don't have any events or meetings tonight. Unable to reach you, I was going home for a much-needed relaxed Friday night. I prefer spending my downtime with you. Can I see you?" he asked again.

Tucker waited through what seemed an eternity as Nichelle thought through allowing him back in, even if it was just to talk and see each other for a few hours. At this point, he would take whatever he could get. He would be okay with her telling him he could drive by and wave from the truck. Yeah, he was a lost cause. He was glad he didn't speak that out loud. Tellis would have crashed the truck after that comment. He laughed to himself at the idea and visual.

"Yes. Do you think it's safe? I mean, what if your wife has someone following you around to get pictures of us or something? You have to think about your bid for Mayor, Tucker. I don't want anything to jeopardize that."

"She's my ex-wife and this is why I love you so much. In the midst of this, you are still thinking of me. I love you for that baby and I don't care is someone is following me around and if so, I hope they get pictures from my good side. I care more about seeing you right now than anything. I can be there in an hour."

"Don't come through the front. Use the underground garage like you usually do. At least no one can get in without a passcode and identification. I miss you, too."

Tucker was ready to dance in his seat. He'd been waiting a week to hear her voice and to see her. His day, his week was officially being made.

"I'll bring dinner. What do you have a taste for?"

"Are you still downtown?"

"That sounds like you want food from the deli," he laughed.

"Exactly. I'll see you soon?"

"Don't blink, baby, or you'll miss me. I'm going to run home, get a shower, change, get our food and I'll have Tellis drop me off in the underground garage. I love you, baby," he said.

"I love you, too."

Tucker waited to hear those words and was glad to know that their love was not spoiled due to Martin's oversight. Hearing her disconnect the call, he looked up and found Tellis shaking his head from side to side.

"I see my balls aren't the only ones a woman is dangling in her bag!"

Tucker laughed so hard, he had to cough out a choke.

"No shame here, brother and I know you have no shame over how Tia's got you. I don't care what anyone says or thinks about men this in love – there is no better feeling than having a solid vibe with the woman you love."

"None for me either!" Tellis laughed along with him. "Did you forget Bailee is coming over tonight for some brother, sister time?"

"Shoot! I did forget. I heard Nichelle's voice and I forgot about everything else in the world."

"You better call her before she heads your way."

Tellis dialed Bailee and she answered on the first ring.

"You're calling to cancel, right?" Tucker heard Bailee say before he could get a word out.

"I'm sorry, sis. I promise I will make this up to you. Can I get a raincheck? I'll be home all-day Sunday. Let's meet at the gym and then I'll buy you lunch anywhere you want to go or we can do Chinese at my house that evening. You know I wouldn't cancel without a good reason."

He hoped Bailee wouldn't ask him why he's cancelling. He didn't want to have to lie to her, but he would. He had no choice.

"Yeah, that's fine. My friends were begging me to hang out tonight. This allows me to stop being anti-social, as I'm being called. I just miss talking to you and we need to catch up. I also need your help with something."

Tucker waited before responding. He heard the hesitation in her voice and didn't know what direction she was leaning it.

"You need my help as your brother or as the Vice Mayor?"

"As my brother. I saw a used car on Carter's dealership website. I want to trade my car in. Do you think you can help me get a good deal through him? I wouldn't usually ask for you to use your connections, but I really, really like it and it can be in the budget I have if you can get me a deal. Can you help?"

Tucker laughed.

"So, that's what tonight was going to be about? You buying me dinner to butter me up? I see you."

"Don't think like that. I really did want to hang out with you tonight and I still will if you want to. You know you're my favorite brother."

"Bai, I'm your only brother, so that won't work, but it's all good. I'll call Carter and see about the car. Text me the information on it and I'll still need the raincheck on tonight. Love you, sis. I'll call you Sunday morning to see if you're up for meeting."

"I will and call Amanda. She's heading to Florida in a month with the kids to visit mom and dad and I think she wants you and me to go with her. I wasn't sure you were free to be gone with all you have going on with work and then the campaign. She said she was going to check with you."

"Thanks for the heads-up. I should be able to make the time, but not in a month, probably the summer though. I'm going to invite mom and dad to come for a big press conference I'll have soon, so we'll all get to visit with them. This summer, I think we should all go to Florida. We can talk about that on Sunday. Be safe hanging out tonight and remember to not accept a drink from anyone and don't leave a drink sitting without your eyes on it at all times."

"Always the big brother. Love you."

"Love you, too."

Tucker ended the call, leaned back against the black leather seat and closed his eyes. Things on a personal level were finally looking up. There was still drama on the horizon, but for tonight, he wouldn't have to focus on it. He could give all of his attention to Nichelle.

Just as he was about to put his cell phone away, it vibrated. Thinking it may be Nichelle, he checked it and, instead, found a text from Omar.

Omar: *'Boss, you coming back or done for the evening?'*

That was an unusual text, but Tucker decided to play along.

Tucker: *'I'm out until Monday – getting a breather. What's up?'*

Omar: *'Nothing. Just checking. We can follow-up with those few action items next week. Just wondering if I should stick around or leave.'*

Tucker: *'Leave and enjoy your weekend.'*

Omar: *'On it. U too.'*

Tucker finally did put his phone away and tried to not focus on anything work related. He had been in the office all day and not once did Omar attempt to have a meeting. There was no way that he didn't know he had left for the day. He pretty much shouted it to his staff well over an hour ago. Omar's behavior got stranger by the day as the week went on. Something was up, but he didn't know what.

If it wasn't for Nichelle, he would think harder on it, but tonight, he didn't want to be concerned about anyone other than her.

He relaxed and hummed a familiar love song by one of his favorite old-school artists, Teddy Pendergrass. The song, *"In My Time"* came to mind. It was a favorite of his and once he'd introduced the song and its lyrics to Nichelle, it was now one of her favorites. He was planning on listening to it with her later.

**

Omar looked around the outer office, happy that it appeared everyone had left for the weekend. He'd waited an hour after he saw the last person leave. Preferring to not run into anyone, he went to the men's room on another floor and waited what he thought was a good amount of time before heading back up to his office. If he was spotted, he would say he left something and had to come back for it. The only person he was worried about was Adrienne.

Though they had always had a great working relationship, she'd been looking at him strange since he told her about what happened to Tucker at the fundraiser when his ex-wife showed up. He felt like extra eyes were on him as if he'd done something wrong. If anyone knew just how wrong he was, he would be in the unemployment line the next day. He needed to be more careful with being so jittery, but being with Roxie did that to him. He would call her Antonia, but that was the reserved side of her; he enjoyed the wild, undomesticated side that taught him a few new things sexually.

He'd been with a few other older women, but none like her and just the thought of her as he walked through the office, had him excited to see her again. He was so excited that if anyone walked up to him, they would see his excitement pressing against his zipper. She did that for him and he couldn't wait to get more. In order to get more, he had to get information for her and, a Friday night when all the staff had gone home, including Tucker, he felt safe knowing that he had the place to himself.

Looking left and right, he walked past Adrienne's desk and opened the door to Tucker's office. If he was going to find out anything, it would probably be somewhere in his office.

Leaving the office door wide open, he looked through the papers and files on the desk, making sure to put them back exactly as he found them after looking them over. Rethinking his strategy, he figured there may not be much in his office that would tell a story. If there was anything to be found, it would be found at Adrienne's desk. She knew everything about Tucker's life, business and personal. He knew that she kept his business calendar, but she also seemed to know a lot about his personal whereabouts and that's what Roxie needed.

Checking for any sound around the office and not hearing any, he left Tucker's office and walked over to Adrienne's cube and started looking around. He flipped through papers and folders and didn't see much. He knew she kept an electronic calendar, but she also kept a paper copy since electronics couldn't be as dependable as a good old-fashioned paper calendar. Checking her office drawers, he found them locked and then remembered seeing her put a taped key under the center desk drawer. Swiping his fingers across the flat under bottom of the drawer, he smiled when his fingers encountered the key. Pulling the taped key out, he looked at it, tossing it back and forth between his fingers. Not many others did the whole lock and key thing, but in her position, she probably held secrets; secrets he need to know about.

What Antonia needed most right now was where Tucker could be reached when he was out of the office. She wanted to know if there was any record of where Nichelle lived or when he was scheduled to see her. Was that something Adrienne would even have a record of? He wasn't sure, but he was about to find out.

Just as he put the key in the lock, he heard the elevator ding in the hallway and he felt a rush of fear run through his bones. Someone was coming. Without time to go any further, he quickly ran the tape back across the key and haphazardly placed it back under the drawer and rushed in the opposite direction, thankful for the rubber bottom shoes he'd worn to work. The sound of him rushing away would be hushed.

Making his way down the back hallway, Omar didn't wait

to see who was coming. If he saw them, they may actually see him too. Opening the door to the back stairs, he closed the door softly behind him and took the steps two at a time. There would be another day and he would get what he needed or he risked not getting another night of wild sex with Roxie and that was unacceptable.

**

Adrienne heard a sound because she was listening for one. She had been on her way home when she received a text from Tucker asking where she was. When she told him she'd finally left the office, he asked her if anyone else was there when she left; specifically, Omar who had just texted him. She confirmed that Omar had said goodnight thirty minutes before she left and she was sure he wasn't in the office anywhere, so she didn't know why he would say he was still around.

Though Tucker didn't ask her to, she had just reached the garage when she decided to go back. Something was bothering her boss about Omar. She could sense it all week and besides that, Omar had been acting really odd, especially with his disappearing acts throughout the week. He had also been asking too many questions about Tucker and Nichelle. They were the only two who knew about the relationship and for months, Omar never asked a question. Now, he seemed to be overly interested in what was going on between them as if he was fishing for information. What she didn't know was why.

When she exited the elevator, she thought she saw a flash of someone rushing away from the office down the back hallway. Staff used those stairs in the back to go between floors quickly because the elevator could take forever, but no one should be on the floor where the Tucker and his staff worked. Other than Tucker, she was usually the last to leave the office on any given day. Who could still be around? Could it be Omar as was suggested?

Walking over to her desk, she looked around and saw no one and nothing seemed out of place. She checked Tucker's office, opening the door slightly and finding it as it was when she left earlier, she shut the door back and this time, she locked it. She wasn't concerned since she and Tucker both had keys. For the first time in a long time, she felt uneasy about leaving the door unlocked. Anyone coming or going from the floor would be seen by the guard once they exited the elevator. If they entered via the back stairwell, there was a passcode for that door that only staff used. If someone had come up after hours, they would have had to use their code.

Checking her desk once more, she was about to leave when something shiny on the floor caught her eye. Moving her chair out of the way, she leaned down and picked up the key that she kept taped under the desk. It had fallen to the floor. For a second, she didn't think anything about it and was about to put it back when she noticed the tape was placed across the key the long way. She always placed the tape across the short way to be sure more of the tape ended up on the drawer than on the key, making sure it stayed put.

Standing to her full height and checking out the key, she knew that her suspicion was correct. She did see someone moving away from the office quickly and she had an idea of who it was. Tucker was feeling some kind of way without saying so and now she was too. Taking the key with her instead of replacing it, she went back to the elevator and asked the guard if anyone from the staff had been lingering around after she left. At first the guard said no, but he mentioned he'd gotten up to get a bottle of water from the vending machine next to the elevator and he thought he saw Omar close the door to Tucker's office. He assumed he was working late.

Adrienne thanked him and got on the elevator and waited for the door to close.

"What are you up to Omar and why are you sneaking around after hours?"

9

Tucker called Nichelle the moment he got in the elevator of the apartment building where she lived. After arriving home after work, Tellis left him to shower and dress. He moved around quickly knowing that though Tellis had left and told him he'd be back shortly, he needed to be ready when he returned.

When Tellis did return and backed into the right side of the two-car garage in the back of the house, Tucker added a black Nike cap to his black and gray Nike sweat suit and matching sneakers. Whether he was dressed up or dressed down, he liked looking good, especially since he was finally getting the chance to see the love of his life. Hopping into the passenger seat of Tellis' black Mustang with dark tinted windows, Tucker now knew why his friend didn't want to wait for him to get dressed. He needed to change cars and without even asking, Tucker knew why. With all the clandestine activities they've had to go through for him to spend time with Nichelle over the past few months, this was another way for them to move about town without being seen.

After getting to the underground garage at Nichelle's building, Tucker paused before exiting the car.

"You know I appreciate how you've gone above and beyond to help me out with Nichelle and helping me spend time with her without too many eyes on what I'm doing. I hate that I have to even do this. I should be able to love my woman, be seen with her and show her off to the world. She's the most incredible, the most beautiful woman I've ever laid my eyes on. I'm lucky to have her."

"You're preaching to the choir. I understand totally. She's just as lucky to have you in her life. I'm pissed that at this time in your life when you are at your happiest and things are going your way, you still have to hide like some criminal. And now, Antonia with her mess is causing you to prolong living your life out in the open. I hope you do get to talk to her soon and get more insight into her angle, but for now, go on and enjoy your night. Call when you need a ride back home and I'll come to get you."

"Nope. We're not doing that. You go home, enjoy your downtime with your wife. I'll figure out how to get home, depending on the time. It's the weekend and consider yourself off for the next few days. I'll see you Monday morning at six and not before then. I'm serious, bro. Don't call me to find out if I've got something I need because I'm not going to need anything. Everything I need, right now, is on the fifth floor of this building. Kiss Tia for me and we'll catch up on Monday. Thanks for doing all this," Tucker said and exited the truck in front of the elevator where Tellis had dropped him off.

Now, in the elevator, he smiled when Nichelle answered on the first ring when he took out his phone to call her. This time, he did use the speed dial.

"Hi, beautiful. I'm in the elevator on my way up."

"Okay. I'm here."

Tucker disconnected the call and held tight to the flowers in one hand and the bag of food in his other that Tellis had stopped to pick up on their way to the apartment. When the elevator stopped, he stepped out and walked past three doors until he got to Nichelle's. Before he could knock, the door opened and on the other side was the most beautiful sight he'd ever seen; his love. With the distance between them for a week, he wasn't sure what to do first, hug her, kiss her or wait for her to decide what should occur between them. He tried to wait a respectable amount of time before seizing the opportunity to do what he'd been thinking about all week, but even that was too long.

Sitting the bag of food down on the small table by the door, he pushed the door closed behind them and pulled Nichelle into his arms. Before she could say a word, his lips captured hers and everything was right in the world. He heard her moan of pleasure, a sound he'd come to love hearing when she was in his arms. Her response to his touch, his caress, his love, his kiss – all delighted him in the best way. Hearing it now brought back memories of the last time he held her this way the night of the fundraiser before the ground opened up and swallowed his happiness with the appearance of Antonia.

What he thought would be a quick, sexy kiss turned into a passionate, fiery one as he pulled her closer, allowing his mouth to mate with hers with exhilarating zeal that he felt cascading over his entire body.

The moment Nichelle's arms landed on his shoulders and

he could feel her lean up on her toes, he held her as tight as he could with one arm and loved her mouth, caressing her lips from one end to the other, kissing and stroking the top and then giving the same attention to the bottom. The moment his body began to react to their closeness, he slowly pulled back and smiled at the look of her now, thoroughly kissed, puckered up lips.

"Hello. I needed that," he shared.

"Wow!" Nichelle said in response.

Tucker smiled when she reached up and wiped his lips, most likely removing the thin sheen of lip gloss that had transferred from her lips to his. That was a ritual between them, though he loved having her essence remain on his lips following a kiss.

"Wow is right and I can't believe I went an entire week without kissing you like that."

"I know and I'm sorry. I guess I was being immature, huh? I'm glad you weren't too angry to be patient with me."

"Baby, I understand and it's okay. It was hard being away from you like that, but I knew you were working your way through what her return could mean for us. Here, I almost forgot I had these in my other hand. My mind was so focused on getting a kiss."

Tucker lifted the yellow and orange roses between them and watched Nichelle's face light up with appreciation. He loved bringing her flowers and from the way she always reacted to getting them, he always flooded her apartment with the most beautiful one's he could find.

"Oh, how beautiful!" she exclaimed.

After she leaned up and placed a soft, sweet kiss on his lips, he watched her walk away into the kitchen. He took in everything about her, not knowing if after today, she'd take another break from him. He needed to get his fill while he could. He smiled at her casual attire for a Friday evening. She was dressed in yellow shorts, a white tank top and her long, wavy hair was pulled up into a tight bun.

"How was work this week?" he asked, not mentioning the fact that he knew she called out sick both Monday and Tuesday.

He allowed his eyes to follow her every move as she reached into the cabinet under the sink and pulled out a vase, one he recognized that he'd given her complete with flowers before. As she moved about the kitchen, he stood still and waited for her to rejoin him.

"Well, I took off earlier in the week and the rest of the week was crazy busy with sessions I had scheduled with parents of some of the kids who require closer monitoring. That was exhausting, but also fulfilling. I didn't realize how much I would love working with children."

After watching her place the vase in the center of her dining room table, Tucker's eyes followed her as she walked over to the sectional and sat down with him close behind her.

The room had a nice soft glow from the lighting from the lamps on the side of the chairs and the one soft light from the lamp at the door. The only other light was from the glare of the television screen. He was still able to see her radiance and that was all that mattered.

"You were meant for that kind of work," he said, sitting and diving into the conversation with her.

"I think I mentioned that my initial plan was to work with seniors and then I changed that and was going to work with young adults and then I realized, I wanted to work with children young enough to hopefully have a positive impact on their journey to teens and then young adulthood. The work can be tiresome, but well worth it when I meet with parents who tell me that my work has helped with improved behavior not only at school, but also at home. That makes it all worth it, even the tiring days like today. How was your week?"

Tucker didn't know if he should go with the work perspective or tell her what his week was like on a personal level. He knew they needed to talk, but he didn't want to jump right into being heavy. He leaned back and watched her movements, which seemed to appear as if she were uncomfortable with him being there. There has never been an odd moment between them and he wasn't liking what he was seeing. They may be conversing back and forth, but her eyes were glued to the television and not connecting with him.

"My week was crazy with meetings and trying to keep up with the large number of homicides the city is still experiencing."

"I saw you on the news a few times this week. That murder rate is getting crazy. I'm glad the people of Chicago will soon have you as the Mayor because I know you want to tackle that. How's the campaign going?"

Tucker didn't want to go through idle chatter as if they hadn't been involved in a hot, heavy and loving relationship for the past six months or so. He didn't come to see her to be distant.

"Come here, baby," he said, extending a hand to her, hoping she would take it and come close; at least slide closer to him on the sofa. They were sitting on opposite ends of the three-seat side of the sectional.

When Nichelle turned her head and looked at him, he let his eyes follow her as she stood, thinking she was going to move even further away. Instead, she walked over to him and sat across his lap. He smiled like a kid on Christmas morning.

"Sorry. I don't know what's wrong with me," she said to him.

Tucker pulled her snug against him and caressed her legs, reminding himself of what it felt like to touch her.

"You know, I didn't realize just how much I really loved you until I spent this week without you. I had many good and not so good things happen this week and I'm used to having you to talk through all of it. Not that I want to drop my bad days on you, but the sound of your voice or a hug or a kiss do go a long way in making my day. I know that no matter what I go through, I have you and you have me. I have to apologize for what happened at the fundraiser."

"I know it wasn't your fault."

Tucker leaned into her hand when she caressed the side of his face with the soft, flat palm of her hand before allowing her knuckles to caress the opposite side of his face.

"I still need to explain something so that you and I can get back on the same page. First, I want to answer any questions I know you've been holding onto all week. I'll explain what I know and let you know what I still have to find out."

"Okay. One of your messages confirmed that you are still married to Roxie or Antonia; I don't know what to call her," she said.

"I am and you can call her whatever you choose. They both apply to her. I was married to Antonia and Roxie is who she became when she realized the attention that outlandish persona got her back in college. She carried it into her career. It worked since she got that role on the reality show because of it. Yes, I am still married to her. My attorney screwed that up and I didn't know the papers were never officially filed because when she signed them, she signed with her stage name and not her legal, married name. I have a new lawyer, someone recommended by Carter and she's already working on getting the final papers signed and filed."

"She's going to fight it isn't she? I mean, she's all over social media talking about how she's about to become the next first lady, the next Michelle Obama. I know she's not talking about the presidency, but about being first lady of Chicago. She really wants it and the way she was looking at you the night of the fundraiser, she still wants you too."

"Baby, just because she may or may not still want me has nothing to do with me. I'm not in love with her, nor do I want her. I love you and nothing is going to change that."

Tucker hoped his heartfelt response was resonating with her. The last thing he wanted was for her to doubt his love. He was trying to contain his lack of patience in dealing with Antonia, at least until he's had a chance to talk to her.

"Have you seen her since that night? Have you talked to her?"

"Neither. I guess I've been avoiding doing so until my attorney gives me more advice on how to deal with her. Antonia has been leaving me messages about wanting to meet up and she keeps mentioning some plan she has that she thinks will benefit us both by staying married through the election."

When Nichelle moved as if she was going to get up from

his lap, he held her steady.

"What?" she asked softly.

"You know this is all a publicity stunt for her television show. It's what they do and she just happens to have an ace in the hole because we're still married. She wants to use that to boost ratings and her stature on the show."

"Well, what if she doesn't get her way? What will she do? You were married to her and know how she thinks. I was on Instagram not long before you arrived and I saw her put up a video asking her fans to answer questions about older men being involved with inexperienced younger women when they have vivacious, exotic, uninhibited women like her. I felt like she was trying to throw shade at me."

Tucker turned Nichelle's body around so that she was now straddling his lap with her legs on either side of his. He wanted to look her in the eyes.

"Listen to me and stop checking social media for things she says. The first thing my new lawyer did was file an injunction to keep Antonia from saying anything about our marriage, the state of it or what appears to be an upcoming battle we're going to have with her trying to stay married and me trying to push the divorce through. There are a whole lot of restrictions included in that injunction that apply to her, the show and its creators and producers. Leslie, that's the lawyer, filed that immediately and had a gag placed on anything relating to the divorce not being final after all this time. I'm sure that pissed her off. Earlier today, Leslie called to say the judge issued it immediately and by now, Antonia's attorney would have been made aware. Leslie was able to get everything done and sealed from the public eye, so for now, we're good. I want you to know that there is nothing in this world that could happen to make me stay married to Antonia by choice. I love you – I want only you," he said.

Tucker waited as their eyes remained locked on each other. He didn't want her to look away, but instead, see the sincerity she could always find in his eyes and in his words. He'd never lied to her and he never would.

"The age difference thing – is that still not a problem for you? I know it's the first thing my sister asked me about and my brother sent me a text on Sunday referencing the same thing. I was hesitant at first myself, but you have been so sure of us from day one. Are you still that sure?"

Tucker laughed. He didn't care what anybody thought about them being together. Their relationship was between the two of them and if he needed to have a sit-down with her family to reassure them that despite their age difference, he'd never met a woman more compatible with him than Nichelle, he would do it.

"Except for the disappearing act this week, I've never had an issue with any part of our relationship, especially not the age difference. I wasn't attracted to you caring about that. I was drawn to you because of the beauty you exuded not just from the moment I saw you, but from the very second that you smiled at me."

"You can have any woman you want. I see how they look at you and ogle you, sometimes openly with me close by as if I'm not even there. Your ex-wife is so beautiful, so exotic, so sexy. Men fall over themselves to be with her and she wants you. She commands a room. I can't compete with her, especially if she's setting her sights on you. The two of you have history."

"Whoa, wait a minute. I think every woman is beautiful in

her own way. There is nothing more or less from one woman to another and I believe there is someone for everyone and for me, there is you. If I was meant to be with Antonia, we would have stayed together and not forced back together in a weird way because of some paper. Do you not know how beautiful, sexy and desirable you are? I know I'm not hearing you doubting yourself. That's not like you, baby. Don't do that. You know my dating life before her and after her and yes, there were quite a few women, but when I met you, I no longer had a desire to see other women and I certainly have no desire to go back to Antonia. Women will ogle me just as men will look at you with desire. My present and my future are filled with you, baby."

"What happens now? My family now knows about us, except for my mother and I can't keep us from her much longer. Your friends all know and if it's left up to Antonia, more people will know. I know you have that injunction, but she'll figure out a way to leak it. It's what celebrities do."

"I want you and me to focus on you and me. I have people to deal with Antonia. I think we need to host a dinner with your family and then we'll have one with mine. My sisters know I'm seeing someone, but they don't know who. I'd love for you to meet them and get to know them. They are going to love you. My parents, who are in Florida, will be ecstatic to meet you. My mom knows when her children are genuinely happy and she'll be able to instantly see that you make me happier than I have ever been and that means more to me than being Mayor or anything else."

"Being Mayor is your dream."

"Yes, but more important than that, I've finally found something, someone who is more important to me than even that dream. My personal life has no place in my political space and I won't allow anyone to taint what I've done or what I can do. My principles in life are no different whether I'm married to Antonia by some fluke while in love with you by choice. I'll let the people of Chicago decide that fate, but in the meantime, you and I are the only ones who can make or break us and I'm choosing make. Any more questions about all this, especially about where I stand with you? I know we were up in the air when I took to the stage instead of coming after you knowing you were upset. It was a hard choice to make, but I had a commitment, which did not diminish my commitment to you. There is room for both. I'm making room for everything that means something to me and you're at the top of that list. I hope you never doubt that. Let me show you what I mean," he said.

10

With Nichelle snug and lovingly close to him, Tucker took both of his hands and placed them on both sides of her face, making sure they remained in a moment where doubt didn't exist. He waited for her response, but didn't really need it. Nichelle's eyes were an open book and he saw the world in them. Right now, he saw pure, uncomplicated love. She finally understood and he saw that understanding looking back at him.

When her face moved closer and closer to his, he allowed his eyes to move from her face to her lips. When hers touched his lightly, he kissed her with all the strength and love he had in him. If there was ever a time to show and prove his love for her, he wanted it to be poured out in this kiss.

Their lips connecting was the gateway to their hearts connecting. Tucker knew that if he could just convince her to see him and talk to him, he only had to look in her eyes and allow her to gaze into his in order to see that nothing was going to come between their love. For now, he didn't want to think about anything; he only wanted the two of them to feel.

The kiss turned hot real quick, the kind Tucker loved. He knew that she often questioned her intimate experience with him, a man she knew had much more experience than her, but he found his equal in their love. Not only did he show her how to love him because she was inexperienced, he was experienced and she in turn, showed him everything about loving her; pleasing and pleasuring her. It wasn't about the wildness of the act, but the connection during the act and he and Nichelle had that. Their intimate compatibility was off the charts. Even now, he could feel her winding hips as they moved around in a circular motion on his lap. They were now on the same page with all talk about anything, but their love, going out the window.

As her lips caressed his, he held her face in his soft, yet determined hold. He suckled at her lips, eliciting the kind of moan from her that drove him mad with desire. Moving his hands down to grip the soft, plump mounds of her behind through her shorts, he held on tight as her arms went around his neck. This is what he needed, what he'd been craving all week. The soft glow of the room added to the ambience of love that encased them.

When Nichelle's hips quickened on him, he knew that she was reacting to the hardness that was his love muscle, proclaiming his need for her. He didn't come to her tonight to make love, but to reassure her of his love and dedication to them. He also never turned down a chance to say and show his love. At this moment in time, their need for each other matched.

When Nichelle leaned back, out of breath and trying to compose herself, he took the time to gather his own breath.

His only thought was how could she ever think that she wasn't enough for him; that she wasn't beautiful enough or sexy enough. He didn't care how many women he'd been with, none had ever reached his heart in the way that she had.

"You brought food," she whispered between kisses.

He leaned forward and kissed along the sexy column of her neck, nuzzling and reacquainting himself with the essence of her that he'd gone a week without being this close to.

"I did and I was starving, but not anymore; not at this moment. Food won't fix the hunger I'm experiencing right now. If you want to stop and eat, there is Chinese food by the door."

"No food."

He didn't care what was next out of her mouth; he only wanted to taste.

Turning so that she was now under him on the sofa, he wrapped her sexy, long legs around his waist and settled in between them. Wasting no time, he reached down and pulled the white tank top over her head, exposing her luscious breasts to his admiration. Before his mouth touched one, he heard a sexy mewl escape her lips because as much as he knew she loved when he feasted on her, the way he enjoyed it heightened the experience for her.

His mouth went to one pointed nipple as it hardened first under his gaze and then under the pressure he applied with the pad of his tongue. Nichelle's hands went to the side of his face, holding him in place where she needed him. Little did she know, he had no plans to move away. He rolled the hardened tip between his lips, licking and suckling, leaving a path of wetness that he blew on and smiled when she lifted her hips and moved under him. He used his hand to caress the other side of her chest as he planted open mouthed kisses everywhere his mouth could reach.

"I love you, baby," he whispered sweetly.

Kissing his way down her body, he kissed across her flat stomach and continued his path down, more intent to give her complete satisfaction than he'd ever been determined to do before. There was something different about their love tonight. He loved her, but he felt the need to make sure she would never doubt that love ever again.

Lowering his hands, he sought out the edge of the elastic band of her shorts and pulled them down along with the lacy black thong under them. Leaning back, he removed them from her body leaving her splayed out before him completely naked as his eyes caught sight of her womanhood staring up at him and glistening with moisture brought on by their love. He quickly removed the jacket to his sweat suit and his shirt. His plan was to make love to her right on the sofa without thinking about any delay by heading into her bedroom. He wanted her more than his next breath.

His heart practically skipped a beat when he watched Nichelle remove the band that held her hair tight on top of her head and allowed her curly tresses to fall freely about the chair. Before him lay an exotic beauty, who was as perfect as every day alive was to him. She was his air – his very breath and he never wanted her to forget it.

Making quick work of removing the rest of his clothing, he remembered to remove a condom from his pants pocket, never leaving home without one when he knew they would be together. They had a tendency to make love at any given moment and until they were married and ready for children, there would be no unplanned pregnancies.

Tucker smiled when the idea of marriage entered his head. Long gone was an old notion that he would never marry again. Nichelle changed all of that for him.

"You're so gorgeous. How did I get so lucky?" he asked sweetly, taking Nichelle's hand and kissing each finger.

"We're both lucky."

Before she could get out another word, Tucker wasted no time going for what he wanted. He opened her legs, placing them over his shoulder and kissed the top of the thin strip of hair that was a map to her sweetness. He loved the taste of her and knew that if he didn't soon get his fill, he would fall over and die from the sheer level of explosive desire he felt for her.

Moving further down, he used his fingers to part her womanly folds and delighted at the pool of moisture, the perfect essence of her that greeted him. Her body never ceased to amaze him at how ready she always was for him — how turned on he made her.

The moment his tongued lapped at her, he had to use his hands to hold her steady or they would both tumble to the floor. Quickly reaching for his shirt, he tucked it under her hips to protect the chair knowing what their coming together would be like after she climaxed again and again, something he was planning on achieving. Messing up her chair was not an option.

As he worked her body, drawing moan after moan of pleasure from her, he knew the moment she was getting close. Her hips moved wildly and he heard her small please of 'more' and he was more than accommodating. He did give her more and more and then she exploded with shrieks of exhilaration and the pure joy he knew floated throughout her body.

He held her still and rode her pleasure out with her, tantalized by the taste of her on his lips. While her body continued to quake again and again, he was focused enough through the haze of his own need for release as he reached for the condom he'd placed on the table next to them and slipped it on without taking his mouth from her. The minute it was in place, he glided slowly up her body until his mouth caressed hers, allowing the taste from her body to pleasure them both.

"Just what I needed," he whispered against her lips. He looked into her eyes, which were half-closed and the glow he saw reminded him of how perfect they were for each other.

Opening her legs even more, he slid slowly into her drenched tunnel, going in a little at a time. Though they had been together a countless number of times, he still loved how tight and snug her body was, yet still ready to accommodate his size that more than filled out the gold packaged condom.

The minute he felt her womanly folds surround him like a well-fitting glove, he reached for her hands, locking them with his above her head while he let his do the work.

As he kissed her, he allowed his tongue to love her mouth as intimately as the lower part of his body was doing. Time had stood still and the world around them had dropped away and the only sound was that of their bodies mating with a dance that was as old as time. As Nichelle locked her legs at the ankles behind his back and as his slim hips surged into her painstakingly slow at first and then when her body encouraged more movement by raising up to meet his lovemaking, he went deeper and loved her more and more. His body and his mind floated outside of his being as he felt her, not just at the point where their bodies met, but all around him. He could feel the impending wave of an orgasm as his legs began to tremble. He lowered his head between her head and her shoulder to attempt to muzzle the screams that were threatening to escape his lips. His body was riled up enough that he was afraid that the roar on his lips could wake a nation.

As his hips quickened even more, he felt her reach her peak and when she gripped his shoulder and then his back, he could feel her nails digging into his back, not painfully, but so erotically that his body could barely hold on any longer.

"Yes!" Nichelle screamed.

Tucker covered her mouth with his, not to shelter her cries of delight, but to have a place to pour his own. Just as she plunged over the edge of the depths of how far and wide their love went, he climaxed as white lights and stars filled his head. There was a blinding light behind his eyelids. He kissed her passionately through their mutual release and took in all of their love as their bodies raced with a mighty power, shattering any doubt or question that they were compatible by heart, mind, soul and especially body.

As their bodies began to calm, Tucker, relaxed his movements, without stopping them. He felt Nichelle's legs fall way due to pure exhaustion of the intensity of the moment because he too felt it. He never wanted to move from their current position.

"I love you, baby," he whispered again and again.

"No more whole weeks without you," she whispered close

to his ear as he kissed his face.

He smiled against the side of her face because he was thinking the same thing. Nothing should be able to keep them apart from each other when their love was so strong. There were issues in his life that needed fixing, but his love with Nichelle wasn't one.

"You know, I wasn't hungry for food before, but suddenly, I have worked up an appetite fit for a king!" he exclaimed and tried to move from on top of her. When she pulled him back down, he moved to the side to take some of his weight off of her.

"I'm starving too, but after not having you like this, I want to enjoy it for a few minutes more before we move to eat. Do I have you all night or do you have to leave before morning?" she asked.

Tucker leaned up and kissed her lips before answering. He wasn't going anywhere.

"Unless you throw me out, I'm all yours for as long as you want me here. I will definitely take all night. Now, I say, let's get up and get a shower, together of course, and then I can heat up our dinner. You're going to need that sustenance for the rest of the night that I have planned for us. This sofa was just the beginning," he said and this time when he kissed her, he let his kiss give her insight into what he had in store for them.

11

Antonia forgot how much she hated Chicago traffic and her driving was made even more erratic by the sheer anger she felt after her attorney shared with her at the start of the weekend that any plans she had of doing some kind of reveal of her private life with Tucker on social media sites were now side-tracked by an order of the court that had been issued on Tucker's behalf. She had to admit, she hadn't expected that, though she should have since Tucker has a law degree and knew how to work the system. She thought she'd be able to get to him before he took any action, which is why she hadn't done much yet. She was sure once he got his eyes and possibly his hands on her, she would be able to work her magic on him like she'd been able to do with so many other men since taking on more of her Roxie persona that Antonia.

As she wielded through traffic on a Monday evening, just before dark, she couldn't resist the need to keep checking her flawless makeup in the rearview mirror, making sure her makeup was still as perfect as it was when she applied it. To her, the lashes she'd added weren't as straight as she wanted, something she could fix once she found a place to park on Tucker's street. She no longer had the convenience of going around the back and parking in the two-car garage where she parked when they were married. She no longer had that type of liberty, something she was hoping to cure.

She trembled when the sky let out a round of ground shaking thunder, a sign that bad weather was on the way. She hoped it wouldn't happen before she got inside of his house. She also hoped that the thunder wasn't some omen that she shouldn't go see him. If the weather held up, she was good. There was no way she'd allow herself to be seen drenched from the pouring rain, which could cause the tight, hair-sprayed curls of her the wig, that had cost her more money than she could actually spare, to fizzle out and have her out here looking like a wet dog. This was one of her favorites and so long that if she didn't move it out of the way before she sat, she would sit on it.

Stopping at a red light, she looked down at her tight, form fitting bright yellow dress that opened so far at the neckline exposing so much of her breasts that one shift in the wrong direction and she'd have nipple-slip. That was something else she had in common with other reality stars. They were on no one's radar if their breasts were not prominently displayed at all times. She found that clause in her contract and knew it was most likely in theirs too. She had no issue with it as long as if her breasts slipped out, it occurred in front of Tucker.

When they were married, she was a sexy 34C cup, but once she'd decided to get some work done, she was now a hot and sexy 34DD and if she thought men found her irresistible before, they clawed at her now; all except her ex-husband.

Being back in Chicago was beginning to make her feel some type of way about him. She had plans of coming back and using him to get what she needed, but instead, she found herself jealous that he had moved on to another woman.

After they divorced, she assumed he'd go back to his bed-hopping days that he'd been going through before they got married. That Tucker she could wiggle her hips at and entice into bed, but this Tucker, committed to a woman for more than just sexual pleasure, she wasn't prepared for.

When they met, it was because they both were interested in a one-night stand that ended up lasting more nights than she could count and eventually led to marriage. Their marriage was a sham – at least on her end. She did love Tucker, but what she enjoyed more was the lust and everything that came with the best sex of her entire life. Years later, she was still trying to chase the kind of orgasms she'd only been able to have with him. That nine and a half inch third leg of his would have her walking with a slight twitch for days and though it could be painful, the remembrance of why she was walking like that only had her wanting more.

She'd had several affairs while married to Tucker, not for the sex, but because she loved the attention. Her dreams no longer matched his and they grew apart. Now, she was back in Chicago, prepared to almost beg for him to let her back in and that move would help boost both of their careers. Issuing her an injunction that forced her to keep her mouth shut until the got to court was a roadblock she was hoping to overcome by dropping by his house.

From information she was able to get from Omar, Tucker should be home tonight after an early meeting with other Mayors and their staff from across the country. She was hoping to reach him before he jetted off to meet his girlfriend, a woman she was liking less and less the more she learned about her. His little school counselor was a problem for her. Usually, no woman could hold a torch to her or get in her way, but Tucker was really into her and that could be a problem.

As she turned onto his street, she looked around for a parking space and found one a block ahead of his house. Pulling her rented BMW into the spot, she checked her makeup again and made sure her breasts were blatantly displayed. No man can resist her when she offered him all of her on a platter. All he had to do was pull up and feast.

Exiting her car in five-inch strappy silver and yellow heels that matched her dress, the minute she closed the car door, she looked around to see how much attention she was drawing. Not seeing many people, she drummed up her sexiest walk and headed toward Tucker's house. When she reached the brownstone next to his, the woman next door, who was living there when she left some when she split from Tucker, and who should be around sixty or so walked up to her.

"Antonia? Is that you?" she asked.

"It is. Ms. Rose, right?"

"Yes, yes, it is. I haven't seen you around here in a long time. You're here to see Tucker? I didn't realize the two of you stayed in touch after the divorce."

"Oh, we're not..."

Antonia caught herself from revealing that they weren't divorced, remembering there was an order in place.

"Not what?"

Antonia held her tongue and smiled, though she was close to spilling her truth. One thing she remembered from living in the neighborhood was that her past neighbor was the neighborhood gossip and giving up too much information could be good and bad for her. Until she talked to Tucker and convinced him to her side of the force, she needed to hold back.

"Oh, nothing."

"You know, I watch your show and you sure are something. I don't remember you being that mean and loud, but I guess that's what you have to do on these shows to make money, huh? You sure do wear a lot of makeup and tight clothes. You're here to see Tucker? Looks like you're on the prowl trying to catch somethin'."

She wanted to clap back, the way she was famous for doing on her show, but she didn't want to cause a scene.

"I'm that person on the show and there's nothing wrong with how I look. When you have it like I do, you flaunt it. Didn't you do that back in your day?" she asked, snidely.

She didn't want to disrespect the old woman, but she was already over the conversation. When Ms. Rose stiffened her stance and cut her head sharply as if she were offended, she knew she needed to apologize.

"Antonia?"

She turned around at the sound of her name and came face to face with Tucker. Seeing him again, her mind immediately went to how fast she could coax him into bed. She checked out his slender yet muscular build and the gap in his legs because of the slight bow to them had her body tingling in places she remembered he took care of in the past.

She turned around and walked toward him, ignoring the neighbor as if she was never there.

"Tucker! Damn you look good. I'm really missing out!" she

declared.

Just as she reached him and attempted to give him a tight hug, he moved out of her reach before she could even touch him.

"What are you doing here?"

"Really? That's the kind of greeting I get? Don't tell me you're not happy to see me. If so, you're the only man on this planet who wouldn't be happy that I'm gracing him with my presence. I'm here to see you; hopefully to talk. I've been calling and then I get this injunction mess."

"Because of the injunction, you should not be here. You can reach me through my attorney."

"Tucker, darling, don't do me like that. You once loved me and loved seeing me. I simply came by to talk one-on-one without lawyers and without speaking of anything that should be discussed with our lawyers present. Listen, I think you and I can work this out and save us both some time and money. Come on, I promise this will be harmless."

"I don't think that's a good idea. You've already stirred up enough trouble to last me a lifetime and it all occurred in the same night. You didn't have to make your presence known that way at the fundraiser, but you needed all eyes on you."

Antonia looked around and saw that Ms. Rose had moved closer to them in order to hear and then gossip about them.

"Look, if you don't want Ms. Rose to tell the entire neighborhood about this conversation, I suggest we take it inside. If you think I'm here for any ill reason, feel free to toss me out at any time. Surely, we can have a civil conversation from husband to wife."

"Don't go there."

"Well, if we go inside, we can work it out and we can both

come out winners. Shall we?" Antonia asked and without waiting, she walked around Tucker and moved up the few steps to his front door. When she turned and found him following her, she turned her head away from him so that he couldn't see the smile that graced her face. She was getting in the door and therefore, she was already winning.

Once inside, she looked around and marveled at the transformation that had taken place.

"Wow. This place looks amazing. It looks nothing like it did when I lived here. I love the brick interior walls and the dark brown hardwood flooring. You have a lot more art on the walls and this is some fancy furniture and décor. What woman did this for you? You didn't have this kind of taste."

"My sister, Amanda handled the redecoration."

"Right. She's the interior designer and she never liked me. She didn't offer to lend her hand at decorating when I moved in. How are your sisters? Isn't one about the same age as the woman you're seeing?"

Amanda knew she was hitting below the belt, but the words came out before she thought through them. She didn't want to start off arguing or throwing insults. There were times when she forgot that she wasn't on the set of her show.

"My sisters are fine and none of your business about the woman I'm dating. Obviously, you already know enough about her to know how old she is or isn't, so if you're digging, stop it now. Feel free to talk about why you're dropping in on me unannounced."

"Do you mind if I at least sit down? These heels are killing my feet."

"Your choice to wear them. Why are you here, Antonia?"

This time, she could see he was already losing patience

with her and she didn't want to get thrown out before they even had a conversation.

"Can I at least get a bottle of water? I'm a little parched," she lied, trying to buy herself enough time to plan her work and work her plan. Tucker was smart and he wouldn't fall for just anything.

"Either get to it or leave. I'm not about your games today. I was on my way out when I heard you outside talking to Ms. Rose."

"Why so harsh, Tuck. I apologize for showing up without calling first, but you have yet to return any of my calls. I came to Chicago to see you and to tell you my truth. You're being hard and mean and I don't like this side of you."

She tried to sound hurt and sad and even blinked her eyes a few times hoping he would lighten up. She wasn't going to get through to this Tucker standing before her, looking uncomfortable in his own home.

"I'm not being mean or hard. You said you wanted to talk and I'm waiting to hear this truth. So, what is it?" he asked.

"I realized I really miss you. Imagine my surprise when I remembered I never got updated divorce papers to sign. I was meeting with my lawyer about something else and she brought it up."

"Really? She just happened to bring up my name after all these years and reminded you that you were still married to me."

"I'm serious, Tuck. I saw that as fate telling me that we should be together and that we shouldn't have given up on our marriage so fast. I know we had aspirations that were taking us in two different directions, but even with the success of my show and me on my way to making it in

Hollywood, I realized my life was empty and I haven't been as happy with anyone since I was happily married to you," she explained.

"Happily? I wouldn't call it that. We were happy early on but at the end, neither of us was happy. It was best to move on and it still is. I have a life now and I'm sure you do and there is no need to go back."

"We're still married, Tuck and I want to stay married, at least for a little while," she admitted.

"Are you out of your mind? We're not staying married!"

Antonia sat back on the sofa, crossed her legs and got comfortable. This convincing Tucker was going to take some hard work.

"Hear me out. You want a divorce and I want to be known as the first lady of Chicago. From what I hear, you are well on your way to winning in the primary and the general election. I'm not saying I want to be your wife forever, but I am saying that I think we can both get something out of this."

"No, we can't. Like I said, I have a life."

"Right – with, what's her name? That won't last. You can't possibly have anything in common with her. How much older than her are you and why? Does she do some kind of tricks and stuff in the bedroom that's got you all hemmed up? She can't possibly be intellectually stimulating, so she must be working her magic in other areas. Remember how good I was at stimulating you? I've learned some new things and I don't mind sharing since I'm still your wife. There is nothing wrong with a husband and his wife getting reacquainted, but you know, there could be a scandal if word got out that we're still married and you've been carrying on with that girl."

Antonia waited and knew the moment Tucker had already heard enough. She was playing too dirty, too fast. His demeanor reminded her of the Tin Man from The Wizard of Oz who didn't have any oil to loosen up his joints. She could see he was working hard to hold his composure.

"She's not a girl, she's a woman and she's my woman. I'm in love with her. Staying married to you for any reason is not an option and we shouldn't even consider it," he said.

"I beg to differ. I think word getting out that you're still married while entertaining a relationship with a woman won't go over well with Chicagoans. You already have a history as a playboy and people could see that stigma resurfacing and not take you serious as a contender. Supporters could second-guess their decision to back you. What I'm saying is, we could still get the divorce sometime after the election, citing that we couldn't work it out and now we're finally going through with the divorce. I can proclaim what a wonderful man you are and how you deserve the support of the people of Chicago while I chase my dreams in Hollywood."

"What do you get out of this idea of yours? It's ridiculous by the way, but humor me."

"Well, I would love for my camera crew to follow us and get some footage I can use in my show as I head toward becoming first lady of Chicago. The ratings would go through the roof and when we finally get divorced, I may be able to have a show about me and how I would be dealing with life after being in the spotlight as first lady. I would be the perfect wife and arm candy at all of your functions. We look HOT together and I know how to be the wife of a politician. I was one, remember. I could do and be whatever you want and, in the end, we both win. You could get mad publicity on my show and I'm talking all good stuff, not the made-for-tv drama that keeps the show in the ratings. My audience didn't know me as your wife and this adds another level to me and could boost my place on the show and I really need that. I don't ask you for anything. We're already still married to each other, so there isn't much we'd have to do other than put out a press release that we never got a divorce because we were hoping we could work things out and now we have. Then sometime after the election, like six-months later, we can say we tried, but it didn't work because my pull to Hollywood was too strong and we decided to part ways. Think of all the nights you'd get extra benefits."

To add to her last innuendo, she licked her lips across her bright red lipstick, hoping that he would remember all of the things she did for him with her lips. She was more than ready to show him now.

"To start with, no and then to end the conversation, *hell* no. Did you not hear me say I'm in love with someone? I don't need a boost to my campaign the way it seems you need for your career. I'm not altering my life and have it based on a lie and some miscommunication about divorce paperwork and signatures. My record as a politician and what I can continue to do for the people of Chicago will speak for itself."

"Really? People like Ms. Rose will understand when word gets out about you traipsing all over town, screwing that woman you're involved with while you have a wife who is begging you to take her back?"

Antonia stood, now ready to play hardball. Playing to his softer side wasn't going to work. It was time to switch from

Antonia to Roxie.

"Like I said, my record will speak for itself and my character won't be called into question. It'll be easy to explain why we're still married if there is a need to do so. Right now, the injunction prevents you from spilling any kind of tea about it."

Walking over to him, she stopped right in front of him, glad that her high heels had them standing pretty much nose to nose in height.

"That's only temporary. I may not leak it, but that doesn't mean it won't get leaked."

Tucker laughed and the way he laughed made her step back a few steps. The laugh gave her chills and not in the sexy way she would like to experience being close to him.

"What's the real angle? What am I missing? This has to be more than you wanting the words, *first lady*" in front of your name and having fodder for your show. Something is missing. You said your truth, so speak it and speak it all."

Exhaling, Antonia decided to play with a little honesty and see where it got her.

"I need to have more focus on me for the show or I won't be asked back for another season. The producers don't think my storylines are attracting new viewers and I need an edge."

"What? You mean, being rude, loud, disrespectful and throwing shade and actual glasses of tea isn't enough?" Tucker quipped.

She wasn't laughing at his attempt to mock her. The show was her life and her livelihood. She wasn't set up like he was. When they divorced, he got to keep what he brought into the marriage and she couldn't get her hand on any of the money he got when his father sold his shares in his company. His father had given him and his sisters a small fortune, which the oldest two received when they turned thirty-five. The youngest, Bailee, would get hers at thirty. That made Tucker a pretty rich man having five million dollars in his pocket, money he didn't need because he was already pretty successful as a practicing attorney and politician. He was also part owner in some gyms and two other businesses that he'd bought into after they divorced. She'd kept up on him from a distance and she realized she was missing out and needed to reclaim her spot. She never should have signed that prenuptial agreement before they were married. She really thought she'd be bigger than him when she reached stardom and her angle was that she didn't want to share anything with him. Turns out, she didn't have anything she'd have to share.

"I need an edge and if my agent can help me wield this story just right, this could be my ticket; the one I've been waiting on. Listen, I don't want to blow up your life, but I will if it means I can finally get the roles I want in television and movies and I think my ride as your wife through the election is the answer. I know you would hate for cameras to start following your little tart all over the place, questioning her and digging into her life. You know it's not hard for people to find out about her and I won't even have to do anything. She looks a little fragile to me. You sure you want that? I'm sure she can wait a year for you. At her age, she's got nothing but time."

She walked back up to him.

"We could have a lot of fun," she added.

To seal the deal with her intentions, Antonia reached her hand up and pressed it against Tucker's chest while locking eyes with him. No man can resist her and she knew he was no exception. Moving her hand downward, she knew he was aware of where her hand was going. As she smiled, loving the power she has over men, she was startled when he took her hand away from him and placed it back at her side.

"Not happening; not today, not tomorrow or any other day. Don't come into my home threatening me or my girlfriend or offering yourself up as a prize. I don't know who you think you're dealing with, but I'm not softer in my self-esteem than I was when we were together. The divorce will go through and I don't plan to wait until after the election. I'm not playing any games with you or helping you build your career on the backs of the people of Chicago by building a false life for them to take in and believe is real. If you had remembered what your name was, we wouldn't be standing here right now. If that's all you came to say, you can leave. My answer is still no and it will continue to be no."

When Tucker turned and walked toward the front door, opening it, she knew it was time for her to leave. There would be another time and she knew that. She was glad he wasn't aware of what she had planned in order to get back into his life. She tried it the easy way by bringing it straight to him and now, she'd have to resort to schemes that Roxie would dish out, which included digging into the life of his girlfriend and seeing how much of a wedge she can cause between them, leaving her as his option to run to. She had time.

"Well, I tried and you're missing out. Do you know how many men would like to be propositioned by me?" she asked as she walked through the front door.

"Really? Is there a line and do you take cash and credit? I don't appreciate you trying to bribe me into doing something that would be a lie of everything I stand for. Sign the divorce papers and head back to California. I wish you well in your career and you'll have to figure out how to up your game with your career, but it can't be at the expense of me and my life. Our time is over. Also, don't show up at my house again. I think we need to keep communication through our attorneys. It was nice seeing you again and you look wonderful. Take care."

Antonia turned around and started to say something. Instead, she held her head up high, hating that she had to practically beg him to take her back even if it wasn't for real. She wanted to tell him that he'd regret turning her down, but instead, she decided it was time to show him. Game on, she thought and walked down the steps.

As she walked back to her car, she noticed Ms. Rose coming back out of her house.

"Good visit? I thought you'd be in there longer looking like that and all."

"Go inside and mind your business!" Antonia spat out and walked more briskly to her car. She never liked her.

12

Tucker walked out of his office and from the look on Adrienne's face, there was something off about his attire. He threw his arms up as if to ask her what was wrong. When she fanned her hands from the floor up to the top of his head, he laughed.

"Okay, I got it. I look like I've been in a cave working all day. That's because I have."

"I'm saying, your tie is crooked and you should have just taken it off since the top button is open anyway. Your sleeves are rolled up like you've been working out in a garden some place and I think I see a smudge of ketchup on your shirt or are you bleeding?" she laughed.

Tucker looked down at himself and shook his head from side to side.

"Okay, you got me. I had some fries and they were good. I shouldn't have, but I couldn't resist. If I didn't get the chance to work-out this morning, I wasn't going to be concerned about what I ate for lunch. Besides, it's Friday and I ate good all week. Weekend plans?"

"I'm going to visit my parents this weekend and I'm

planning to spend it relaxing. What about you?"

Tucker watched her look around as if she were looking for someone. His eyes landed where hers landed, right on Omar who tried to look like he wasn't listening to them.

"Omar, what are you up to this weekend?" Tucker asked.

"Nothing much. Catching up on some reading and may check out a festival or two. You have big plans with your lady?" Omar asked.

There it is, Tucker realized. For the past two weeks, every conversation with Omar seemed to lead right back to Nichelle which bothered him. He also remembered that Adrienne said she caught Omar snooping around the office after hours. Little did Omar know, he was on their radar; they were watching him since it appears he's watching them.

"Well, I did plan on making a few appearances in place of the Mayor because he was taking a few days off, but he changed his mind and decided that he wanted to show up as much as he could since this is his last term. I'm planning on staying in all weekend to catch up on some games I've been recording and look over some campaign stuff that Carter sent over."

"It's good to see you relaxing. You've been burning the midnight oil all week this week. You could use the break," Adrienne said.

"Yeah and I'm sure Nichelle has been missing you. Are you still seeing each other?" Omar inquired.

Tucker didn't bite.

"This weekend is all about me and the many ways I plan to relax alone at home. We could all use the break because next week, there are sessions all week long. The finance session will get heated, so get ready for that. I'll see you Monday morning," Tucker said and escaped back into his office, followed by Adrienne who came in and shut his office door.

"You see it don't you? Why is Omar so interested in your personal life with Nichelle all of a sudden? He's known like I have that you 've been seeing her, but lately, since the fundraiser, every conversation gets steered in that direction. I don't like it and to top it off I found out he was snooping around another day, earlier this week. What do you think is going on?" Adrienne asked.

Tucker sat on the corner of his desk and asked her to come closer.

"I'm going to tell you this and you can't reveal it. I think I know why he's doing it, but I won't let on to him just yet that I know."

"Okay."

"I think Omar is looking for dirt to share with my ex-wife."

"Why? I don't understand. He knows her like that? Why would he do that and why would you think that?"

"Adrienne, when I was married to Antonia and shortly before my marriage ended, the two of them were having sex."

Before Adrienne could shout out her surprise, he encouraged her to cover her mouth, since Omar was still in the outer office.

"He what! Are you sure? How do you know?"

"You didn't know? I don't think he knows that I know. I know my wife and I peeped them a few times and the looks between them. I had Tellis check her out one night and he followed her where she met up with Omar and they had sex in his car. I suspected, but wasn't sure until then. Tellis thought I would be upset, but I wasn't. I think the love between us had already fizzled out. I don't know how long it was going on, but it was. Not long after, she and I split up and she moved out and I no longer cared."

"Oh, my. That is crazy. He was sleeping with your wife and you're explaining this to me real calm like. Did you want to kill him? Fire him?"

"No, not at all and I can't fire him for sticking it to my wife. I can fire him if he is leaking any information about me to her to help with her cause to get back into my life prior to the election."

"That's what she's trying to do? I never liked her."

Tucker laughed.

"Tell me something I didn't know."

"Nichelle is a perfect fit for you. She makes you happier than I have ever seen you. I hope you don't let Antonia get to you and don't let her back into your life. She doesn't deserve a good man like you. She deserves a snake like Omar. Do you know what he's telling her about you? After knowing he was snooping around last week, I've changed where I lock your paper calendar up. The locked cabinet at my desk doesn't have anything in it but office supplies now. If he gets in there, he won't find anything."

"I'm glad you left the key taped where it was. If he's looking for something, I want to catch him doing it. Antonia showed up at my house last week and I'm sure he told her where I would be. I also found out that it was Omar who gave the okay to allow her into the fundraiser that night at the casino. I wasn't going to worry much about it because everyone knows her, but without a ticket, it should have been hard for her to get in without going through me, Carter or you. He tried to hide it, but he gave Antonia his plus-one ticket. I'm getting closer to finding out his end game, but for now, I want to see what he's up to. At first, I thought it had something to do with my opponent for the Mayor's race, but it's actually all about Antonia. We'll keep an eye on him and at the right time, I'll confront him on it."

"Let me know if there is anything you want me to do. I know some really good places we could hide a body," Adrienne whispered and then laughed out loud.

"You're hilarious! No longer keep my off-hours schedule. Send an email to me at the end of the day and I'll add appointments to my iPad, especially when I have plans with Nichelle that I don't want to forget about."

"Got it. Let me go take care of that right now. You heading out soon?" Adrienne asked.

"In a few. I have a call to make first."

"I'll give you some privacy. See me before you leave to be sure you have what you need for weekend stuff. I think you cancelled just about everything, but I want to confirm that's the case."

"Will do."

Tucker took out his cellphone after Adrienne left and shut his office door behind her. He smiled as he dialed.

"Hey beautiful," he said, speaking low for any ears that may be on the other side of the door or wall listening.

"Hi to you," Nichelle replied.

"I was thinking about you. Do you have weekend plans? I actually have an open weekend, something that never happens and I wanted to see you. I had a pretty full calendar and now it's empty."

"Aww. I was hired as the makeup artist for a movie shooting in Indianapolis tomorrow and Sunday. I'm driving up tonight since they provided me a room through Sunday evening. If I had known you had a free weekend, I wouldn't have agreed to the job."

"Nonsense. You rock as a makeup artist and they're lucky to have you. Never pass up an opportunity that we can work around. I didn't get a chance to see you this week."

Tucker wasn't happy that he wasn't able to get in as much time with her especially since he felt like they were in a fragile state. He wanted the momentum back that they had before Antonia showed up.

"I know and I miss you. I was happy to talk to you every day even if I couldn't see you," Nichelle said.

He had an idea. He still had a free weekend and nothing was keeping him in Chicago. If there was an emergency, he could be reached by cell or by dialing his office and leaving a message. The service would then call his cell and alert him to anything that needed his immediate attention.

"Am I imposing if I join you? I won't get in the way and I'll stay away from the set. I just want to be able to see you during your downtime. I'll make myself comfortable in a room and you can come and swing by when you can. Doesn't that sound sexy?"

When Nichelle laughed out loud, he knew she was thinking the same thing.

"Every moment with you is a sexy one. You sure you can get away for a few days?"

"Baby, for you, yes I can. My calendar is clear and I can meet you there later tonight. I would say I would pick you up and drive, but you're still forcing me to play mission impossible to see you."

"You know why and, yes, I would love for you to join me. Don't get a separate room – stay with me and stay naked the whole weekend. That last part is a deal breaker, so if that doesn't work, you'll have to stay home," she laughed.

"Me? Naked? All weekend? I can do that. Ready and waiting for my lady? I can do that all day, every day, sweetheart."

"Okay. I'll text the hotel address to your phone. I'm about to hit the road. How long will you be?"

"I can't leave right away. I need a few hours, but I'll call you when I get close. That's a three-hour drive, so I'm thinking I'll be there by ten. Are you working tonight or does it start tomorrow?"

"Tomorrow. Tonight, I'm going to drive to the location so that I know where it is. They said I'm in a hotel about fifteen miles away, but I want to check so that I know where I'm going. I was planning to relax in my room tonight, order room service and watch movies or something."

"Well, now, we can find something to do together. It's been a long week without you."

"Damn right which means you have a lot of time to make up for."

Tucker laughed out loud.

"Your wish is my command, baby. I'm going to get out of here and get some things in place and then I'm on the road in about two hours. I love you, Nichelle. I love you, baby."

"I know and I love you, too. I love you so much," she replied.

Tucker put his phone back on his hip and called for Adrienne to come back into his office.

"You need something?" she asked, entering.

"Close the door. I'm going to be out of town this weekend, but only about three hours away. Make sure all calls are forwarded to the service and leave specific instructions that I should only be reached in case of an emergency."

"I can also stay on call this weekend. My parents are only an hour away," she said.

"No, no. I want you to enjoy your weekend and I plan to do the same thing. I'm going to meet Nichelle in Indianapolis for a few days. You know what this week has been like and I haven't seen her since last week. I don't think I'll be needed. The Mayor will be around this weekend. Omar shall remain in the dark about where I am," he explained.

"Do you think he and Antonia are watching you or perhaps she has someone watching and following you to see where you are or to find out about Nichelle?"

"I don't know and I'll do everything in my power to protect her. I'll work it out. If you need me, call my cell.

"Gotcha. Enjoy your weekend and tell Nichelle I said hello."

"Gotcha."

After Adrienne left, he called Tellis.

"Hey. I'm heading down in a few minutes and I need a big favor."

"I'm listening," Tellis replied.

"I've got ears here in the office as it pertains to my personal life. I'll get into it more when I get in the car. I need to get away this weekend, incog-negro!" he joked.

"I hear you. What do you need me to do?"

"I need your car, not the new one – the black Accord with all the tinted windows. After you drop me off, and do it out front of my house, can you come back with it and pull into the garage? I'll drop you back off at home. I need the car until Sunday. Is that possible?"

"That's all? Of course. I thought you were going to ask me to rob a bank or something!" Tellis jested.

"Nothing that drastic, but I know you have my back if it was. I'm heading down in a few minutes and I'd like to get on the road around seven. That work?"

"That works and I can't wait to hear why we have to do all of this. See you in a few," Tellis said.

13

"Roxie, what's the deal? It's been weeks since you landed in Chicago and I'm not getting any information on your progress with your husband. What is he saying? Is he onboard with your plan until after the election? I can get a camera crew there asap."

Antonia knew she should not have answered the phone and she hated that she had to remind her agent again and again that she was only Roxie when she was on the set. In her off time, she was Antonia.

"Nancy, I really wish you would call me Antonia. I know I'm Roxie and Antonia, but when I'm not in California, I'm trying to get back to be Antonia and no, I haven't persuaded Tucker yet. He's playing hardball. He really wants the divorce to happen right away."

"What's gotten you in a snit? I always call you Roxie."

"I know, but I'm finding that people don't like Roxie. I mean, fans like Roxie, but people who know me here in Chicago do not like the Roxie character I play and I think it's starting to get to me. I tried to connect with some old friends and they all want to tell me how much they hate the person I have to be on the show to make money and how they prefer me as Antonia over Roxie. Is my character really that bad?" she asked.

She had been in the dumps as far as her mood, all week. Everyone she's reached out to has treated her like she has the plague after reading her the riot about the horrible person that show has turned her into. She spent a week of trying to reconnect with old friends and having to remind them that she is Antonia, not Roxie.

"Your character isn't the kind a woman anyone would want as a friend, but it's called acting. It's what you're supposed to be doing. When you think about it, you tell everyone's business, even those you claim as really good girlfriends, you criticize everyone's life and decisions and you flirt with everyone's man, but that's what will get you the big bucks. The more horrible you are as a friend, the more the producers will love you. It's all about the show. Don't sweat it. Say, did you go see your family? Call your mother? The two of you have lots of drama and I would love to make the love-loss between the two of you a part of the show. You also said your family pretty much hates you and that could be some good stuff for television too. I know you were thinking of doing that. Where are they or at least your mother?"

"They're in Atlanta and some are here, though I don't know them that well. I called my mother and she asked me not to come visit right now. She says she's gotten flack about me being on the show and she doesn't want to have to explain me to people if I come to visit. She said maybe another time."

Antonia would like to hear someone have a sympathetic ear and heart to her plight and she wished Nancy would. She has a feeling that wish wouldn't be granted.

"Really? Oh, well, don't worry about it. When you're making the big bucks, she'll want you to come visit then. Stay focused on Tucker for now. We need to get cameras into your life while on the campaign trail. No luck with that yet?"

"No and he hit me with an injunction. I can't say anything publicly about the fact that we are still married until after we go to court which isn't for another month from now. I can't hang around that long living in a hotel room. I was hoping to be back in his house by then and living off of him. I'm spending my money on a hotel and I have outstanding bills that need to be paid. I got a call earlier today from the bank about my car. They want to repossess it if I don't catch up on my payments. I had to use most of my money for the last appointment with my plastic surgeon. I'm running out of funds. Even my roommate, Shadow, is bugging me about rent," she explained.

"I told you I can get you an advance on the next season if you get Tucker onboard. Work harder and throw some of those new and improved body parts at him. Do whatever you have to do, but get him onboard. My agency wants to continue representing you, but the powers that be are reminding me that if you don't produce more, they will have to drop you which means I can't be your agent. Get it done, Roxie; I mean Antonia. Let me know when it's all done. You led us to believe that you would have this in the bag by now. Do it and call me in the next few days with some good news or I don't know how much longer I can put this off. We promised the producers some juicy stuff and so far, we haven't given them anything."

Antonia flopped back on the bed in the hotel room that

she was barely able to afford for much longer. She needed to get in touch with Tucker again and this time, she would try harder to make a move on him. This time, she'll have to try and find a way to get close to him and get photos of it – something to use against him to get him to see her way.

"I'll call you," she said to Nancy and then ended the call.

Rolling around on the bed in frustration, she didn't know what to do. She had a lifeline and she needed to use it tonight.

Dialing, she waited to hear the familiar voice.

"Where is he?" she demanded.

"Uh, Antonia?"

"Fool, you know who this is. Where is he? Is he at home tonight? What are his weekend plans?"

Antonia waited through Omar's attempts to get words out as his stuttering took over.

"He..he..he is at home. I saw him leave and he mentioned staying in and watching sports or something like that. He has a free weekend. You going over there?"

Antonia sat up straight. She didn't like to be questioned.

"Why? You concerned that I'll have sex with him? He's my husband! I can have sex with him if I want to. Just be lucky that I'm still throwing some of this good stuff your way. If you come through for me, I'll do the Tiffany Haddish grapefruit thing from the Girl's Trip movie that you said you wanted to try. Now, you're sure he's at home?"

"I think so. I mean, I can't be sure. I can only tell you what he said and that is, that he was going to relax at home. I asked about his girlfriend and he said he was spending the weekend alone watching sports. He should be home. I followed him like you asked me to and I saw Tellis drop him off and leave and Tucker's car is parked out front of his house. You don't need to have sex with him. I can come over later if you want me to," Omar said.

"I will let you know when I want you to drop your trousers for me. In the meantime, make sure you know where Tucker is at all times and if he has plans with his girlfriend, I want to know when and where they are going to be. I need to know where she lives. I'm still waiting on that."

"I'm trying. That's not easy information to get. I'm trying," he said.

"Try harder!"

Antonia ended another call, wishing she was on a landline phone that she could hang up loudly like years ago before the cell phone. She'd seen that many times in movies.

"So, he's home. I've got something for you Tucker," she said out loud.

Getting up, she looked through her sexiest underwear and laid some options out on the bed. Deciding on something white and sexy, she went to the closet and pulled out a sexy black wrap dress, something she could drop and give Tucker and eyeful he won't be able to resist. She knows he asked her not to drop by again, but for this, he would be happy she did. If he's not spending the evening with Nichelle, something must be wrong in their relationship. She could only hope.

She smiled as she headed to the shower. Tucker had better be ready for her because she was coming with everything she could muster up and perhaps within a week, she'll be able to move out of her hotel room and into his house and definitely into his bed.

14

Nichelle walked around the living room of the suite that she'd upgraded to once she found out that Tucker was going to be joining her. She was more than willing to pay the difference in the room that the production company was paying for and what the large suite she ended up getting cost. Tucker was well worth it. This wasn't their first time stealing away for some time alone, but this was the first time that she was going to treat him to a great weekend away.

Checking out the setup, she moved the bottle of 2009 Alexander Valley Vineyards Temptation Zinfandel around in the pitcher of ice she'd requested from the hotel. With Tucker arriving any minute, their late-night dinner should be on its way up to their room. She was excited about the dinner she ordered of stuffed lobster tails and braised lamb chops, garlic-smashed roasted potatoes and his favorite, grilled asparagus. She ordered something simple for dessert, double chocolate cake, topped with cherry glaze. There were battery-operated candles all over the room and the bedroom. She stopped at a Pier One store on her way and picked up over a dozen candles, all they had in-stock. There was soft jazz playing throughout the suite. She was proud of the ambience she'd set. She felt the need to take their romance to another level after feeling insecure and letting him see that she was insecure about Antonia being back in town. For an entire week, she kicked herself for letting Tucker's ex-wife get under her skin in the short interaction she had with her at the fundraiser. She never should have doubted Tucker's love and now, she never would again.

Looking at how nice she'd set the table up, including flowers as the centerpiece, she was happy with herself. During their time of dating, Tucker loved planning their getaways and he always thought of everything. This was her chance to show him that she could be just as romantic as he was.

She'd dated back in high school and even in college, but this was her first time being in love. She'd gone through an experiment phase when she thought she was attracted to women, but then found she was just testing the waters. No one, not a woman or a man had ever made her feel like a precious queen the way Tucker has. She was still troubled by the secret she kept from him that for a few weeks, she dated a woman, though that didn't go far other than some kissing and fondling. He knows that she was a virgin when they got together, so there was no way for him to think that she may have experimented with a woman before. She believed everyone should find their soulmate, wherever that may be and for her, that turned out to be Tucker.

Rushing into the bedroom, she stopped to check herself in the mirror. She loved the silky, soft, pink robe that came just below her behind with a sash tied around her waist. Underneath was a matching two-piece, lace and silk demi-bra and thong. She'd let her hair flow down around her shoulders with little makeup and a sheer pink lip gloss that tasted like strawberries. She couldn't wait for Tucker to taste it. Looking down, she turned her foot to the left and to the right admiring the high-heel pink and white thong slippers she'd borrowed from Reese, thankful that she was able to catch her while on her way out to Indianapolis. This weekend, she wanted to be sure Tucker had the time of his life in-between her times of being absent because of work on set.

If the job had not been paying such a large amount for two-days of her service, she would have cancelled. After working all week as a counselor, she looked forward to her wind-down weekends, but more and more, she was being drawn into the world of a makeup artist.

She had picked up a knack for doing makeup back in high school and once she reached college, she made money on the side doing faces at school. Realizing she had a talent for it, she took classes her last year of undergraduate and officially began doing makeup professionally. Thankful to Reese, she had been connected with some high-profile people and jobs had been flooding in. She'd recently been offered a contract to do a new twenty-something television show with sixteen episodes for the first year. The job was going to pay her four times what she was making as a school counselor and it would mean taking a leave of absence from the school.

She loved working with the kids, but the entertainment world was calling her. She wasn't interested in being in front of the camera like an actress would love. Instead, she preferred behind the scene, still a part of the team making magic on the screen. She had a few weeks to consider the offer, but she was already close to accepting the job.

Life was going well for her. She was in love, she had a job she loved and a side hustle she really loved. She was living her life and basking in the glow of being in love with an incredible man. Every time she thought of Tucker, she found herself sporting a silly grin. That was how he made her feel.

Hearing a knock on the door, she raced to it and saw Tucker. She flung the door open, excited to see him and before he could even get inside, she threw her whole body into his, happy that he knew what to expect and was ready for her launch.

"You're here!" she shouted, kissing him all over the face. Before he could get a word out, she kissed him full on the lips as he held her body in his arms, his large hands holding her behind caressing it softly. She loved the way he did that.

Devouring his lips, she wanted him to feel how happy she was to be with him after another week of being apart, this time because of their work schedules. He'd had appearances all over town and she'd had parent conferences after hours to accommodate working parents. Seeing him now brought their love into focus.

She heard moans of pleasure and smiled knowing the sound was that he was happy to see her and then she realized, he wasn't the only one moaning out loud at the heady kiss. There were moans coming from her too as their tongues dueled passionately.

"Mmm, someone is happy to see me," Tucker said, moving into the room and kicking the door closed behind me.

"Yeah, and I was willing to give the other hotel guests a show because that's how much I've missed you and I don't care who knows it."

Kissing him one last time, she put her feet back on the ground and pulled him further into the room.

"I won't tell you how fast I got here from Chicago. I had one goal in mind and that was to get to you. You look amazing! Damn – I could get use to you greeting me like this. Pink is your color, but so is every other color you put on and allow me to take off," he suggested to her.

Nichelle smiled as he beamed looking around the room and the work she'd put in for them. His look of appreciation and surprise was all she needed.

"I've been looking forward to this ever since you called earlier and asked to join me," she said.

"You've been very busy and I love it. I can't tell you how much I need this time with you. I hope you're okay with me never leaving this room and I may sleep the whole time you're gone, but always wake me when you get back. I don't want to miss any of our time together," Tucker said pulling her into his arms again.

Nichelle felt her body melt into his as he placed soft kisses across her face, teasing her lips to open for him. Inhaling, she did just that and took pleasure in the love that flowed between them. No one could have made her believe that she could be this happy with someone – this in love that everything about another person made her feel so complete. When their lips parted, she reached up to wipe away the rest of the lip gloss and he moved her hand away.

"Your lips are shiny," she said.

"I like it like that."

She stepped back and looked at him.

"You're still in your work clothes. You didn't get a chance to go home?" she asked while helping him remove his suit jacket.

"I did, but just long enough to grab some stuff for the weekend away and to wait for Tellis to bring me his car. I drove it here."

"You did what? Is something wrong with your car?"

"No, but, well, there is a lot I need to tell you and I need to start with that before I explain the car."

Before he could start, there was another knock on the door.

"That should be our dinner. I wanted to wait for you. I know it's late," she said getting up.

"I know you are not about to answer the door dressed like that," Tucker joked. "I'll get the door while you save this view of you all for me."

Nichelle giggled and ran to the bedroom to be out of sight as their food was brought in. Once the cart full with food was left for them and the door was again shut and locked, she came back out to check each covered dish.

"This looks delicious. I hope you like it all," she said.

"I love it and thank you for doing this. I didn't get a chance to eat. I started to grab something on the way here, but with thoughts of getting to you, I forgot to stop and now I'm glad I did continue on. I want to enjoy every bite. I need to grab a shower first and then we can eat."

Tucker grabbed his duffle bag and walked into the bedroom with Nichelle followed close behind him.

"What were you going to tell me about what led up to you driving Tellis' car here?"

She had a feeling the conversation was about to steer to something unpleasant if he had to switch cars.

"Well, I saw Antonia. I should have told you earlier this

week, but I wanted to talk to you in person. She showed up at my house unexpectedly. I was about to go out and I heard her voice out front talking to my neighbor."

"What did she want?"

"Me."

Nichelle felt like the wind had been knocked out of her. She was finally getting a whiff of Antonia's plan for being back in Chicago. She was right in her thinking that his ex-wife wanted him back and not just in name only.

"She wanted you? She actually said that?"

As Tucker unpacked his bag, Nichelle sat on the side of the bed and watched as she listened.

"She said a whole lot. Without wasting a whole lot of time on talking about her, I'll give you the short, yet thorough version. She wants me to take her back through the election. She wants to use the platform to increase show ratings thinking being the first lady of Chicago will skyrocket her status on the show and even lead to some new show all about her. In return, she agreed to not blow my life out of the water or to send the media your way to harass you. She didn't use those exact words, but that's what she alluded to. She wants me to let her accompany me and tell the media that we were separated and never divorced because we want to give our marriage a try. After I win the election, which she is sure will happen because she'll be on my arm, six months later, we'll announce that our attempt to make our marriage work failed and she'll head back to Los Angeles with a whole new fan base. Oh, did I forget to mention that she also wants a camera crew from her show to be able to follow us around and record our reconciliation?"

Nichelle caught the quotes Tucker made with his fingers

when he said, reconciliation.

"Well, what did you say?"

Nichelle knew she'd asked the wrong question when Tucker stopped taking clothes from his bag and looked to her with a dull expression on his face.

"Really? You should already know the answer to that, but if you need to hear me say it, I told her no. Her angle is her own career and she's holding not signing the divorce papers over my head."

"I apologize. The question just slipped out. It was in my head. I'm just concerned about what she could do to your career and your run for Mayor. Can anything hurt you? Can seeing me while you're officially still married hurt you? I don't want that."

"You would want me to give you up to save my career? Would you want that?" he pleaded.

"Of course, not. I also don't want to be the cause of you losing the election."

"Nichelle, you have nothing to do with my losing the election , if that happens, and if the people find out that I'm still married and that I've been seeing someone that I'm madly in love with at a time when I didn't know I was still married, then perhaps they don't deserve me, if that's what they choose. I'm not going to sweat it. I'm going to let my attorney deal with the divorce, I'm going to continue my campaign and if any of my personal life around my marriage, divorce or even dating you comes out, I will address it and move on. What I don't want to do is stop seeing you. That's not an option for me and I hope it's not an option for you."

Nichelle stood and hugged Tucker from behind, laying her head against his back.

"That would never be an option for me. I'm really thinking about you and about us," she explained.

"I know, baby, and I'm thinking about you, me and especially about us and in all of this, I choose us. You make me happy and that goes a long way. Life is too short to let someone else control your life like Antonia is trying to do. She doesn't hold the cards, though she thinks she does. She's spent too much time on reality television thinking that crap is real life. Real life is me and you. I wanted you to know that she showed up at my house."

When Tucker paused and didn't move to finish what he was doing, Nichelle leaned back but held her arms around him.

"What else?" she asked softly.

"She made a sexual inuendo toward me, as if that was going to persuade me. Before you ask, I shut that foolishness down immediately. My lady, right here with me, is all I need in a woman. I also want you to know something she doesn't think I know what she's really up to, which is why I asked to use Tellis' car. Antonia has been screwing Omar who works for me. She was doing so back when we were married and I believe she's been doing it since she returned to Chicago. Omar has been acting weird at work and I believe he's been snooping around trying to get information on my life with you."

"What!"

Nichelle sat back on the bed and all she could think was what she was hearing sounded a lot like that happens on that show Antonia works on.

"Yeah, you heard me and I didn't care then just like I don't care now. What I do care about is whether they are planning something together that could compromise your life and if they are keeping an eye on me or having someone else keep an eye on me, especially to find out where you live," he explained.

"She's that devious? That's crazy!"

"She is and I wanted to be careful. My car is parked out front of my house and I have the timers on my lights. I told Tellis that I saw Omar's care out front of my house before he came back to pick me up. It was parked a block away in a parking space right before I left to come here. Luckily, Tellis came the back way to my house and picked me up in his personal car. We drove back out the back way and I dropped him off at his house and got on the road here. Tellis sent me a text about an hour ago and said that Omar's car with him in it was still sitting up the block from my house. I have no doubt Antonia sent him there. He was in a different spot, so he may have left and come back."

"I'm sorry you're going through this and to have someone disloyal working for you. Are you going to fire him?"

"No. I can't fire him because he hasn't done anything. I need to keep him around to keep an eye on what Antonia is doing. I did alert my attorney to the latest and she said not to worry; she'll take care of it. All I want to do is spend this weekend not thinking about any of that and hoping there isn't some emergency that would send me back to Chicago before the end of the weekend. Are we good?"

Nichelle smiled and knew that she didn't have a care in the world. She would never doubt his love and if he said he will deal with it, he will.

"We're perfect."

"You know that I will protect you by any means necessary.

I won't let Antonia hurt you in any way. All of our cards are on the table and we have no secrets. I will always tell you how I feel and what I'm thinking. No secrets," he repeated. "I'm going to get a shower and join you and all your sexiness at the dinner table. Keep it hot for me and that's not just about the food," Tucker said. Nichelle accepted the kiss he gave her, nodded her head. No words were needed.

She watched as Tucker walked into the bathroom. She didn't want him to think that she was worried about anything. He said he would protect her and she had no doubt that he would. She wished there was something she could do to protect him from Antonia. Letting him know that she was his safe place was all that she needed to do. He wanted a weekend away from craziness and work and that's what he was going to get.

She stood and began putting his clothes away for the short time they would be at the hotel. The minute she heard the shower turn on, the idea of him being naked and glistening from the downpouring shower elicited thoughts of shower love. Not thinking twice, she grabbed a condom from his bag, dropped her robe and as she walked to the bathroom, she removed everything she had on underneath. She had packed plenty more that Tucker could take off of her slow and methodically, the way he loved doing. Right now, she needed to help him relax.

Walking up to the glass shower door, she could see his silhouette behind it. He was standing still with his hands braced against the wall in front of him with his head hung low. To her, he looked like a man with the weight of the world on his shoulders. Tucker was a man with a big heart and an even bigger job of trying to make life better for so many people, including her. For a change, she wanted to be the one to take the weight off of his heart and allow him to just feel; to only feel the loved she had that could carry them both through life's ups and downs.

She reached for the shower door. The minute the air whooshed in, Tucker turned around and like her, knew that no words were needed. When he moved over to make room for her, she moved back against the cold shower wall, a contrast from the heat of the water. With the door closed behind them, her head went up and his came down as their hot, powerful kiss added to the steam encasing them in the shower. She let her hands roam all over his muscular body, reacquainting herself with the feel of him. Her hands went from his firm, yet taught chest, down over his flat six-pack abs to the strong protruding, swollen member that stood at attention against her belly. She looked up into Tucker's face and realized that though he put on a brave face for her all the time, she saw the pressure that has been building up and he was overwhelmed. His face was emotionless, even a little strained, though his body recognized her.

"Close your eyes," she whispered and caressed both sides of his face. "You try so hard to be strong and in control of everything. It's okay to be vulnerable. It's okay to let it all go, especially when you're with me. Remember I told you that you will always find a safe place here when you're with me. Close your eyes, baby, and let me help you relax. All I want you to do is concentrate on this moment and nothing else. For the next few days, the rest of the world doesn't exist. Until we go back to Chicago, it's just you and me. Agreed?" she asked sweetly and placed a soft kiss in the center of his chest. She looked up to see him shake his head yes and then she didn't want any more talking.

Kissing her way down his body, she let her hand travel to the space between them to his hardness which was standing at full attention. She smiled that he was blocking out the world and letting himself live in the moment.

Taking his hardness into her free hand, she continued kissing his chest as the water from the shower pummeled against their bodies. Stroking him, she allowed her movements to be slow and precise as Tucker moaned out his pleasure. When his hips moved in sync with her movements, she gripped him tighter, the way he loved. Pleasuring him was the only thing on her mind and she focused on his reaction to her to be sure he stayed in the heated atmosphere of pure desire she was creating.

"Baby," he groaned out, sending pleasure throughout her senses.

"Just feel, baby," she sighed just before she began moving further down his body, bending her own body at the knees.

When his flesh rubbed across her lips, she placed several soft kisses around the large mushroomed head of him before taking him into her mouth slowly. As Tucker's hips moved in a circular motion, she increased her sucking motion and took as much of him in as she could. Moving around him with her tongue, she could feel the powerful veins along his stiff maleness vibrating in her mouth. As his hips began to move a little stronger, she was ready to feel his hardness inside of her, not only a place he loved to be, but it's a place she longed to have him, forever.

Quickly opening the condom packet, she sheathed him and then felt her body being lifted off of her feet and placed snugly between him and solid wall behind her.

"I love you for loving me," Tucker uttered against her lips.

She moaned her pleasure out in the kiss they shared as he wrapped her legs around his waist, kissing her so deeply that her toes tingled. As she felt the thick head of him easing into her body slowly, she held her breath, taking in every bit of pleasure her mind could encompass.

"Love me," she uttered, as she felt his lips brush across hers before seeking out other parts of her face and neck. Her body grew hot as Tucker's teeth playfully dragged against her chin as she shivered with euphoric need. She tried to take in deep, savoring breaths, but her need grew stronger and a scream she tried to suppress came out as she gripped his neck tighter as their bodies danced to a rhythm that he had set and her body raced to keep up with.

"That's it, baby," Tucker groaned out in an emotion-rich voice that drove her want for more of him higher and higher.

Nichelle felt her body rising as her release was coming on hard and fast. Her mind, like her body, was in a frenzy and with the arduous, strenuous way that Tucker was stroking inside of her, she knew that he was just as close as she was. Without any warning, a sensual pleasure, more powerful than any she'd ever experienced before turned her body into a mass of quaking spasm as her mind and body felt as if she had flown off of a cliff, leaving her with a feeling of weightlessness along with a searing, highly intense level of ecstasy that shouldn't be foreign to her because she'd made love many, many times with him, but this time was different. The wall behind her appeared to have disappeared from behind her and to her, she was floating with Tucker still encased within her body giving and giving her so much that her body couldn't come down from the illuminating high even if she wanted it to, which she did not. She never wanted to let go of the moment.

Knowing that Tucker was with her and climbing as high as she was, she held on to him tight and with the help of strong womanly muscles, she allowed the slippery folds of her womanhood to grip him tighter each time he surged into her body. When she felt his powerful strokes go deeper and stronger as his hips rolled around and around and then forward driving her body further up the water cascading wall, she held on, never wanting to let go. She rode him, pouring more and more of her love into her rhythmic strokes which matched his. Tonight, they were one and it was just them and their love. Their desire was immeasurable and then she felt it. Tucker's body rocked into hers and with them being chest to chest, she could feel his heart palpitations and his inwards groans exit his mouth as a loud, animalistic growl.

Opening her eyes, she was surprised to see that Tucker's eyes were opened and locked on hers. The moment his orgasm slammed into him, she saw it in his eyes and she couldn't look away. Even as she continued to ride out her own pleasure, she delighted in seeing the world slip away and he allowed himself to just feel and be felt. This was the kind of moment she never wanted to forget or be without. She almost did a double take as his eyes widened and without words, his eyes screamed out his love for her the way his growl of satisfaction hit a precipice of heights of pleasure she wasn't sure she'd ever seen in him before.

She relished at how time stood still as they mutually floated through the most delightful and gratifying experience.

As her body calmed and the movement of Tucker's hips slowed, they never turned their eyes away from each other. They were experiencing a pause in time where only love resides.

"It's just you and me. Remember that, Nichelle," Tucker breathed out softly. "Remember this moment when you and I are tangled together like this and we let everything go until there was this. Our bodies joined together in sync with our minds and our hearts."

Nichelle nodded as he leaned his forehead against hers.

"Just you and me. Just us two," she said as tears fell from her eyes; tears of so much joy that she had to let some out in order to make room in her body for more.

15

Antonia was running out of time and Tucker was starting to be a problem. She'd been calling and texting him for almost a week and he had ignored her. Undoubtedly, his attorney told him to stop talking to her just as her attorney warned her about any more unannounced pop-ups. This latest one could not be avoided. She needed him to agree to what she wanted and needed and there wasn't much more time to waste.

After finding a parking garage two blocks from City Hall, she made her way to his office, again wishing she had worn reasonable shoes. She was still a block away and was ready to take her heels off and walk barefoot to the office. She was so determined to get her way that the pain in her feet turned secondary to her need to talk to Tucker and have a final showdown.

The day before, her roommate called to say that a car repossession company had been by their place twice looking for her car. She was glad she'd convinced another friend to allow her to store it in their garage while she was gone, buying her some time to come up with more money. If she didn't soon make magic happen in order to get an advance check on her next season, the hotel would soon realize that the credit card she is using was about to be overextended. She barely had enough money to get a plane ticket back to Los Angeles if she had to do that as a final resort. She found herself running out of not just money, but out of time.

Reaching the doors of City Hall, she marched in, straightening up her flowery red and white dress as the security guards all looked her way. She was hoping to see someone who had worked their when she was married to Tucker, but all of the faces were new, though the looks they gave her were not. All eyes went straight to her cleavage and she decided to play that up.

"Hello," she said.

"Hello. You are here to see whom?" one of the guards asked.

"Oh, this isn't a public building?" she asked.

"No, it's not. Do you have an appointment? I need to check for your name," he said.

"Daniel," she said leaning over to read his badge, making sure to stay leaned over a few extra seconds. "My name is Antonia Glass and I use to be married to the Councilman Tucker Glass. I'd like to see him please," she said.

The way Daniel looked at her, he appeared to not be phased by her obvious attempt at flirting with him. Apparently, she wasn't the first to try using her womanly ways to gain access.

"Right. Is he expecting you?"

"Not exactly, but it should be fine. I used to walk all around these halls. Lots of people know me."

"That may be the case, but unless your name is on the list, you can't have access to any part of the building. If you'd like to call his office and have them send me your name, I'll let you in immediately. You can use this phone right here or one of your own. I would need that email to come directly from his assistant, Adrienne Patterson."

Antonia was furious, but she didn't allow it to show. She decided to try another angle as she leaned closer to him while others walked around her and used badges to get into the building.

"Do you know who I am? You don't recognize me?" she asked.

"Well, you just said you were once married to the Councilman Glass. Did you know he's actually Vice Mayor as well? I don't know how long ago that was that you were married to him, but I don't think it's been since I started working here about six months ago."

"No. I'm saying, you don't know me from anywhere else? My face isn't familiar?"

"Ma'am, are you going to make the call? If not, you're sort of in the way of the traffic flow into the building."

Antonia stood to her full height and held her head up high.

"I'm Roxie Hall. I'm the star of the reality show, *The Next Big Queen of Hearts*. You don't watch it?"

"Hey, I know you!"

Roxie turned when a woman interrupted her conversation.

"Excuse me?"

"I know you. You asked if he knew you, but I know you. You're Roxie Hall, the backstabbing bi... Oops, I almost cursed in a government building. I love you on that show. No one is time enough for your clapback. I love it. I can't believe you're here in City Hall. You are my favorite person on the show. I know that no one understands you or even likes you, but we are kindred spirits. We are two peas in a pod. If you lived in Chicago, I think that we'd be best friends," the woman hollered.

Antonia looked her over and knew that if she had a best friend or even a friend in Chicago, it would not be the colorful woman in front of her who was wearing an outfit that should be burned it was so old, and, she even had stains on the shirt that looked like someone's grandmother should have it on. Looking down at her feet, she saw that the woman's were practically hanging out on all sides. Her hair was weaved up and had to have been done by a blind woman it was so poorly done. It was so kinked up that there was no way she'd even get a comb through it. Why was it that it was the fans that looked like her that always pulled her up and wanted to be her best friend?

"Thank you for watching the show," she said.

"Oh, I watch replays again and again. I really loved earlier in the season when you slapped that chick Tyrika knocking her sunglasses off of her face. Sometimes, you have to check a trick like her! I can't wait for the next season to see who you'll dog out!"

"Well, again, thanks for watching the show."

Antonia tried to turn back to the security guard, that is, until the woman tapped her on the shoulder with long pink and yellow painted nails that showed she was weeks behind with a fill-in on her fake tips. The bawdy rings on every finger did not add to the look at all.

"Can I get a picture with you? My Instagram account will blow up when I post a picture with you," the woman asked.

"Uh, sure."

She waited while the woman pulled out her camera and smiled like she'd just won the lottery as she shoved her camera phone in their faces. As soon as one picture was done, she thanked the woman again and this time was able to get away from her and back to the security guard.

"Miss, if you're about to ask me again, I'm serious about needing that email in order for you to get in."

Feeling defeated, she didn't feel like arguing anymore and was about to leave when she spotted Omar coming her way. She noticed that he tried to walk back in the direction that he'd come in and she called his name, waving him over.

"Omar, this security guard won't let me in to see Tucker," she explained.

"No one is allowed in the building without prior notification from Tucker's office. Does he know you're here?" Omar asked.

"Of course not, but it's imperative that I see him. I'm getting desperate," she whispered.

"Desperate? What's wrong?"

Antonia leaned back, wondering why he was asking so many questions.

"Don't worry about that. Just get me in!"

"I can't, but if you want me to call up to see if Tucker will have the approval sent down, I can. I can't even bring visitors into the building in these post-911 days."

"Whatever. At this point, I might as well just wait around here until he leaves and catch him then. He will never allow me up to his office."

"That wouldn't work either. He doesn't leave by this entrance."

She sucked her teeth at him.

"Don't be an ass, Omar. I need to see Tucker," she pleaded.

"Call him."

"Call him for me and tell him I'm here and you ran into me here in the lobby and see what he says.".

"That's not a good idea. I don't think he should see us together or know that we're talking to each other. He might get suspicious."

"Of what!" Antonia yelled and then covered her mouth, apologizing to the security guards who looked her way after her outburst.

"You call him and he might let you up. He's in his office."

She thought about it and knew that Omar wasn't going to be any help. She would make him pay for this, adding this moment to her memory.

"Fine," she said taking out her phone.

"I'm going to leave. Can I see you tonight?"

"Maybe. I'll call you if I'm free. You know, when I'm back with Tucker and he wins the Mayor's seat, we can't see each other anymore. I have to maintain an image and in that kind of a position, all eyes will always be on him and me."

"You were with him before and with me. I don't like being used."

Antonia stopped dialing and moved to the side, away from people and pulled Omar with her.

"You don't what? Do you not realize that the only connection we have is give and give? You give me what I want and then I give you what you want. There has never been anything more than that. It's called I use you and you get to use me. Don't start acting your age and getting all clingy. If you can't get me upstairs to Tucker's office, you are no use to me right now. I said I would call you later and if I have time and I want to see you, then I will call you."

When Omar turned and walked away, she exhaled.

"Whatever," she heard him say.

Finally dialing Tucker's number, she waited for him to answer and then changed her mind and hung up. Instead, she asked the security guard for the number to call in order to get someone in Tucker's office. Dialing what he gave her, she sneered when Adrienne answered the phone, a woman who she never liked and who never liked her. She'd been working for Tucker since he first became a city council member.

"Council President Tucker Glass' office, can I help you?"

Antonia cleared her throat, ready for a show-down.

"Hello. This is Antonia Glass. May I speak with Tucker, please."

"One moment."

Antonia was shocked that Adrienne didn't hit her with a million questions.

"Antonia, whatever the reason, you are treading on thin ice calling me here," Tucker said when he jumped on the line.

"I need to talk to you and it's important. I'm serious, Tucker. We need to talk and resolve some things."

"We have lawyers for that and I know you've been told to stop contacting me. You're becoming borderline stalkerish now. I've already told you that your plan is a no-go for me and thereby, rendering any further conversations mute."

"Don't talk all legal like and stuff with me. I'm in the lobby downstairs. Either let me up or I will make a scene down here and you're not going to like it!" she yelled.

"Really? That's your threat? You can make a scene if you

want to. You're in a government building. The first sign of any problem and they'll have you in handcuffs being escorted out of the building. What do you want? How can I get rid of you so that you understand that the court needs to deal with this?".

"Give me just five minutes of your time. Five minutes is all I'm asking for. Surely, you can give me that."

"Ugh. Wait in the deli next door. I'll be right down, but you're not coming up."

Antonia was about to say thank you when he hung up on her. Turning around, she didn't look at any of the security guards as she exited the building and walked into the deli next door and grabbed a seat in the back-corner booth. She then waited.

**

Tucker stormed out of his office with purposeful strides. He knew he never should have agreed to meet with Antonia again, but maybe this time, he could make his point clear and concise and she will move on. He didn't want to hurt her and he wished her nothing but great success, but it wasn't going to be with any help on his end.

"Adrienne, clear my calendar for the next hour. I'll grab lunch on my way back and eat during my next conference call after lunch."

"Doing it now. Good luck," she said to him.

Tucker smiled.

"From your lips to God's ears!" he chimed and rushed to the elevator.

Thankfully, he was able to get an elevator that didn't stop until he reached the lobby. Moving swiftly, he exited the building and went next door. As soon as he entered, he saw

Antonia sitting in the back and joined her.

"Thanks for coming, though we should have been able to talk in your office. It's not like I'm a stranger or anything. You were married to me."

"The key word here is, were, something you can't see to understand. On paper, we may not be officially divorced, but we have been done for a long time and there is no turning back," he reminded her.

"Tuck, I'm going to be completely honest with you here so that you can understand why I can't let this go. I need this. For me to succeed in my career, I need this. My producers are saying I must come up with a juicy story about myself to bring in more viewers and the idea of us not being divorced fell in my lap. You're running for Mayor and this is the kind of stuff good television is made of. I want to be a part of it and I don't think I'm asking you for much since, as you stated, on paper, we are not divorced. I got that you don't want me and you're all in love and stuff, but we were married and you should still care enough to want me to be successful. Our marriage wasn't all bad. There were a lot of good times; enough that you and I can work together and both come out winners."

"I don't need dramatic flair to get elected like you need it for your television show. I'm running on a positive platform that deals with real issues that don't need to be mocked on a show. The answer is still no and it's not going to change. Nothing you say or do can make me change my mind."

"When did you become so unreasonable?"

Tucker leaned back in the brown leather seat, trying not to lose his patience.

"I'm not unreasonable. I'm trying to live my life and run a

campaign. I don't have time for drama with you at this point in my life. I left that back in the past," he explained.

"You must really love this girl. Will you love her if your little fling with her causes you to lose the election? I know you don't want that. I have a chance to get an advance on next season if you will just give this a chance and I promise that six-months after you win, I will quietly go away and back to my life in Los Angeles. You won't ever have to hear from me again."

"Antonia, how many ways can I say no!"

"I haven't heard enough of them yet. I'm not going to sign the divorce papers and then what will you do? I can drag this out. I'll tell the judge that we've had sex during this time apart making the separation and divorce null and void. See, I know some legal terms too," Antonia huffed.

Tucker laughed out loud. He laughed so loud that the people in other booths looked their way and he didn't care that they knew who he was.

"Don't test me. You won't like the outcome."

He waited while Antonia huffed again, knowing she wasn't gaining any ground.

"Look, I'm broke. I need that money. I need that advance check and I need a storyline or I'm not on next season. I will never get the kind of roles I want if this show tanks. My career will be in the toilet and I will have nothing. I don't want to, but I will blow your little relationship out of the water and you will be just as done as me. You're still married to me and you're screwing someone else," she scolded.

Tucker smiled sinister-like and leaned over the table.

"And you're screwing Omar and was doing so back when we were married. You want to bring up mess, let's bring that up when we get to court and you try to prolong the divorce proceeding."

Leaning back he took in the look of horror on Antonia's face. He could tell she was looking for words to come back with, but had none, unlike her Roxie character who was always ready to spit back words in someone's face.

"Wha...What are you talking about?"

"Don't try it and if I wanted to, I could have Omar in here with one phone call and he'd admit it because he wants to keep his job, but I won't hold your knack for seducing men over his head. He is young and impressionable."

"Just like your girlfriend," Antonia shouted.

"The difference in our scenarios is that I'm in love with her and she's in love with me. You're using Omar to get information on me and Nichelle and let me be very clear – if you try to hurt her, I will bury your career. If you're smart, you'll sign the divorce papers and go back to Los Angeles now. I don't care anything about being Mayor over my love for her and your desire to destroy me, even if it means hurting her is disgusting. Don't go there with me. I am not to be played with when it comes to the woman I love."

He took a minute and calmed his spirit. The thought of someone trying to use Nichelle to hurt him set him off and he wasn't going to sit or stand for it.

"You loved me at one time. You love her more than you loved me? You don't care that I could lose my car, my place, my show and my career, but you care if your little girlfriend gets a little hurt? Who are you? You cared about me at one time. I can't believe you can't sacrifice a little time, a few months of your life so that I can thrive like you are."

Tucker exhaled and prepared to leave by standing.

"Look, I'm not responsible for what happens in your career or in your life. I can't help you by sacrificing all that I've worked for professionally and especially personally. I'm in love. I'm happy. I will not curtail my life to help boost yours. I deserve a life and I deserve one with Nichelle. She deserves to be my first lady in every part of my life," he said.

"You're going to marry her?" Antonia questioned.

"I am and no way would I ever disrespect her by playing out some script with you for ratings. Let it go and stop popping up on me. Your little visits are not welcome."

Tucker didn't wait to hear anything else Antonia had to say. He turned and walked out of the deli and hopefully for the last time, he was leaving his old life behind him in that booth.

**

Antonia sat stunned and fumed in her booth. Never had she been turned down by a man. She thought that she had enough of a history with Tucker that he would help her get her life back on track.

"You'll regret choosing her over me. Trust me, you will regret it and so will your little girlfriend," she said to herself.

16

Nichelle walked up the two white and gray marble steps of the home that Alyssa, a friend of her sister Reese, shared with the love of her life Dexter and their son, Devon. She was nervous about the possibility of the job Alyssa wanted to offer her.

After her weekend way with Tucker, she'd been living on cloud nine. Other than the times when she had to be on the set of the show which was recording in Indianapolis, she and Tucker could barely keep their hands off of each other. They'd made love all over their hotel suite and she hated each time she had to leave out and leave him looking hot and tempting in bed. When she returned, she'd find him asleep and she was happy about it. She knew he wanted her to wake him, but she would return, close the bedroom door where he was sleeping and watch television in the grand room part of the suite. When Tucker woke, he would pretend to be mad that she'd let him sleep when he could have been enjoying having her in his arms.

That weekend they ate without worrying about gaining weight. The suite had a kitchen and she even grabbed a few things from the store and cooked for them. They watched movies, danced in each other's arms and talked about everything except work. They had a weekend of bliss and didn't regret that they had to return to the real world. That weekend owed them nothing. They would always have that time and others that they were already planning, including trying to get in a week's vacation away someplace like a resort or an island. She didn't care where they went as long as they went together and had more days and nights like they did back at the hotel.

While there, she'd received a call from Reese that her friend, Alyssa had inquired about her skills as a makeup artist. Calling her while out of town, she and Alyssa set up a time to talk and she agreed to come to Alyssa's house since she had a small child.

Ringing the bell, she beamed when Alyssa opened the door. She was immediately mesmerized by how stunningly beautiful she was. She found it hard to believe that Alyssa would need any makeup on her unblemished face.

"Nichelle!" Alyssa chimed and hugged her tight.

"Hi, Alyssa. I haven't seen you in a while, not since one of my sister's parties. I think you came with Dexter, Carter's best friend. She told me you and Dexter have a son," she said walking behind Alyssa into the house.

"We do and I'm glad you remember me. I wasn't sure you would. Dexter is at work at one of the auto body shops he and Carter own. Devon is taking a nap."

She walked behind Alyssa, watching her pick up one toy after another, tossing them into a large toy chest in the middle of the living room decorated in white with gold accented décor.

"Your house is beautiful. Did you do your own decorating?

I love the white theme in this room and your décor is unique."

"Thank you. I did decorate it and I'm still doing so. Dexter and I are still getting used to living under one roof and with the baby, he keeps me pretty busy. I get a lot done when he's asleep, but when he's woke, he wants my full attention – that is when Dexter isn't home. When his daddy is home, he only has eyes and wants attention from him. I become that woman with the breast milk!" Alyssa joked.

Nichelle followed her across the light oak wood floors and into the kitchen where a tray of fruit, cheese and crackers sat in the middle of the small kitchen table to the right of a large white marble island that sat eight.

"Okay, now you're showing off with this kitchen. This looks like something only an actual chef would enjoy from the brass cookware that extends from the ceiling to the restaurant style stove and ovens. Who does the cooking?".

"We both do. Dexter loves to cook more than me and the kitchen is his baby. I wasn't the best at cooking once we got together, but I've learned a lot having a kitchen like this and well stocked pantry. Feel free to have some fruit and cheese if you like. I thought I'd prepare us a snack. I also have wrap sandwiches and tea."

Nichelle watched Alyssa move about the kitchen and she could tell domestic life was something she loved.

"Thank you because I'm starving. I didn't get lunch today at work and I left and came right here."

"You're a school counselor, right?"

"I am and I love it, but I love doing makeup a lot more."

"That's good to know. Did Reese tell you much about my photoshoot?"

"No. She only mentioned that you asked about me because you know it's a great opportunity and you enjoy helping others come up!"

"That's true. I'll give you a little background of what you may or may not know about me. I used to be a part-time photographer and one day a woman saw me and told me that I was so beautiful that I should be in front of the camera and not behind it. She talked my ear off about doing a mini-photo shoot so that she could show me how much she already knew the camera loved me, and she was right. I never really thought much about it, but those photos took my breath away. I starting booking small gigs and now, after having the baby and getting back into shape, I've started getting back into modeling on runways and sitting for magazine layouts."

Nichelle took one of the sandwiches and opened one of the jars of tea.

"Wow. You still do all of that with a baby? How do you manage?"

"Dexter is how I manage. Though he is busy with all the businesses he and Carter have from the dealerships, to the autobody shops to the auto customization business, he still makes sure that I get to live out my dreams. I do a lot of work around Chicago and sometimes I travel. My mother may fly with me to help with the baby or Dexter's foster mother will travel with me to help with him. A lot of time, Dexter will come along because other than my mother, his mother and Sienna, he doesn't want many other's looking after Devon."

"You have a good man. Reese talks about him all the time. She calls him and Carter her other brothers from other mothers."

"They are all very close from back in their college days. I

have heard some stories about them from those days. They are closer than most blood siblings I know."

Nichelle shook her head in agreement. Reese has shared a lot about her college days and most stories involve Dexter, Carter, Sienna and Reese's fiancé, Torrence. She loved hearing about all of their shenanigans.

"That they are. I've known most of them all of my life," Nichelle acknowledged.

She stopped talking when the doorbell rang and Alyssa jumped up to answer it.

"Ugh, I hate that loud bell. It can easily wake the baby," Alyssa said running to the door.

Nichelle ate her food while she waited. After biting into the shrimp salad wrap, she wondered if she'd made them or bought them because they were delicious.

"And who is this?"

Nichelle turned and looked into the face of a man who looked like giant and it wasn't because she was sitting. The man was tall, well over six feet and he was broad like a boxer. He reminded her of the wrester turned actor, Dwayne The Rock Johnson. His features even favored him and not just his stature.

"Nichelle, this is my brother Joey. This is Reese's sister. She's a makeup artist."

"It's nice to meet you, Nichelle. I hope I'm not interrupting?" he asked Alyssa.

"You are, but you're here now. What are you doing in Chicago? I thought you were back in Vegas."

"I was, but I'm here because Torrence is hosting an upcoming wrestling match at his casino and I'm going to take part in it."

"Where is Carlos? Is he in town with you? Nichelle, I have two brothers and they are semi-pro wrestlers and they also operate a private security company."

"I'm actually hoping to go pro after the wrestling match that's happening here. There will be some scouts in the house that night looking for some professionals and I plan to be someone they're looking for."

"How long are you here for?" Alyssa asked.

"A few days and then I'm heading back to Las Vegas. I have a show there next week."

"I'm glad you stopped by," Alyssa said sitting down at the table.

Nichelle watched the exchange between brother and sister and it reminded her of how she interacts with her own brother, DJ who some also call Black because he has always been known to wear all black clothing since he was a young boy. She still preferred to call him DJ especially since he hates being called by his given name of Delvin, after their father. Though he and their father have tried to patch up their rocky relationship, he still didn't like being named after a man who spent a lifetime cheating on their mother before finally leaving them all to live his life.

"Well, the last time I was in town and didn't stop by, you berated me over the phone like I was a little child as if I'd committed a crime," Joey quipped.

"I consider you coming to town and not calling or coming by to see me and your nephew is a crime," Alyssa retorted.

"I listened and now I'm here. Where's Dexter? Working?"

"Yes, but he should be on his way here soon. You waiting around? I'm in the middle of a meeting with Nichelle, but you know you are welcomed to chill here if you want."

"I was actually hoping to spend the night. Think Dexter will be okay with that?"

"Oh, sure. Even after you hit him and almost knocked him out in Las Vegas, he has completely forgiven you!"

"What? You knocked out Dexter?" Nichelle asked.

"Not really, but I tried to. I didn't know the full story of him and my sister. I thought he got her pregnant and then kicked her to the curb and my sister failed to set me straight before we ran into him. I went off on him based on the information I had at the time about him, which wasn't much. Turns out my sister failed to tell my brother and me that he didn't kick her to the curb, but she had actually left him before telling him she was pregnant. He's a stand-up guy because as soon as he realized she was pregnant with his baby, he focused on claiming his child and ultimately proving to my sister that he loved her. We're good now."

Before any more conversation, they all heard the whine of a baby through the monitor on the counter. Alyssa stood to get him.

"Go ahead and have your meeting. I'll get Devon. I want to spend some time with him anyway."

"I'm sure his diaper needs to be changed."

"I got that. Any milk in that fridge you keep upstairs?"

"I do and there is a bottle warmer in the changing room. Thanks for looking after him so I can have my meeting."

"That's what brothers are for!" Joey shouted and ran up the stairs to Devon who was now screaming at the top of his lungs.

"Gotta love brothers!" Alyssa stated pointedly.

"Yes, you do. I have one and I love everything about him."

"Now, back to our chat about the shoot. This is not just a

job doing my makeup. I recommended you for the full set. There are twelve models and there are several clothing changes, which also will mean constant makeup changes. It takes place over a two-day time span and we're local here in Chicago."

Nichelle took the folder Alyssa handed her and opened it.

"Inside you will find photos of all of the models on the left. Get to know them and what works and doesn't work on their skin. You'll find that information on the back of each of their photos. The job pays very well and you'll see information about that and a contract on the right side of the folder."

Nichelle pulled that out and her eyes bulged in shock.

"Is this real? This job pays that much? This is for two days of work?" she asked. "This is almost more than I make in a year."

"I told you it pays well and when I found out, I asked your sister about you. The agency trusts me and I've heard great things about you. I showed them your Instagram videos and they were very interested. I asked if I could reach out. I want you to be comfortable and to know what to expect. I know you work full-time, but that shouldn't be a problem because the job is on the weekend. I don't want to take away from your personal life, but I'm hoping that weekend, you can free up some time for this. It could lead to big things," Alyssa said.

Nichelle thought about Tucker and knew that he was just as busy as she was and he would encourage her to take the job even if it meant cancelling any plans they may have together.

"I see the dates and this is fine and yes, I want the job. I need to order some new MAC and Fenty products, but I have plenty of time to do that. This is major!" Nichelle declared happily.

"I can see the joy on your face. You really enjoy this. Do you think you'll ever give up being a counselor and consider doing makeup full time? I know how heavy my schedule can be as a model and I'm sure it's just as hectic as a makeup artist. I would love to bring you on as my personal makeup artist for all of my gigs. I know more offers will also pour in after this shoot. Your life can become this job and I'm sure at your age, you're still hanging out with friends, going to clubs, partying. It's a lot of dedication."

"Actually, I don't really hang out much. I've never been big on parties. I prefer quiet evenings at home, especially on the weekends. I would like to focus more on makeup if the opportunities keep coming my way and I would love to be your personal MUA. I've been doing a lot more jobs lately than I've ever done. I'm now making more money than what I make on my full-time job. It's something to consider. I was asking, my...a friend and he agreed that I should consider a career change."

Nichelle almost let Tucker's name slip out.

"Tucker?"

Her eyes lit up.

"What?"

"Don't worry. Your secret is safe with me. I know about Tucker and I'm happy for you. He's a great guy. I don't know a lot about him personally, but Dexter and Carter speak highly of him and from what I hear, he's in love with you. I take it that feeling is mutual?" Alyssa asked. "I hope I'm not prying," she added.

"No, not at all. I didn't know you knew."

"I was at the fundraiser and Sienna and Reese told me what happened behind the scene. I hope that hasn't negatively impacted your relationship with Tucker. I hear he and Antonia are probably still married, but it's only paperwork. Real, true love can conquer anything."

"Is that what happened with you and Dexter? There had to be some craziness if your brother tried to knock him out."

"It was a crazy time. I was so in love with Dexter and then he broke up with me right when I was about to tell him I was pregnant. Did you know that there is an age gap between us like you and Tucker? Not as wide of an age gap, but there is one. I felt like he broke up with me for that reason and because he didn't want to give up his playboy status. After that, I high-tailed it out of Chicago and went to stay with my brothers in Las Vegas. One day, near the end of my pregnancy, Dexter happened to be in Vegas with his friends and saw me and saw my belly. He put it together that the baby was his. We had a rocky road to where we are now, but I will tell you that it was all worth it. We had our ups and downs and my lack of faith in him almost kept us apart. I learned to let nothing stand in the way of me having the man of my dreams and that is Dexter. Do you feel that way about Tucker?"

"I do. I love him so much. He came along at a time when I wasn't sure about being heavily involved with someone. Can I be honest with you?"

She didn't know why, but talking to Alyssa made her feel comfortable. Perhaps it was because Alyssa was being open and honest about her own struggles in her relationship and how keeping the secret of her baby from Dexter could have caused her to lose him. Reese also told her that Alyssa was close to her age and she may be able to relate to her.

"Absolutely and nothing you say will leave this room."

"Tucker is everything to me. I never thought a man could make me feel like a queen every single day. He's so good to me. We share everything. Before I met him, I dated a woman for a little bit. I was into what I saw going on in college and I fell into the *'fluid'* type of lifestyle of being open to dating men or women. That phase I went through wasn't for me, but still, it's a part of my past; a past I haven't told Tucker about. I don't know how he feels about that kind of stuff. Still, I haven't told him out of fear that he'll be turned off by me after hearing about that. I don't want to lose him. I fear losing him that way more than I fear losing him to his ex-wife, who I am sure he has no interest in. Still, he's big on honesty and I have a secret. I don't want someone to make the connection between me and the woman and it comes out while he's running for office. Right now, we've been keeping our relationship out of the public eye, but as things heat up, there will be deeper looks into his private life as much as his public life. I don't know what to do."

Nichelle exhaled loudly feeling like she'd dropped pounds with that admission.

"A lot of people go through a phase of discovering who they are and what they want and don't you dare shy away from any part of your life. If Tucker is the man I believe him to be, he won't judge you. I think he'll be happy that you love him. Right now, your life is private, but if your love becomes public, trust me, your past will come out and you don't want Tucker to be surprised by something that you should tell him about. Secrets can destroy a relationship. I almost lost Dexter and I would have regretted that forever. I don't think you'll lose Tucker over this, but don't keep anything from him. Be as open and honest with him as you say he's being with you. This mess with his ex-wife may get crazy. Is he keeping you in the loop about her?"

"Yes. He's telling me everything, even the fact that she tried to seduce him by showing up unannounced at his house. He wants me to know that he is all-in."

"Do the same thing; be the same way. Hold on to that love and don't let anything or anyone keep you from having it."

"That's good advice. I'm glad I came by here today and just in case I haven't already said it, I definitely want this job. Can you go over this contract with me? This is the biggest dollar amount in a contract that I've ever signed. I want to be sure I'm understanding it all and you're familiar with this."

"Of course. Then you have to tell me about how you met Tucker. He is one of the hottest bachelors in Chicago and there aren't too many women who wouldn't want to be in your shoes. I've known him to be a friendly-friend, if you know what I mean and that's not a dig on him. What I'm saying is, he loves you and that's big. I want to hear it all, but first, let's go over your contract and then I can answer any other questions you have about being on a set that big," Alyssa offered.

Nichelle nodded her head and was ready to dive in.

"First, tell me if you made these shrimp salad wraps or did you buy them?"

"Oh, I made these. I got a recipe from Dexter's foster mom and now Dexter wants them all the time."

"Mmm, I understand why. This is delicious. I hope you have enough that I can take one home with me for later."

"Absolutely. I have more in the fridge for Dexter to have

when he gets home later. Let's eat and talk and get you this money!" Alyssa shouted as they laughed and ate together.

Nichelle smiled for more than just the job she was getting out of this. She had found a new friend.

17

Carter walked out of his house and onto the expansive brick patio and straight to the grill to check on the steaks that were looking and smelling good.

"Y'all ready for these steaks? I think I missed my calling as a Grill Master! I'm serious, catch that aroma," he joked to Tucker, Dexter and Torrence, who were gathered around the bottle green, felt top, Metro reversible poker table that he usually kept inside of his mancave on the lower level of the sprawling house he shared with his wife Sienna and daughter Symone, but today was a beautiful weather day and they wanted to be outdoors to smoke their favorite cigars, something Sienna did not allow in the house.

"Bro, you may be good at grilling, but not as much as you are at selling cars and making deals," Dexter said.

"Thanks for the invite," Torrence added. "I could definitely use a good steak and a break away from all things casino for a night."

"How's everything going?" Carter asked.

"Booming and the new casino is still on track to open on schedule in a few months. This will be Montiel Avage, 3, for our third location. We're also expanding the casino in Las Vegas. The property to the left and right of us are both up for sale and Horace and I made an offer that was accepted. He's thinking of moving here to Chicago to oversee operations at the new location, which would great. Overseeing the one location has me running ragged some days. We already have one of the managers who we are thinking about training to run the Vegas location. I'm heading out to Vegas next week to check on that deal," Torrence explained.

"Living that dream!" Dexter shouted.

"That I am and I'm not the only one. I heard you and Carter are being invited onto a new night-time talk show to talk about black wealth because the two of you are successful and how you're mentoring other young black men to reach for their goals. Y'all are doing it," Torrence said.

"Yeah? That's dope," Tucker added.

"It is and we're also going to be on all three of the national morning news shows as well, later this month. How we got those interviews was crazy. I reached out in response to them wanting to get Tucker on their shows to talk about his run for Mayor after he was listed as the number two African American politician to watch. The strides he's made here in Chicago as Council President and Vice Mayor have been heard about and felt around the country. Some believe that's why the current Mayor isn't running again. He sees that Tucker can bring the change that we've all been wanting for the city we love. The country is taking notice too after the Mayor did an interview and credited Tucker with implementing major initiatives that have benefited the city – ideas that people assumed came from the Mayor," Carter said.

Closing the lid on the grill, he rejoined them for another quick hand of poker before they shifted to the covered glass top table to eat. Beside the steaks, there were ribs that he'd been cooking slowly since early in the morning and hand made from scratch burgers made by Sienna. Along with that, she'd pulled together a large bowl of potato salad, deviled eggs and his own favorite, corn on the cob.

"I'm thankful for the platform I've been given. I never thought that one day I'd be this deep in politics. I thought, like my dad did, that I would join him in business, especially when I decided to go to law school. I know he wanted me to join the family business, but public service was a harder tug," Tucker explained.

"Was your dad disappointed that you didn't join him in business?" Torrence asked.

"Not even for a second. When I told him I wanted to go into politics, the first thing out of his mouth was how could he help me. He and my mom and my sisters were in my corner from day one. I thought his plan was to retire one day and have me take over, but he said his only dream for his children was that we find love, happiness and careers that made us proud of ourselves. I've done good on the career side, but the love and happiness part I'm finally getting to at thirty-nine. I'm okay with saying better late than never at all," Tucker acknowledged.

"Ah, so you're finally where the three of us are?" Carter asked.

As Dexter dealt the cards, Tucker looked around the table and found all eyes on him. Other than talking with Carter about the Antonia situation the night of the fundraiser where they all also found out that he'd been seeing Reese's sister,

Nichelle, he hadn't spoken with the other fellas about it. They all played pool recently, but his private life never came up; none of theirs did. They talked a lot of sports and future business plans, but nothing persona.

Through his friendship with Carter spanned many years, he was brought closer into the fold of his friends and knew that they were a close bunch, some would say closer than some real brothers were. He had a lot of friends, but he was cautious of how close to have those friends knowing the influence he had as a politician. Carter, Torrence and Dexter he trusted unconditionally and he had no problem letting them in on what he's been keeping a secret for months.

"I am and it actually is a relief to be able to say that I'm in love with Nichelle. I know you were all shocked to hear I was seeing her, but it wasn't kept on the downlow because of me. I was protecting Nichelle's right to her privacy considering the high-profile stance which is my life. I was ready for her to meet my family after the first week of us dating and I wanted her family to know about me. I fell that hard for her," he admitted.

"Damn! Not you? Y'all fools don't know that, if we thought we were something when it came to the ladies, Tucker had us all beat and the thing was, he wasn't making a commitment to any of them and they didn't care. He was putting something down on these women out here, especially after he and Antonia split up. You're one smooth guy, Tucker," Carter joked.

"Yeah, whatever. Antonia took me through some stuff and though I didn't really think we were in a forever marriage, I did love her, but she was a handful and our lives were not going in the same direction. With Nichelle, it's pure, unconditional love. I knew it from the moment she agreed to eat her lunch with me at this deli I like to go to downtown," Tucker said.

"That's where you met her?" Dexter asked.

"No. I met her at the school where she is a counselor. Carter and I were there for career day and she was my escort for the day. Check this out – she actually shot me down when I asked her out."

"What?" Torrence and Dexter questioned at the same time.

"I bet that was a shock to your system," Carter said.

"It was. You know how we can be so self-assured. She broke a brother down when she said no, but then I ran into her again and I guess my charm worked. I've been in love with her ever since. She's the first woman that has made me see that I can love forever. I want to marry her and have a million kids and just live happy. I love politics, but she's made me see that there is more to life and I can actually have both politics and a happy personal life and I can have that with her and, with her full support, we can be unstoppable. I will also always give her that same kind of support in all that she wants to do."

Tucker looked around as none of the guys commented but looked at him like he had food in his teeth.

"Did you say marry? You're going to propose to her?" Carter asked. "That's big since you said you never wanted to marry again."

"I didn't think so until I met her. I'm telling you my love for her is no joke."

"Reese will be happy to hear that," Torrence said. "She had some reservations when she found out about the two of you, but then she talked with Nichelle and what you're saying matches what she told her. She's in love with you. I'm happy for you. You plan on proposing sometime soon?"

"I will after our relationship is public. I was going to introduce Chicago to her at the fundraiser and then the rug was pulled out from under me when Antonia made an appearance announcing the fact that we weren't actually divorced. I need to take care of that first. She signed the divorce papers with her stage name and not her actual name and then my lawyer, at that time, didn't follow-up and have me re-sign new documents. It's crazy, but Carter put me on to a new lawyer and she's getting things done. I have a court date in two weeks where the papers will hopefully finally be signed and I can move on with my life with Nichelle. I've decided that I'm not going to wait on that to make my relationship public. There is no reason to. I have nothing to hide and me still being married was all about a paperwork glitch and not about me cheating on my wife," Tucker explained.

"Yeah. Antonia is trying to use that as an edge to try and stay married to him so that she can be first lady of Chicago and then use that platform to boost her credibility in the acting world. It's a mess, but y'all know Leslie. She is not about any foolishness. She's been my lawyer for a long time. When Sienna divorced me, Leslie actually tried to convince me to not give in so easily, but Sienna wanted out because I'd cheated on her and I wanted her to be happy. When Sienna and I got back together and remarried, Leslie was the first to send us a big bottle of champagne, which Sienna couldn't drink because she was pregnant, but I appreciated the gesture," Carter said.

"Yeah, I used Leslie when I thought I was going to have custody issues with Alyssa after I found out she was pregnant and then didn't want me to be a part of my son's life. Leslie helped me draw up papers to protect my son in case anything happened to me and she also encouraged me to work with Alyssa to co-parent and that turned into us realizing we loved each other and I hope you all will be in the place for our wedding next month. It's going to be a small gathering, but we need to get to it quick since she's two months in on our second baby," Dexter said.

"Congratulations!" everyone at the table chimed together.

"That's what's up. That's what it's all about," Torrence said.

"When is your wedding with Reese?" Dexter asked. "The two of you got engaged before Alyssa and I did," he added.

"We were trying to plan something big, but now, with our busy schedules, Reese wants to do a small wedding in Vegas. I think we'll be doing it the month after your wedding to Alyssa, so be on the lookout for plane tickets to join us," Torrence said.

"That's great!" Carter said. "Sienna said that Reese was coming over tonight to talk about something going down in Vegas. I guess they are about to wedding plan. You know we're there. I'll get either my parents or Sienna's parents to watch Symone. Now that Sienna is over the severe morning sickness, she'll be good to fly. Look at us sitting around talking about love, marriage and kids and not once have we mentioned man stuff like sports and cars!" Carter joked.

They broke out in a loud round of laughter at the thought.

"What's so funny?" Sienna asked from just inside the house.

"Nothing, babe. You good?" Carter asked.

"I have the corn and salads ready for the table. Can you come get them? Reese just got here and we're going to talk girl stuff and this is the last of your food. If you all need anything else, you'll have to get it yourself," she said and turned around.

"We see who runs things around here," Dexter joked.

Carter stood and walked toward the house.

"Don't think I haven't been to your house and heard Alyssa barking out instructions and watching you jump to get it done before she has to say it twice," Carter yelled over his shoulder.

"We've all experienced that," Torrence laughed.

"I look forward to being this blissfully happy with Nichelle," Tucker said.

"Got a ring yet?" Torrence asked.

"Not yet. Where did you get Reese's ring?"

"I have a guy who will design something unique. It will cost you, but he's the best," Torrence explained, taking out his cell phone to get the number.

Tucker took out his phone and added the name and number to his contacts.

"That's for the connection."

"He'll even come here to Chicago to see you all the way from Vegas. If you and Nichelle come to Vegas for the wedding, if that's not too far off for you, set up a meeting while you're there."

"I'll do that."

Tucker started to say more when Carter came back out of the house with his arms loaded with food. To help, he got up and walked over to take a bowl from his arms.

"Hold up. Look, Reese is here to talk with Sienna and guess who showed up with her?" Carter asked.

Tucker took a few seconds and knew right away.

"Really?"

"Yup. She's in the house. I got this. Go see your woman. You don't need to hide your relationship when you're around us."

"Cool. I'll be back in a few minutes," Tucker said and headed into the house.

18

Tucker heard her before he saw her and the minute their eyes locked, he didn't have to say a word to explain how happy he was to see her. Nichelle was amongst the other ladies, but all he saw and focused on was her. His eyes never left hers the moment she looked over at him and didn't look away. He saw the moment her eyes lit up with recognition and instead of awkward surprise, he saw happiness. His heart immediately leaped with an overwhelming desire that was far beyond love. In this space and time, there was only them. As if in a fantasy, even the walls of the home fell away along with everything else physical and all that remained was the two of them, allowing their eyes to fall in love again and again.

The air was getting thick and all he wanted to do was pull her into his arms to kiss her until he needed to come up to breathe more air into his body. There was no doubt Nichelle was the love of his life and he saw that same kind of unwavering love staring back at him.

"Tucker? Reese called out in question.

Tucker shook his head like in a cartoon movie to bring his

mind back to the present. He finally looked away from Nichelle and turned to her sister, who had just called his name.

"Oh, hey Reese. Good to see you," he said, feeling slightly embarrassed that he'd been caught by a group of ladies as he openly ogled Nichelle.

"Likewise. I see that you and Nichelle only see each other. Perhaps you can take all this love-staring into another room," she joked.

Tucker coughed with even more embarrassment and looked to Nichelle for help in rescuing him from the penetrating stares of the women in the room.

"Sorry, sis. I'll be right back," Nichelle said standing and putting her hand in Tucker's outstretched one.

Tucker turned and walked away like a man with a purpose, holding on to Nichelle's hand as if his life depended on him never letting go. He was focused; he was determined and he was with his woman and while it wasn't a shock to anyone else and he didn't care if it was, he would have loved all over her in front of them, but he decided the moment Nichelle got up and walked with him, he would spare her the embarrassment of how he wanted to devour her with the kiss that his mere life now depended on. He needed to have her in his arms that much.

Tucker didn't talk as he looked for a quiet place for them to talk. Seeing stairs that led downstairs, they walked down them and found themselves in what he was sure was Carter's man-cave. There was a large movie screen at the far end of the room in front of three rows of two sections of love seats. The screen covered the entire wall. On the side of the screen were four smaller, yet still large screens, a sports fan's dream. There were two more poker tables that matched the one they were using outside and a music sound system with speakers throughout the entire room.

"Wow. I'm missing out!" Tucker said checking out the space and all it included. His lack of taking the time to man-cave his own space proved that he spent too much time at the office.

"I've been here before. Carter loves this room and Sienna always says she never comes down here. It's a place where he can go to get away from everything and to hang and be loud with his friends. She has a similar room that's more girlie than this upstairs in the back of the house," Nichelle said.

Stopping and pulling her flush against his body filled with need for her, he didn't want to chit chat or talk about anyone other than them. Just when she was about to say more, he covered her lips with his, a kiss he wasn't prepared to wait until later to experience. They had made plans for him to stop by her place after he left Carter's house later that night, but since they were together now, he saw no reason to wait to douse the fire blazing. Releasing her lips, he kissed her quickly again when she smiled up at him, just as happy with their connection as he was.

"I didn't know you were going to be here," he said.

"I didn't either. Reese called me and said she wanted to hang out. I thought we were going out to eat at this Ethiopian place she loves and then I look up and we're here. I think she planned this because you told me Torrence and Dexter were going to be here too, and Reese would have known you would be here. This bar is new," Nichelle said, looking behind where Tucker was leaning.

Tucker turned and scoped it out.

"There are some spots that don't have bars this big and is there a brand of liquor that is not on the shelves on the wall? Wait, I see another room in the mirrored wall – a reflection," he said, thinking that the area he could now see appeared to be even more private.

Tucker took her by the hand and led them inside the room where they found a gigantic black leather sectional, the size of two king-sized beds. There was another wall-sized television that wowed him."

"I like this room with the red walls and black furniture. It's nice," Nichelle noted.

"Carter is living the life! I love the life he has with Sienna," Tucker said, once again pulling Nichelle close as he braced his back against the wall inside of the space. "It's quiet in here," he added.

"We need quietness?" Nichelle asked.

He saw the questionable look on her face and chuckled. For what he had in mind, they actually needed the house to themselves, but this room would do. He knew what he needed and there has never been a time when their needs didn't match when their bodies were this close. He looked down, and with one of his hands, he lifted her chin up to hold her eyes. He knew what she would see in them and he wanted his intentions clear.

"I need you," he whispered softly.

"No more than I need you. I'm happy to see you, though I will scold my sister for this setup. I guess she's making it known that she's tired of us not being able to date openly around them."

"We're all friends and we should be able to be openly in love just as they all are. Remind me to thank your sister for bringing you and let me start with thanking you for wearing this sexy ass dress! Your body was made for form fitting dresses like this and the open neckline makes it easy for me to do this."

Leaning down, he slowly swiped his lips along a path from her shoulder and up her neck to her ear where he kissed the lobe and bit it playfully. When Nichelle moaned just enough that he could hear her, he smiled against her cheek.

"I like when you're like this. Being this close to you makes me miss you when we're not together," she said.

Tucker leaned back.

"I want to always be together and not just behind closed doors. I know we're being cautious, but I don't want to do that anymore. I'm tired of hiding, baby. My parents are flying in for my upcoming press conference that I told you about. It's going to be a big night and letting all of Chicago know how hard I will work for them. My sisters will be there as well as other family. My friends will be there including Carter, Torrence and Dexter and their ladies and I want you there with me, by my side. I can't keep hiding you like you're some secret."

Tucker lamented about having this chat now because he was hoping they would be alone where they could really talk things out and at Carter and Sienna's house wasn't private enough, but the words just wouldn't stay in him.

"But what about Antonia and her threats? What happens when people find you're still married and knowing that you are, you are still seeing me? What would you say when questioned?" she asked.

Tucker could hear the worry in her voice, but his love for her outweighed any need to worry about what outsiders thought about their love, even if it meant the election not going his way. He'd waited long enough to love the way he and Nichelle loved each other. He was done living his personal life for everyone else to have a say in.

"I would say that you're the woman I love and that I didn't know I was still legally married until recently and that the issue is being handled by attorneys. That's it. People don't deserve more information into or explanations about my life or yours. What I need to know is, are you comfortable if I do that? I don't want to put you on the spot or put your life out for people to dig all into, but this is my life. I'm a politician and people want to know all about me and that will include you. I don't mind sharing small details, but I don't want to give into any pressure to share specific details about us despite anything my ex-wife way leak to the press. I don't want to live like that. Are we in this together, baby?"

Tucker only cared what Nichelle thought. He could deal with other people's negative thoughts about how he lived his life, but he needed to know that he and Nichelle were on the same page. He needed her with him for their love to work. He searched her face for any doubt as he waited for her to speak.

"I love you and if you want me with you that day at the press conference, I will be there and like you, I don't want to hide anymore. I don't even care about Antonia and her tricks. Let her come with whatever she has. At least we will know all that she's working with and she'll see that people won't care that she is the reason the divorce didn't happen and I believe they will understand. Reese and I were talking about this very thing on the ride here and she told me to stop hiding my love for you and to not let anything or anyone keep us from living freely. You know she's ready to jack Antonia up – you know my sister. I'm the cool sister and she's the scrapper! She will take her heels off, whip out a ponytail holder for her hair now that she's letting it grow out even more and then throw down if she needs to."

Tucker laughed out loud. He was picturing Reese doing just that and found humor in the visual of it.

"Yeah, I know about Reese and how she can set things off. There won't be a need for that. I just want to be able to share with the world that I have the perfect woman in my life. We're good, then?" he asked.

He needed her reassurance and then they could move on to what was next or at least, what was up for them in the next moment.

"We're better than good. I need to find something to wear for that night. I'll get Reese on that. She knows all of the fancy places to go to shop for events like that. I'm so happy for you and I'm proud of you. If I could, I would reward you for being a hot, sexy boyfriend who knows how to make a woman feel like she's queen of the world. That's how you make me feel all the time."

Tucker leaned close to her ear and he knew what she felt when he did. He felt her tremble in his arms because his desire for her was unmistakable between them.

"I would say prove it because I'm already feeling the proof and from the look in your eyes and the slight moving of your hips from side to side, you feel it too."

Tucker had a plan in mind, but didn't want to make her feel uncomfortable about what he wanted to do considering where they were. He tried to will his body to calm down so that they could rejoin the others and take up the rest of what was on his mind when they were together later that night.

"Oh, you feel that? I can feel you," Nichelle leaned up and whispered close to his ear.

Tucker was about to explode the moment she licked her tongue across his lips and across the hair of his beard.

"You're killing me and what I had in mind when we came into this room is starting to control my actions, but we're not at your place or my place. I guess I'll bring this up again a little later, sweetheart," he swooned and kissed her sweetly.

When Nichelle moaned sexily against his mouth and with the gleam now in her eyes, he knew where her mind was going even before she said the words.

"Oh really? Later? What about right now?" she challenged him.

Tucker started to question her intent, but it was already becoming clear when she reached for the belt of his blue denim jeans. Reaching for her hands, he held them still even as his body reacted to the slight touch of her fingers, which brushed against him, causing him to harden even more. He loved how even the slightest touch or gleam from her beautiful brown eyes could ready his body to explode. The fact that his jeans suddenly felt a lot snugger didn't surprise him and he couldn't rejoin the fellas with a hard-on that was stiffer than a light pole.

"We are in Carter and Sienna's house. You know we can't. Okay, I admit, I came down here with the intention of enticing you into a little quickie, but then I regained my sensibility, even with the way my manhood is about to break the zipper of my jeans. I'm thinking we should make an excuse and leave early; together," he suggested, though his body was aching to follow her lead and his lower head and not the head on his shoulders.

"Is that so? I guess you're no longer the most adventurous one in our relationship. I need you right now. I want you right now and you're going to make me wait? You are the one who turned me into a woman who can't get enough of her man and now I'm being denied," Nichelle said sheepishly. "I don't know how to feel about that."

When she looked at him and batted her eyes, Tucker was close to giving in, but he tried to let his more sensible head lead his actions.

"You know how irresistible you are and that's twenty-four, seven. I would love to be inside of you right now, but come on – you know how loud you are. I'm trying to be a gentleman now, though my intentions a few minutes ago were anything but gentlemanly," he explained.

"Not as loud as you, but I'm willing to risk it. How risky are you willing to be for this?" Nichelle said, spinning her body around and making sure to stop with her back to him, teasing him to see things her way.

Tucker was about to lose his mind when she bent over, giving him an even greater view of her perfect behind. He licked his lips in potent desire.

"You are dangerous!" he exclaimed, reaching for her.

"I bet you have a condom or two in your wallet since you were already planning to come see me tonight. Stop holding out! I want to celebrate no longer hiding our love."

He loved how deep their passion ran for each other and he never liked denying her anything, especially when it came to loving.

"What will everyone upstairs think with all this time we're gone?" he questioned, not really caring, but giving Nichelle a chance to save face. He knew what their friends would think and he would take the brunt of their ridicule – he just didn't want that for her.

"They'll think that you're loving me up and Reese set us up. You know that's what she did. We slipped away to the lower level away from all of them. They know what's going on and I don't care what they think. Like you said, they're our friends and we don't need to hide and believe me, they are freakier than you and me. I can't tell you the number of times Reese and Torrence have been caught in a closet or in the car in the driveway at someone's home. If we stop talking and get to some action, we can have this quickie and rejoin the living upstairs before they remember we were missing in action."

Tucker laughed when she again reached for his belt buckle with the zeal of a woman who didn't want to hear the word, no. Now his body and his mind were both screaming yes and this time, he didn't stop her. Instead, he reached into his back pocket and pulled a condom from his wallet.

"I can never resist giving you your way," he said, shaking his head from left to right knowing they should both be ashamed of themselves for what they were about to do, but he didn't care. They had already gone beyond the no-return zone. He was on the edge and the way she was working his buckle and zipper, so was she.

"Good, then drop these pants, lover boy, because I see something I want and from the look of things, that something wants me just as bad," Nichelle slurred and purred like a she-devil in heat.

This is how he loved seeing her – wanting him with as much zest as he always wanted her.

Tucker followed her eyes, even though he didn't need too. He knew how hard and ready he was. He was so anxious to feel her wrapped tight around him that his hands shook in his rush to get the condom on.

He leaned down as he slid it on and moaned as he kissed her with eagerness, devoid of any move to hold back.

"I love when you're a bad girl. Hands against the wall baby as if you're under arrest and make sure you spread those legs wide for me," he whispered close to her ear.

When Nichelle bounced and moved in place, he laughed out loud and had to cover his mouth because he couldn't hold back. He loved her enthusiasm as she moved to his left, next to the doorway, bent over slightly, lifting her dress up over her hips and showing him her bare cheeks with the thin strap of her yellow thong underneath the black dress."

"That ass and thong; you're trying to kill a brother!" he exclaimed against her neck.

"Don't die before you get to this quickie," she responded and he laughed harder.

Nichelle said it with such fervor, that he knew they were about to have an explosive couple of minutes. Moving up behind her, he quietly shared a few words of how much he wanted her and if she could feel how excited she made him when he rubbed back and forth against the soft cheeks of her behind. When all she could do was moan, he smiled and knew that this was only one of many, many more sexy adventures they would have. He couldn't wait to make her his forever love.

Allowing his body to delight in being this close to her, Tucker rubbed his hands across the exposed flesh of her thighs and behind. Caressing her softness as she wiggled in response to this touch, he reached for the thin strip that covered her womanhood and slid it to the side. Reaching between her legs, the fact that she was wet and ready for him was no surprise. From the beginning of their relationship, following the first time they were intimate, he had come to expect that her desire matched his. Bracketing her hips and plump behind in his hands, he held her steady as he stooped down and easily slid into her body. He savored the feel of her, tight and inviting – to the point where he was already seeing stars behind his eyelids. When her hips moved, he moved with her.

Finding the crook of her neck, he kissed her there and down to her shoulder. He knew if he didn't find something to do with his mouth, he wouldn't be able to keep what they were doing a secret from those who were one level up, right above them.

Pressing closer and surging deeper and deeper, Nichelle let go in his arms as her body gave way to the pulsing outpouring of her release. Following her, his jaw clenched and he groaned out his own powerful release. Their breaths came out in short, aromatic emissions as their bodies rose and then slowly calmed.

"That was an incredible quickie and I needed that," Nichelle uttered.

He held her up when he felt her legs begin to buckle in front of him.

"Always with us. Every part of you and me together is like this, which is why I love you so much. It's not just the great sex, it's because of the incredible love."

There would never be an end to his love for her. Now that they were free to love in front of others, he knew that what they shared was ready for the next level and knowing they were in this relationship together and on the same page was all that he could ask for. He stood with her in his arms with her head against the wall and his head against the back of hers. He could stand like this forever if it were not for the fact that they were in someone else's house. He just wanted to cherish this moment and he secretly prayed that nothing would ever be able to tear their love apart. He wasn't sure he would survive being away from her. Nichelle was his air; she was his every breath in and out. He needed her; he loved her and nothing else mattered if he didn't have her.

**

Nichelle walked back into the living room and sat down while Reese and Sienna continued talking about wedding plans for Las Vegas. She was excited for her sister because Torrence was a great man and she couldn't wait to call him brother-in-law.

"Is daddy coming to Vegas to walk you down the aisle or is DJ doing it?" Nichelle asked, as if she had been a part of their conversation from the start.

She smiled when she saw Reese and Sienna look around for Tucker, she as sure of that, but he had entered the kitchen from another entrance, thereby, avoiding eye contact with the ladies after what had just occurred downstairs. There is no doubt in her mind that Reese and Sienna already knew. When Reese cleared her throat for no reason at all, Nichelle giggled to herself. She couldn't even make eye contact because her mind was still on what she and Tucker had done and even though she had cleaned up on before coming back upstairs, her body could still feel the essence of her powerful orgasm and she shivered at the remembrance.

"Daddy is doing it and DJ is fine with that. He and daddy are making good strides in repairing their relationship and don't you dare jump in the middle of the conversation like you didn't just slither in here! Did you remember to put your panties back on?" Reese asked nonchalantly.

Nichelle was surprised that Reese asked her that so calmly as if it was the most natural thing in the world to say. She looked between the two women as they laughed out loud and what Nichelle knew was a look of pure shock and amazement on her own face. Nichelle was trying to think of how to respond to move the moment beyond Reese's question.

"Don't mind your rude sister. Reese is one to talk. You should be familiar with her antics by now and trust me, I know you have caught her in many uncompromising positions over the years because I sure have and I've gotten my share of an eyeful and not just an earful. You and Tucker are not the first to get a quickie in a room in my house, is she Reese?" Sienna asked.

Nichelle, like Sienna, turned her attention to Reese who almost fell out of the chair as she doubled over with laughter.

"Girl! Trust me – I was thinking about texting Torrence to meet me in the guest room and to come up with an excuse for his absence," Reese declared. "You know how we like to get it on in your house and don't act like you care. You know how we do!" she added.

Nichelle wasn't surprised, but still shook her head in amazement at the things she's caught Reese and Torrence doing. Reese was a big freak and wasn't ashamed of it, especially when it came to wanting Torrence whenever and wherever she chose.

"You and Torrence just do it anywhere you please! Sienna,

I once had to go for a walk when they were helping me move into my new place. He disappeared into the bathroom and then I looked up and she was gone too. Then I heard the sounds of moaning and knew what they were doing and they weren't ashamed. They weren't even trying to be quiet. The things she was saying to edge him on were disturbing knowing they were in my bathroom and not at their own home. Reese is such a freak!" Nichelle boasted.

"Oh please! That was nothing! I could tell you some stories about me and my man, but I won't. I'm saving that for the erotic book I may write one day! Like sister, like sister!" Reese yelled.

"Your sister is my best friend because she keeps everything in her life real including loving on her man at any time," Sienna added.

"Panties? Did you remember them?" Reese asked again.

Nichelle held her head down, embarrassed. She had hoped that Reese had forgotten she'd asked that question. She knew there was no way she'd get away with not answering. Exhaling loudly, she leaned back on the chair and shook her head.

"I cleaned up in the downstairs bathroom and while you were talking, I slipped them in my purse which I'm glad was still sitting here on the floor by the chair," she admitted.

This time, she did laugh with Reese and Sienna who laughed even louder when they looked up and saw Tucker look through the doorway and wink. Nichelle blew him a kiss, since they were all being all open and honest about their stuff.

"See, you have learned so much from your big sister!" Reese declared. "In the future, take a spare thong with you, just in case. I keep a pair or two in my glove compartment in a zip-lock bag, just because," Reese added.

"Are all of you like that? Are you just doing it all the time, wherever?" Nichelle asked. "Cause, I never wanted to as much as I have lately with Tucker. We've been sneaking around so much, but we seem to not care when and where."

"No worries. I get it in with Carter when and wherever I can. I am use to having to slip drenched panties into my purse. Like Reese said, the trick is to have a fresh thong in your purse when you're out with your man, just in case. We have some virile men!" Sienna shouted.

Nichelle had to laugh and agree along with them. She made a mental note to buy extra underwear and zip-lock bags the next time she was out at the store.

**

Exiting the kitchen, Tucker walked toward the table where the fellas were already digging into steaks and ribs. He went to grab a plate from the small table Sienna had set up near the door when Carter rushed up to him and grabbed a plate and added food to it though he knew Carter already had a plate in front of him at the table before he got up.

"The next time you sex your woman up in my house, check your zipper to be sure your shirt isn't sticking through it."

Tucker turned around and looked down.

"Damn. I thought I checked that," he said.

He looked over at Carter who tried to stifle a laugh as he turned his back to the other guys at the table.

"Tell me you did not screw your woman on my sectional. I went looking for you and Sienna said she thought you and Nichelle had gone downstairs. I'm use to that from Reese and Torrence and even Derek and Alyssa, so it's no sweat. I don't know what it is about that sectional, but seriously, there were wipes down there and I hope you used them to clean my chair if you used it. What is it about my house that makes people want to randomly get their freak on?" Carter asked, jokingly.

This time, Tucker laughed at finally feeling like a true member of the group. He stopped long enough to explain.

"I promise I didn't do that. Your sectional was safe from me, but before I leave, if you give me some Lysol, I'll spray your wall down. That's one part of your house that witnessed it all, up close and extremely personal!" Tucker joked.

Carter laughed out loud and walked back over to the table.

"I got a bunch of freaky ass freaks for friends!" Carter hollered back at him.

Tucker had a smile so big on his face, he didn't care who knew what he and Nichelle had been up to. He did fix his zipper before joining them at the table.

He had to remember to go back down and wipe the wall down, though he had already checked it before cleaning up in the bathroom after Nichelle had done so and gone back up the steps ahead of him.

Sitting at the table, he went right into devouring the food he'd worked up an appetite for and he joined in the conversation they were having about naming their top five professional basketball players.

As the night drew on, he'd caught several glimpses of Nichelle in the kitchen and each time she looked his way, he winked at her. When she and Reese finally decided to head out, he stood when Nichelle came out to say good night and instead of ignoring any show of affection like they had been doing for months because of the secrecy around their love,

Tucker pulled Nichelle into his arms and kissed her like a man who just come back from war. He didn't care who saw and didn't see. He loved his woman and he wanted everyone, especially those closest to him to know that he loved her and he would no longer keep anything about their love hidden. The kiss was hot and sexy and when he finally let her up for air, he had to take a few minutes to catch his own breath.

"Damn, are you letting her breathe!" Dexter shouted.

"Oh, like you don't slobber Alyssa down every time she's within arm's reach!" Carter hollered.

"Whatever!" Dexter declared and sat back down.

"Tonight?" Tucker asked Nichelle before letting her out of his arms.

"I'll be waiting," Nichelle replied.

As she walked away, Tucker was ready to leave, but he didn't get the chance to unwind with beer, food and poker, so he held onto the notion that he'd have her in his arms again before the night was over – that he was sure of.

As Reese and Nichelle walked back into the house, Tucker felt like a new man. He was ready for the newness that was about to enter his life. That newness would be no more hiding; no more secrets. He was ready for what was ahead of him with telling the world about being in love with his beautiful lady.

19

"Roxie Hall?"

Antonia turned her head around quickly in the direction of her stage name being called and lowered the large, dark sunglasses that covered her face. She should have told Omar to tell his friend to call her Antonia. No time to make corrections now. She forgot to be more cautious about her identity and she knew changing her look wasn't enough. On her head, she wore a baseball cap with her wig pulled back into a bun at the nape of her neck. Sliding further down into the booth to not be seen, she looked up into the face of the friend of Omar's who had been doing her a favor by looking into Nichelle's life all week via the internet. People didn't seem to understand how much of an open book their lives were once they created social media accounts and nothing ever went away.

After no longer being able to get a response from Tucker and knowing that their court date was coming up in a few days, she had to use every trick she could think of to get Tucker's attention and getting something juicy on his girlfriend is the only thing that would make him take note of how dire her situation was and how much she needed him to help her.

"Yes. Sit down quickly. You look suspicious standing over me talking," she bemoaned quietly at her guest who seemed to appear out of the nowhere and ended up right next to her without warning. She thought she had been doing a good job of looking out.

"Yes, ma'am. Omar said to meet you here and show you what I found."

"Okay. I hope it's good. I need something good to go my way. What do you have?" she asked, impatiently as he opened a laptop computer in front of her and began talking.

"I went through her social media like you asked me to and she has a lot of followers and friends. She does this makeup stuff that thousands of people love following. Anyway, I didn't get a lot from her page, but I checked some of her friends' pages and I found this," he said.

When her guest was taking too long to turn the computer around to show her, she turned it around herself so fast, it almost fell to the floor. Thankfully, her mysterious young guest caught it before that happened. This could have all been over before it started. Deciding to calm down, Antonia inhaled and quieted her excitement. She looked at the screen and didn't know what she was seeing.

"Sorry about that. What am I supposed to be looking at?"

"Oh, right. Well, her name is Sasha, something, and she was in a relationship with the woman you had me look into. I think she was a lesbian before she met your husband."

Antonia's sunglasses clashed to the table when she lifted her head suddenly.

"Who said anything about her and my husband? Did Omar tell you that?" she blurted out annoyed that he assumed anything.

"Uh, well, he said something about her and your husband. I did ask him what he wanted me to look into her accounts for and he sort of said she was messing around with your husband. Isn't that why you wanted the information? What are you going to do? Is it stuff for your show?" he asked.

Antonia wasn't happy about his level of excitement and she hoped Omar told him about how discreet he needed to be. Deciding to not play along, she tried to focus on what was in front of her.

She looked back down at the screen and scrolled through several posts, reading as much as she could.

"Don't worry about what I need the information for. You say they were involved? Do you know when it ended? Is it still going on? Could she be cheating with this woman? Who is she? Sasha who? Who is Sasha?" she asked loudly and anxiously.

Antonia was getting pissed that she wasn't getting information as quick as she wanted it.

Her excitement was through the roof. There was no way Tucker knew that Nichelle had been or could still be seeing a woman while seeing him.

"Her name is Sasha, but I don't have a last name. She doesn't give one. She's some dance instructor or something. I only found those two pictures of them, one at a night club over three years ago and the other wasn't too long after that. In one, they are clearly kissing. That's hot, right? Two women? I mean it's hot to me and they're both hot chicks."

Antonia was losing her patience. She didn't care what he found hot. She only needed to know if it was still going on and if so, how she could use the photo to her benefit to get her away from Tucker.

"How old are you?" she asked.

"Nineteen. I'll be twenty soon. I know Omar from the neighborhood. I was always the nerd everyone came to for computer stuff," he said.

"Well, you did good for me. How can I get pictures of this? Can you text them to me somehow? I need these and if you can add in the posts that would be good."

Antonia rubbed her hands together because this is the kind of stuff she needs to get Tucker to see the light. He would never survive a scandal of his girlfriend messing around with women and seeing him too.

"Sure. I can send anything to you that you want. Just give me your cell number and you'll have it really quick-like."

Antonia handed over her phone and told him the number.

"Was there anything else on her? This is good but I need more," she exclaimed.

"From what I can see, she's a pretty cool person. She loves working at some school with little kids and she's being sought after for jobs doing makeup for television shows and movies and stuff. She may be as famous as you soon. She also talks about finding real love, but she doesn't mention a name. She's kind of a private person."

"I hate private people. I see nothing to gain in not sharing your whole life with the world. People would have nothing to admire. I live off of the attention my stardom has gotten me and now that's being threatened."

She looked up and realized she was sharing too much information about herself.

"The posts are now on your phone."

She took her phone back and put it in her bag and then retrieved it. She would start with these pictures and see what happens. She quickly dialed Omar.

"Where is he?" she immediately demanded when he answered.

"What?" Omar asked.

Antonia was now beyond annoyed. Who did Omar think she was talking about? She never inquired about any other man. Grabbing her focus back, she held her frustration back.

"Where is Tucker? Is he home? Does he have a meeting? Where is he right now? I need to find him and see him. I have something I want to show him. You work for him – so, where is he?" she demanded.

When she looked around, Antonia found that she was drawing the attention of those around her. She no longer cared. She had some of what she needed and that's all she cared about.

"Again, with this? Didn't we have this same back and forth recently? You need that information right now?" Omar asked.

Antonia wanted to leap through the phone and strangle him for the way he was stalling her.

"Omar, stop acting like I'm not speaking English. Your guy came through and got me some information and I need to confront Tucker with what I found, which means I need to find him," she scolded.

When she heard Omar huff on the other end, she knew he was about to give in.

"We're at a press conference. It's been the talk of the town and all over the news. You don't watch the news?" he asked.

"Press conference? About what and where?"

"McCormick Place and everyone is here including his girlfriend. I think he's going to say something about her tonight. His family is all here, all the staff and a bunch of his friends. There is a seat reserved for her on the front row along with his family. I think their relationship will soon no longer be a secret."

Roxie thought quickly and tried to remember where she was compared to where she needed to be, which was at that press conference. She was the diva of making a scene and so adding another one to her list was not a thing for her. She was ready. Tucker would be made for a little while, but not long.

"I'm not far from there. Do I need a ticket to get in?" she asked.

"No, but you have to go through a security body scanner. A lot of the public and press are here."

Antonia grinned facetiously. She loved hearing that there will be press around. She lived off of the press.

"Omar, why the hell wouldn't you tell me about this? You were just at my hotel and all up in me and yet, you failed to tell me about this. I need to try and confront this woman and hope that she'll walk away before I tell all of her business. I need to do something with my hair and thankfully, I always have makeup on. How long before the press conference starts?" she asked.

"About an hour. People are still gathering. If you plan to get here before it starts, you better hurry. Tucker hasn't come out yet, so no one has seen him and his girlfriend together. He only told me to make sure there was a seat for her, front and center."

Antonia jumped up from her seat and left the Subway restaurant she had been waiting in for the past hour, leaving her guest sitting and probably wondering if she was going to sit back down or leave him sitting alone. She chose the latter and never looked back.

When she reached the street outside, she stopped and looked down at herself. She had on tight jeans and a long sweater and sneakers. She was trying to make sure she could move about unnoticed, not that many people paid her much attention. Looking around, she saw a boutique where she could get attire more suitable for the soon to be, almost first lady of Chicago.

Running across the street, she darted inside the store, looking for anyone who could help her.

"I'll be there shortly. This is going to be big, so get ready!" she told Omar and hung up.

"Can I help you?" a woman who looked to be in her sixties asked. Antonia looked her over from head to toe and knew immediately this woman couldn't help her with anything when it came to fashion.

"I don't think so. Do you have anyone working here who is about forty years younger than you and has better style? Seriously, look at me and then look at you and then ask yourself, could you really help me out fashion wise," she blurted out.

No shame for her bluntness, Antonia saw another much younger woman loading clothes on a rack and dismissing the older woman, she walked over to her.

"Can I help you?" the younger woman asked her.

Antonia smiled.

"Yes. You look like you might have some taste in clothing. I need a top to compliment these sexy jeans and it has to showcase my ass really good and some high-heels, the highest you have. On second thought, get me a suit. Maybe something red or pink – I have to be the talk of the room. I'm going to an event and I need to stand out. I also need a place to fix my hair and makeup. Do you have a dressing room I can use for about ten minutes while you find me a suit? I need to be out of here in fifteen minutes. Here is my credit card. Find me something and when I like it, charge it. I'm going to wear the clothes and the shoes out of here. You can throw away everything I leave in the dressing room. Perhaps give it to that old woman who tried to help me when I came in. How can she work at a place like this and look all old and frumpy?" Antonia ask and didn't even try to talk low. When the older woman walked away, she knew that her words had been heard.

"Well, she owns the place," the girl said.

"Oh, hell. That's even worse. I hope there is always someone young like you working here or she'll never make any real money. Get me some options in suits and make sure they're nice. I wear a medium to large, if it's a button down to accommodate the girls here and a size eight high-heel. Get to it!" she shouted and walked toward the dressing room. She needed to transform and do it quickly. By the end of the night, she plans to be on camera and she needs to look her best. Tucker won't know what hit him. With the pictures and the story she's going to make up about the pictures, she'll have him eating out of her hands by the time he gives his speech and that seat on the front row will be hers.

**

"You have about twenty more minutes, Tucker. Are you ready?"

Tucker looked his assistant over and wondered if she was as on edge as she appeared.

234

"Adrienne, are you nervous? This is the tenth time you've asked me that. I'm good. You know public speaking is my thing and Carter and I worked for two days straight on these speaking points with the writers. I'm more than ready. How's the crowd?" he asked.

"The place is packed."

"What about my family and Nichelle?"

The door to the green room, where he was supposed to be relaxing, opened and in walked Carter.

"Your family is here and Nichelle is also and she looks amazing. You look stressed. Are you stressed? What's going on?" Carter asked.

"I'm good. Adrienne is the one on edge. I'm as cool as they come. You know that saying as cool as a cucumber? That's me. I'm doing better knowing my woman is here. This room is nice, but there is too much food. I thought I mentioned bottled water and some fruit. What's with the sandwiches, large veggie tray and dip and all the other stuff?"

Tucker had walked into the room when he first arrived after being whisked away by his staff before he had the chance to check to see if his family had arrived. When he got to the room, he saw the spread and he assumed it was for them all, including his family, to then be told the room was only for his benefit; a place for him to chill until the press conference starts.

"Hey, don't sweat it. Just because it's there doesn't mean you have to eat it. Also, your tie sucks and luckily, I brought a batch from home," Carter said, snickering.

Tucker looked at his tie in the mirror that ran from one end of the wall to the other in front of the table that had food laid out from one end to the other.

"I like my tie. I have on a black suit and black goes with everything," he said adjusting it.

"It sucks and take it off. I told you to wear a power tie, not a black tie. You look plain. The image consultant told you what to wear and you show up in a black tie. I knew that you would which is why I stay one step ahead of you at all times. Look at these."

Tucker removed his tie and looked at the ten or so that Carter displayed on the black leather sofa.

"Paisley with shades of purple? How about that one?" Tucker asked.

"Yup, go with that one. This is your night, so look like you came to claim it. Where's your iPad? You won't really need it, but I understand when you say you want it as a backup. The teleprompter has been checked and rechecked. Remember, no more than fifteen minutes of questions at the end or we'll be here all night. Your plans for the city are aggressive and will garner lots of questions. We have press kits that provide information on where follow-up questions can be sent. If they get too personal once you introduce Nichelle, try to stay away from that. I'm still not sure this is the time to add your personal life in, but you're in charge."

Tucker heard his concern and at one time, he would have felt the same way, but not anymore. Yes, his career was on the line, but so was his relationship with Nichelle and he saw no reason why he couldn't have both.

"Carter, you've told me that a few times and I know what you're saying. I've had enough of trying to hide my personal life from everyone as if I don't have one. My divorce will be final soon and I can put that behind me. We're about to hit the streets hard with campaigning and Nichelle wants to be by my side where I want her to be. Now is the time. I'm not trying to let Antonia get me all tangled up with her mess. The only woman I ever want to be tangled up with is Nichelle. Do I have time to see her before we begin?"

Tucker didn't want to hear any answer that was an affirmation of what he wanted. He just needed to see Nichelle to know that she was actually here and by his side.

"Of course. I already asked Sienna to bring her to the room. They should be here any minute. I wanted to drop in first to check on you before things started. Place is full, lots of media are here, including every national broadcast network and your support is here and ready to back you up. Don't forget that another reason to not drag this press conference out is because I made reservations to celebrate at *Shallots Bistro* for the whole family and your close friends. We have a private room and that gives you a chance to relax after what will be a controversial press conference. Everyone has been calling this primary in your favor and even the general election appears to be in the bag. You have a lot of support and the citizens of Chicago love you and what you stand for. You bring the moral factor, the desire to bring change and the fight to make that change. You got this!" Carter chimed.

"You're the best Carter and I couldn't have gotten this far without you. We're going all the way. The press kits include my proposed approach to fighting crime? I'm spending most of my time focused on that and how we can revitalize the south side," Tucker said.

"I got it covered and yes, that is detailed and included."

"Sounds like you have it all under control, campaign manager. I knew I asked the perfect person."

Tucker smiled when he heard a soft knock on the door.

"I know who that is," he said and practically hopped and skipped to the door with excitement. His love was on the other side of the door.

When he opened it, the moment Nichelle walked in, he couldn't take his eyes off of her.

"I'm going out to rally the staff. Do you need anything else from me before I go?" Adrienne asked heading for the door after greeting Nichelle and Sienna.

Tucker shook his head, but didn't take his eyes from Nichelle.

"I'm good and thanks. Make sure that all staff members remember our celebratory luncheon is next week," Tucker said.

"Got it. See you out front."

"I'm heading out too," Carter said as he took Sienna by the hand and the door closed behind them.

Tucker was ecstatic that he was now alone with his love.

"Alone," Tucker said, pulling Nichelle close.

"Are you ready?" she asked, smoothing out his suit jacket.

He loved her more than he could ever say with words.

"I would say no because I need a kiss, but I don't want to mess up your lip stick. If I got a sexy kiss from you, that would make me ready. You look stunning tonight. Purple is your color. Now I see why all the ties Carter brought me to choose from have some shade of purple in them."

"He did good and thank you. Reese went with me and I found the perfect wrap dress and heels to match. Sienna was with us and he may have asked her what I was wearing and she told him about this dress. I hope I'm representing you well," Nichelle said.

Tucker could see her nervousness and wanted to help her relax.

"You never have to worry about that. You being you is all the representation I want and need and I mean that so that it lasts until the end of time," he explained.

"I love you," Nichelle said.

"And I love you, baby."

"I'm so nervous," she said, winding her hands together.

"Baby, don't be nervous. Just keep your eyes on me and if anyone tosses questions at you, just smile. They can talk to me since I'm the candidate. Did you meet my mom and dad yet?" he asked.

"I did and they were both so nice and sweet to me. Carter introduced us. Your mom gave me a big hug and thanked me for loving you. I wanted to cry, but I didn't want to mess up my makeup. Reese would kill me after she paid some woman too much money to do it considering I'm a makeup artist and could have done it myself. She wanted this to be a special night for me too and it is. I also love your sisters! They held me in a three-way hug and welcomed me to the family. I guess they're okay with us."

Tucker hadn't told her that he had called his family a week ago and told them all about her and how much he loved her. He told them all of the things about her that are wonderful, which is everything there is about her and his family never questioned his love for her. They only told him that they couldn't wait to meet her. Everything was falling into place and he couldn't be happier.

"I told them about you on a family conference call and they were happy for me. That's all that matters. We're still going to see your mom tomorrow?" he asked.

Tucker was ecstatic when Nichelle called the day before to say that her mother invited him over for dinner to finally meet the man who put the permanent smile on her daughter's face.

"We are and I told her you wanted to know her favorite kind of wine so that you could bring it. She would have been here tonight, but she has a friend in the hospital and she promised her friend's daughter that she'd sit with her until more family arrived in town."

"Oh, you know I understand and I look forward to meeting her and we'll get the best of her favorite wine tomorrow," he said.

"I didn't want you to worry about it, so I picked it up this morning. Just pick me up looking as good as you do right now and the night will be perfect. My mom has really mellowed out now that she's all in love and stuff. I'm going to head back to the ballroom to get ready for your amazing speech. I know you're going to kill it tonight and I'll be right there supporting you. When you need a friendly face, besides the others in the room who are in your corner, you can look to me and I'll always be smiling and winking at you."

Tucker pulled her close and took both of her hands into his.

"You're so good to me and for me. To the top together, baby," he said.

Without messing up Nichelle's lipstick, Tucker settled for kissing her on the cheek and then slipped one in on her neck. He laughed when she stepped out of his embrace.

"I'm watching you and I should have known you would try and pull something. Tonight, I got you," Nichelle said. "I have the perfect seduction planned for you."

"Yes, you do and I look forward to being the recipient of all that seduction and love. Nothing can possibly ruin tonight and I look forward to tonight and the entire weekend with you."

Tucker had so much planned for them for their much needed downtime after his speech tonight. After dinner with her mother, they were heading for a much needed road trip.

"You still want to take a road trip for the weekend after dinner tomorrow night?" she asked. "I didn't know how exhausted you would be," she Nichelle added.

"Yes, I do and all you need to do is pack and be ready. I'm never too exhausted when it comes to you. Be ready for me and I'll be ready for you," he said and kissed her again, this time lightly on the lips without messing up her makeup.

"You're perfect, you know that?" Nichelle said.

Tucker knew he was looking at perfection.

"You are my perfect woman and this is our perfect night. I'll see you out there in about ten minutes."

"Good luck, baby."

Nichelle's parting words gave Tucker that extra boost he needed. Nothing could ruin the great mood he was in.

Alone to prepare for the biggest night of his career so far, he looked in the mirror and tightened the tie he'd selected. It was the perfect complement to his lady love. They were one tonight and he knew they always would be. Having her with him and sitting right where he needed her, he would look to her throughout his speech because in her gaze, he knew he would find the encouragement he would need to get through the night of not only his plan for Chicago, but to get through the questioning he knew he was going to have to endure. Though he wanted the focus to be on the campaign and his plans, he knew that at some point, when he introduced Nichelle, he would have to address questions about his private relationship and he was ready for that too.

Tucker checked himself fully in the mirror and he was now ready to go. He turned to the door just as it opened again and Carter walked back in.

"Ready?" Carter asked.

"I've never been more ready. Let's chat about a few things and then we'll head out," Tucker said picking up his iPad and looking for the last minute questions he figured would get asked and he wanted to be prepared with answers. Nothing could ruin this night for him; nothing.

20

Nichelle was on her way back to the main ballroom in preparation for Tucker's press conference, feeling as good as she looked. Before getting to the main doors, she decided to stop in the ladies room first since she had some time to spare. She wanted to be just right for her place as the woman that Tucker loves. Their relationship was about to become front page news right next to the other main topics for the night.

Going inside, she stopped in front of the mirror and noticed that only her lipstick needed a slight touching-up. Placing her bag on the dark red counter between two sinks, she pulled out her favorite MAC gloss and eye shadow just as the bathroom door opened. Since there were several stalls, she wasn't bothered that the door had opened or that someone else would be entering. What bothered her was when she looked up at the woman who had entered, her eyes locked with Antonia's and her hand stopped midway to her face with the lip gloss in it.

"Well, well. Look who I ran into," Antonia said to her, flippantly.

Nichelle didn't move, but exhaled and decided to not get into any kind of battle of wits with her. When Antonia didn't move or say anything else, Nichelle placed the lip gloss down on the counter and looked at her through the mirror.

"Hello," she replied.

Nichelle didn't want to say that and she definitely didn't want to give her more than that. The woman looked like she was waiting for some kind of greeting.

"That's it? I don't get a hello along with my name? Let me help you out with that. You should have said, hello Mrs. Antonia Glass. You do remember that I'm married to your boyfriend or has that slipped your mind every time you slip and slide with my husband?"

Realizing this encounter was not going to go well, Nichelle turned around and faced her. If she wanted a happenstance, she would give her one. Antonia had been playing with their lives for too long and she was sick of it. She wasn't backing down from the likes of a woman who practices being a bitch to make a dollar.

"I don't slip and slide with anyone. Tucker and I are in love and the fact that you're still married is a technicality that will be handled next week," Nichelle said confidently.

Antonia laughed and the dark, scary tone of it was disturbing.

"Is that what you think? Little girl, marriages don't just go away because you wish them away or did your fairy godmother tell you that last week when you wished upon a star? I know you think you've got Tucker in your clutches, but you have no idea what I'm capable of. If he knows what's good for him, he'll wave you off like all the other women he's ever had in his life who thought they could claim the status of wife like I did and that I still have, technically or not. Either way, I'm still Mrs. Glass and you're the tart he's using to entertain him for the moment. He needs a cultured woman like me by his side, not some young girl who's still trying to figure out if it's boys or girls that she likes."

Nichelle started to come back at her but was put off by her comment. She was ready for the conversation to end.

"What do you want Ms. Hall?" she finally said and turned back around to the mirror. "Clearly you being in here with me is no coincidence, so what do you want? I have someplace I need to be."

Nichelle didn't feel the need to explain more and if she did, it could prolong the conversation and she was already done.

"Oh? Is that place in the front row next to *MY* in-laws? Runaway little girl. This is a grown woman you're standing in front of and I'm not giving my husband up to you for anything. Once he finds out all about you, he won't want you anyway, especially if he plans to win the election. I will ruin him with so much gossip that the people will be sick of hearing about it and look for someone with a lot less drama. I told you, this is a grown woman you're dealing with. It's time you and Tucker recognized that."

Nichelle sighed in a show of her lack of patience and caring.

"You claim to want him, yet in the same breath, you're willing to tank his career for what? For ratings? Surely not because you love him. There's no way you could love him as much as I do if you're willing to sacrifice his career for your own advancement. That's sad," Nichelle said in response, still unmoved.

"Sad? Let me tell you what's sad. Sad is talking about loving my husband while straddling both sides of the fence. Does he know you dabbled in some lesbian behavior?"

Nichelle's hand that had reached for her lip gloss again stopped midway to her mouth and then she let it fall back to the counter where the tube clicked loudly on the marble top.

She looked at Antonia through the mirror, not sure she heard what she'd said.

"What did you say?" Nichelle asked as she felt a nervous ping at the nape of the back of her neck signaling this interaction was about to turn really bad.

"You heard me. I bet he doesn't know, does he? I know he doesn't. I tried to have a threesome once for his birthday and bring in another woman and he was disgusted by it. He doesn't support that lifestyle and I know he would hate to think that he's been sticking it to you and you've been giving it to other girls," Antonia said snidely.

Nichelle's anger started to rise. She grabbed the items she took out of her bag, threw them back in and turned around. She didn't want to entertain a conversation about her very personal life, now or in the past, with the likes of Antonia.

"You are a vile woman and Tucker is not like that. He's not a homophobic person. He believes in letting people live their lives their way. You're trying your hand at whatever works as if that's going to drive him into your arms. My past is my past and it's none of your business. My life right now is Tucker and that's all that matters," she explained.

Why she felt the need to give Antonia any explanation was beyond her, but she was feeling defensive and thought it was warranted.

"This revelation may not drive him into my arms, but I bet

it will drive him out of yours. For now, I'll settle for that. I was able to get my hand on a few pictures of you from a few years ago with your lips locked with Sasha. Remember her?" Antonia asked and waved her hand in front of Nichelle's face.

If she were a violent woman, Nichelle would have slapped her hand away. It was times like this that she wished she were more like Reese. By now, Reese would be rolling around in the floor getting the best of Antonia.

"We all have a past and I'm sure you do too. How's Omar?" she tossed back at Antonia.

Nichelle reveled in the look of surprise on Antonia's face. She'd just hit her below the belt, hitting tit-for-tat.

"What?" Antonia screamed.

"See, we all have a past and yours is nasty. You're trying to fight to get a man back while you slept with his intern while you were married to him. That's right, Tucker told me about it."

"Why you little..." Antonia screamed.

"Little what? I don't have time for this."

Nichelle tried to get by Antonia to get out of the door but she blocked her way.

"I'm going to show him this picture and in fact, I'm going to show everyone this picture and think of the mess that's going to cause. How do you think Tucker will look at you then? He'll see you as the woman who kept a secret that will be plastered over every internet, blog and social media site. Don't you know who I am? I already told Tucker that I would blow your life up and I will if you don't back off and go on home. He won't miss you. I promise you that I'll take good care of him by being the perfect host as his wife tonight and then later, I may reward him with loving from a real woman.

I bet he hasn't had that since he started playing around with you. Go run home to Sasha! In a few minutes, this picture will be all over the internet and then what will you say? I think the timing is perfect. While he's making a speech about family values with his lesbian girlfriend on the front row, I wonder how that will work."

Nichelle was imagining her personal life being all over the internet and how that would hurt Tucker to have to focus on explaining that and not being able to deal with the real issues at hand of concern to the people of Chicago. The last thing she wanted was to bring any drama his way. She walked past Antonia to the door.

"You're a horrible woman. I don't understand how Tucker ever thought he loved you!" Nichelle shouted.

Before Antonia could reply, she opened the bathroom door and headed, not to the ballroom door, but to the door that led outside of the building. She needed to think. If Antonia followed through on her threat, that could ruin Tucker's event.

When she bumped into someone, just as she could feel herself on the brink of crying, she looked up into Reese's face.

"I was just coming to look for you. Sienna said you were missing in action. She thought you would be in your seat by now. Tucker is coming out in five minutes and you need to where he wants you. I'll be in the seat right behind you," Reese said.

No words, came out, but Nichelle broke out crying and didn't know if she could stop. When Reese moved her to the side, she struggled to explain through her tears.

"I have to leave," she said and Reese held her in place.

"What? Why? Tucker is expecting you on the front row. He'll be looking out to you for support. Why are you crying and why are you leaving? Stop crying and talk to me!" Reese shouted and looked around to be sure no one was looking their way.

"Antonia found out about Sasha and she just threatened to release some old photos she found on the internet of me and Sasha kissing. That was years ago, but it could ruin Tucker's night. She said she's going to send the pictures out over the internet if I don't leave him alone. I have to leave. I love him and I don't want his night ruined."

Nichelle waited as Reese reached in her purse, grabbed a tissue and handed it to her.

"Where did you see her?"

Nichelle did stop crying when she heard the low, momma-bear tone of Reese's voice. That would mean trouble and that wouldn't help anything. She looked wide-eyed up at her big sister and knew what was coming.

"No, Reese. Leave it alone. Let me go and tell Tucker I'm sorry," she said.

She tried to move again and Reese grabbed her by the arm and held on tight.

"If you move from this spot, it better be to go into the ballroom. Where is Antonia?" Reese asked again.

Nichelle pointed.

"In the ladies room."

When Reese looked at the closed door, Nichelle felt a fear that wasn't for her or for Tucker, but was for Antonia because now that Reese was involved, she only prayed there would be no blood shed. If it was, it would be Antonia's.

"Find another restroom and fix your face up, right now.

Go in that room and take that seat that your man has reserved for you. Don't you dare back down from any woman, threat or no threat. You have nothing to be ashamed of. So you kissed a woman – who hasn't. We all have things we've done that we would like to stay hidden, but I don't want you to ever run from your past. You face it head-on and deal with it. I can guarantee you that there will be *NO* pictures for anyone to see. Go get yourself together," Reese demanded through clinched teeth.

"You don't understand. I didn't tell Tucker about that part of my life. He will be hurt," she said.

"Hurt by what?"

Nichelle was frustrated. Reese wasn't paying attention because she was pissed off.

"Are you listening to me?" she asked.

"Sis! Look, I won't even get into the fact that you can live the life you want to live and do it by your own rules whether it was with a woman in your past or a man in your present. You chose Tucker and he chose you. Don't let Antonia win by allowing her to intimidate you. Stand your ground and stand with your man. I'll take care of Antonia. You know I love you and I will shut a trick down before I will *ever* let her hurt you. Got it? Now go fix your face and go be with your man. Do you really want him to arrive, look out expecting to see your beautiful face and instead, he'll encounter an empty seat? He'll be more concerned with where you are than on the topic for tonight, which is his campaign. You've been by his side all this time and you've fought to have his love and now you're willing to toss it aside because some woman wants to do what she thinks will expose something seedy? I've been up against women like her and they are all talk and no action. You came this far and you only have to go the rest of the way with your head held high. Antonia can kick rocks! Go ahead because you're running out of time. I'll be there in a few minutes. This won't take long."

Reese turned around and headed for the ladies room and while Nichelle wanted to stop her, she let her go. She was right. Tucker was her priority and not threats made by Antonia.

**

Reese opened the bathroom door just as Antonia attempted to exit.

"Oh, no you don't! You're not going anywhere," Reese screamed and pushed Antonia back inside the restroom and locked the door behind them.

"What? Are you out of your mind? Who are you?" Antonia asked.

Reese smiled at the terror she saw on Antonia's face – probably the same feeling she got from Nichelle when she tried to scare her with her threats.

"I am out of my mind right now since you've threatened my sister. I am now officially out of my mind and crazily pissed off! I'm the sister you don't want to mess with and I am the sister of the woman you will wish you had not threatened and tried to intimidate!"

Reese glared when Antonia took several steps backward until her back was against the wall.

"I did no such thing. Who is your sister and I don't feel safe being locked in here with a crazy woman!" Antonia screamed.

Reese calmly walked toward her slowly, still keeping distance between them. She knew if she was too close, she wouldn't be able to reach out and grab, which she was very tempted to do.

"My sister is Nichelle and I don't take kindly to people who mess with her. You see, she is the one that people think they can walk all over because she's so soft-spoken. I, on the other hand, don't have anything soft about me other than my big ass. I'm the aggressive one who will have no problem snatching that trashy wig from your head, dipping it in the toilet and then shoving it in your *mouth!* You like to be on television? Okay, here it is."

Reese took out her phone, hit the record button and propped it up on the counter.

"You are mad! Let me out of here," Antonia screamed.

"Oh, I will, but not until you explain to me how you threatened to release pictures of my sister kissing a woman she was involved with years ago like that's some big revelation, all because you want to get your husband back who you are supposed to be divorced from but didn't sign the papers correctly. Why don't you tell your followers about the young intern you were screwing when he was nineteen years old and you were married to Tucker back then? How about how you're currently giving your goodies up to the producer of your show who is married and his wife is six months pregnant? Shall we tell them that your mother got pregnant with you by her sister's husband and that's why your family doesn't bother with either of you? Wait, let's go a little bit further with how you paid your rent the first few months after moving to Los Angeles. Does *Mae-Mae's Massage Parlor* sound familiar? Did you know there were cameras in some of those rooms when you made a little extra money on the side for the extra's you gave both men *and* women you serviced in what you thought was a private room? Did you think you were the only person who could look up someone's life and find dirt? I knew you would come for my sister and Tucker one day and I'm ready for you. The moment I heard you were in town trying to stir up trouble, I started looking into your life. As soon as you try to tell anything about my sister to Tucker or anyone else, you'll never get another job anywhere. Do you remember the joy ride you gave your producer's twenty year old son on the beach one night? Did you know he had a friend recording everything? I suggest you go back to your life and leave my sister and Tucker to theirs. You do *not* want to tangle with me. I'm the sister you never want to come up against," Reese hollered and waved her hand in front of Antonia's face for good measure.

Reese knew there was never a time that she wanted to be this person, but if she had to be in order to protect those she loved the most, she would in a heart beat and Antonia was prime for the taking.

"I...I...Where did you get all of that? No one knows...I mean, none of that is true. It's all lies!"

Reese laughed when Antonia, who can't resist a moment of being on camera said that while speaking right into the cellphone camera on the counter.

"You are certifiable and I have more proof than you can ever think of coming up with when it comes to my sister. Do not try to tangle with my sister because you will have to deal with me. You know everything I just said is true and if you want to doubt it, try me. Please, give me a reason to *really* get you the spotlight in Hollywood. You'll be untouchable. You won't even be able to get a commercial in that town. I love my sister and I will go to jail before I let you and anyone else ruin the happy life she's living. Do you understand?"

To make her point, Reese walked close up to Antonia and pressed her head against the wall.

"Stop touching me!" Antonia screamed and tried to get away.

Reese held her in place and grimaced close to her face.

"I said, do you understand me?" Reese asked again. "Nod your head if you understand me."

When Antonia followed her instruction, Reese let her go and grabbed her cell phone. With this footage and what I've been able to have a private investigator find out about you, I could ruin your entire being. I know people too and if I tell my people to reach to your people, you're done. Oh, and by the way – tell Nancy I said hello. I did the marketing and promotion work for the past three years for her firm in California. She may be your agent, but not after I give her a call and let her in on what I know. She may be helping you with your shenanigans, but that's because she doesn't know who you're hurting. She works for a company that I've made a lot of money for. I would love to tell them what you and Nancy have been up to. Try me, trick; try me!"

Reese didn't wait for an answer after screaming at the top of her lungs. She turned toward the mirror and made sure her red suit was still neat and that her hair was still in place.

"I never said I would do anything to your sister. She must have misunderstood me. I only wanted to congratulate her on her life with Tucker. If she thought I was threatening her I some way, that wasn't my intention," Antonia stuttered out as she tried to move around Reese.

Moving backward to keep Antonia from leaving before her, Reese smiled and turned toward her as she shrunk back against the wall.

"You have a nice life, but do it someplace other than here in Chicago. Your presence here is no longer tolerable. I'd like to not have to have this conversation again, so be warned – stay away from my sister. I was actually nice this time; I won't be a second time. You like looking information up on people? I suggest you check my name. Ask around and you will find that I do not play, especially when it comes to my sister."

Reese left the bathroom and once she was on the other side, she took a few seconds to gather herself as she walked into the ballroom. She didn't wait to see what Antonia would do. She didn't care. All she cared about was seeing her sister where she was supposed to be.

When she entered the room where the press conference had already started, she didn't want to interrupt things by taking her seat. She did walk toward the front of the room so that Torrence and Nichelle could see that she was in the room. When her sister smiled at her, she winked.

Seeing Nichelle with that bright smile on her face made her day. She leaned against the wall and listened to Tucker.

"I've taken up the last fifteen minutes giving you all highlights from my written plans for Chicago if you elect me as the next Mayor. I would love to hear your questions, but before we get to that, and I know you have many, I want to address something very important. As most of you know, I was once married and without saying, you know who I was married to. I can't speak ill of her and our time together because I believe that every person you encounter is someone who causes you to be better even if you don't know it. They could be good for you or bad for you but what you take away from the encounter is what matters. I know that the media has been asking about my personal life and rumors have been going around and I'm here to put my life on the table so that we can move on and focus on the campaign with the love of my life by my side. Nichelle, can you join me up here please?" Tucker asked.

Reese clapped loud and uncontrollably before anyone else did. When she didn't stop, others joined in, though she started to realize that it wasn't a clapping kind of moment – at least not yet. She was happy for her sister, so she didn't care.

"This is Nichelle Michaels and she has made me happier in my life than I have ever been. We started a journey some months ago and trust me when I say at the end of this journey, no matter the outcome, she will still be the love of my life. I'm going to ask that if there are questions, that you pose them to me and not to her. You will find out more and more about her as the months go by because you'll see her with me every step of the way as we make our way to the Mayor's office. I wanted to show off my beautiful lady tonight because it was getting harder to have a personal life while trying to keep it from everyone's prying eyes. Here we are and most importantly, she believes in me and what I'm trying to continue doing for the city of Chicago, but this time as your Mayor. Now, if there are questions, let's get to them."

Reese watched her sister walk back down to her seat, still with a smile on her face. Looking around, her eyes darted to the back of the room as the door opened and in walked Antonia. The minute they locked eyes, she used hers to issue her last and final warning. No words were necessary. When Antonia turned around and left, she felt proud that her job was done and her sister would hopefully no longer have to live in fear of the happiness that Tucker brought into her life. She didn't care where Antonia went as long as it wasn't the press conference. This was a day for Tucker to shine and for her sister to glow and be happy. That's all she ever wanted for her Nichelle and her brother, DJ. Their lives haven't always been the best, but they've always had each other and if for some reason, Antonia decided to come and try again, she would be ready. This time, she wouldn't be as nice as she was in the ladies room.

Smiling, she went back to clapping along with others in the room. She didn't know what had been said, but it must have been good because everyone was smiling and for that, she was smiling brighter too.

21

Primary Election Night
Six Months Later

Nichelle leaped into Tucker's arms the minute he walked into their hotel room at the Montiel Avage casino. She was so excited, she didn't think she'd be able to get any sleep. It was well after midnight and she was glad that Tucker had finally made his way to their room, a complimentary gift from Torrence for a night together at his casino.

"I am so proud of you! You did it! You won! Next up is the general election and polls already show you have ninety percent to your opponent's ten percent. You are on your way to being Mayor, baby! You looked so good out there on that stage tonight and when you first came out and the thunderous cheers that went up, it showed how serious people are about their support for you. How do you feel?" she asked excited for not only him, but for them as a couple. Their lives had only gotten better since he announced their relationship months ago and no one asked uncomfortable questions about their life together. People understood that there were bigger issues on the table for Chicago than the personal life of the man who would soon be their next Mayor.

"I feel like a winner and having you here to celebrate this night with me is everything. We won – not just me, but me and you! This is truly just the beginning," Tucker said and danced around the room.

Nichelle watched and clapped as he showed her his winning dance moves.

"How are your parents? Did they get settled?" she asked.

Since his family was in town and his sisters and brother-in-law were here, Torrence provided rooms for everyone to go to after the party celebrating Tucker's win, which was held in the grand ballroom of the hotel part of the casino. She was glad they didn't have to drive anywhere because champagne and wine flowed freely all night. From what she heard, Carter and Sienna, who was fresh off of having their son, Kingston, and already back to her pre-baby weight after giving birth two months ago were also spending the night. Even Dexter and Alyssa, who was close to giving birth to their second son were also staying at the hotel.

"My parents are down at the casino. I went to their room after I left the party to see if they were good and they had already changed and were heading down to gamble. They have more energy than me because I am exhausted, but not too exhausted for my fiancé," he crooned next to her ear.

Nichelle trembled having him close as she moved to the beat of the music in their heads, but not in the room. They didn't need any music because they were always in-sync.

She danced around more, even while in his arms as he swung her left and then right while humming some tune in her ear.

"Want to see my ring? The man who bought it for me must really love me," she said and sidled back up against him when he spun her out away from him and then back close. She waved her perfect, big and shiny engagement ring in his face where he laughed uncontrollably with happiness. They were on cloud nine.

"Yes, he does. He loves you very much."

Nichelle nodded in agreement.

"You know, I fussed at my sister for not telling me that you were going to propose to me a week ago. We tell each other everything."

She shivered when Tucker leaned close to her ear and whispered into it.

"I'm glad she didn't. She helped me design the ring and I swore her to secrecy. You're not the only person who can keep a secret," Tucker exclaimed.

"Yeah, I see that. Reese even told me she was giving me her brand of payback for not telling her a year ago that were seeing each other. Either way, I'm happier each and every day we spend together," she said.

"Baby, I hope you didn't mind the timing. I wanted to propose months ago, but after Antonia disappeared and never reached out again, I didn't know what was up her sleeve until my lawyer told me she finally signed the papers and signed them correct this time. I was shocked. She spit out a lot of drama over what she was going to do and then nothing. I'm just happy that I could finally propose with no drama over our heads and your whole family, including your brother and his wife, Avalon were there. I hear they're pregnant. There must be something in the water in this group of friends I'm now forever connected to," Tucker quipped.

"I know. Now that my sister is married, I wonder if she

and Torrence are going to start having babies. That would shock the hell out of me. Can you imagine my sister having babies?"

Nichelle kicked her silver high-heels off and began unbuttoning her black dress by the zipper under her right arm. When Tucker moved close to help her, she giggled when she felt his hands caressing her back as he slid the dress down her body.

"I can't imagine that. That baby will come out talking trash to everyone!" Tucker joked even more.

"You're right about that."

"What about us?" Tucker asked.

"What?"

"Babies. We're getting married in eight weeks. Do you want to have babies right away or do you want to wait?" he asked.

Nichelle turned around in her bra and panties and walked up to Tucker to help him remove his tuxedo. Tonight, she wanted him as relaxed as possible.

"Well, let me say this - I have wanted to be your wife since the moment you first said you loved me. Right after that, I began imagining what our babies would look like. I want a ton of them. I hope that's not too much," she explained.

"We can have as many as we want. When?" Tucker came right back with.

Nichelle got the feeling that he was more than ready to have them as soon as she was ready.

"No birth control the moment we are married and we'll let nature handle the rest. The way you can't seem to keep your hands off of me, I'm sure the first baby won't be too far after that," she responded excitedly.

"That's good to know. We have so many plans to make and getting married before the general election is important. I want our life solidified before any political moves. I know I'm picked to win that race and that would make me ecstatic. If I know I have you to come home to no matter what, I'm already the biggest winner in life. Watching your belly swell with my baby one day will be a great bonus."

When Tucker sat down on the edge of the bed and pulled her to him, she held his head tight as he placed his ear against her stomach where one day, their child will be nurtured.

"This was the life we were meant to have. That day in the deli when we saw each other again, that is what was supposed to be. Life is perfect as long as we're together and nothing and no one can come between us ever again. I meant to ask you something. I saw Adrienne and the rest of your staff at the party tonight before I came back to our room, but I didn't see Omar. He's been front and center since that mess with Antonia and now he doesn't show up? What happened?" she asked.

Nichelle knew that something had changed. There was no way Omar wouldn't stand and be counted amongst those who helped him win tonight, even after Tucker approached him about having sex with Antonia and helping her scheme once she returned to Chicago. She was happy and surprised that Tucker still kept him on his roster at City Hall and on the campaign.

"Omar will work for the next Council President. I don't want him working for me directly. He broke my trust, but I still want to see him succeed. I think Councilman Thomas Hanks will be the next Council President and trust me, he will keep Omar in line and help him get to the next level of his career without any distractions. I think he thought Antonia really cared about him. I talked to him and he knew what he was doing was wrong, but she roped him in. He's immature and needs to grow up and being away from Antonia is best for him. He has a lot more women to go through and I'm sure he will. He's handsome and smart. He'll go places and women will throw themselves at him. He needs a mentor and I've agreed to still do that when I can. Omar has great potential. Antonia was a virus to him, but she's gone now and he's getting his head back on straight. He is taking some much needed time off and decided to visit his parents in Minnesota. Antonia really did a number on him," he said.

"I see she's still on that reality show. I just can't believe her mother has joined the show. The two of them are just wretched."

Nichelle was shocked when Reese called her one night and told her to turn to the show to see Antonia as Roxie in full bitch-mode. What she wasn't expecting was to see Antonia's mother on the show being as ornery as her daughter. They turned out to be the boost Antonia needed to her career.

"Yes, they are, but that's the kind of show people like. Enough about everyone else. Let's talk about your plans. You signed on to be the lead makeup artist on that new show being filmed here in Chicago and you have decided to be Alyssa's personal makeup artist after she gets back to work after the baby. The show alone pays you several times over what you make at the school. Are you changing careers?"

Nichelle removed the rest of her clothes while Tucker did the same thing. She was moving around, but she knew he wanted an answer and knew that whatever she chose, he would support her.

"I'm going to give my resignation at the end of this month, but I will stay through the school year since the show doesn't start taping until June. That is my calling and I will have my degree to fall back on if I ever need it. I can't wait to do makeup full-time, but only until we get pregnant. I want to be home full-time with our baby. I know we haven't talked about it, but that's what I want to do. I can still be Alyssa's personal MUA and that pays more than some full-time jobs. She brings her baby on set to all of her shoots and she said she will encourage me to do the same with our baby if I want to. What do you think?" she asked, now completely naked and ready for whatever was next. She was hoping for an all-nighter of mad, passionate love.

They were already planning to stay in their hotel suite until at least the weekend. After a busy campaign, they deserved this time together. Leading up to this day, all of their time was spent focused on politics and she only wanted to focus on them for as long as she could before they had to again focus on the next phase of his career, the general election coming up in November.

"I'm proud of you and I'm glad you're giving your resignation at the school. I know you love working with the kids, but I see a special glow when you talk about makeup. Before the wedding, ask Reese to help you find us a new house. We need a new beginning. Find something that we can grow our family in and where we can build you your own studio if you want to take clients at home. Think about something like a studio with a separate entrance. That studio can be whatever you want it to be. If there is anything else that you want, I got you. It takes two to tangle baby and finally, that two is just me and you."

"I love you, soon to be Mayor Tucker Glass."

"And I love you, soon to be Mrs. Nichelle Glass. Are you ready?" he asked.

"Oh, I'm more than ready. Can I ask you a question that I hope won't put a damper on our night?" she asked.

Nichelle knew that they had discussed a very personal issue months ago, but she wanted to make sure that he didn't have any outstanding questions that she needed to answer before they soon committed their lives to each other when they got married.

"You can ask anything and everything at any time. No secrets between us, right?" he asked.

"Right. About my past. Are you sure you don't have any questions about my old relationship with Sasha? I know you said you had no qualms with my past because everyone has one, including you, but I want to be sure you're not repulsed by that time in my life," she said.

Nichelle stood naked and vulnerable to his gaze and wanted to once and for all put the issue behind them.

"Baby, you've told me everything about that time in your life and your life was and is still your life. I have no issues with any of it. You know that I stand by my beliefs and they are that everyone is entitled to live and let live and that means you too. I could never be repulsed by anything about you and I'm sorry that Antonia tried to extort you with that information. She was willing to use it against you in order to get you to disappear from my life. I'm glad you didn't fall for that and I'm even happier for what Reese did to make sure Antonia never bothered you again. I met Sasha at one of the fundraisers a month ago and she's a nice woman. I am your life now and you are my life. Thank you for sharing your life with me and that includes your past and your present. I look forward to our future. There are no secrets and nothing that is left that is questionable. I love you, you love me and you make me happier than I have ever been in my life. All of you is everything to me. I never want you to doubt my love. If there is anything that I say or do that ever makes you question that, you tell me and we will work it out. It's me and you, right? Until the end of time?" Tucker asked.

"You and me forever. It takes two to tangle and I'm ready to be entangled with you until my last breath," she responded.

"I'm happy to hear that. Now, I'm not leaving back out tonight. I want to shut the world out and have this time alone with you and that sexy body. I'm already over tonight's celebrating. Though I appreciate the win, I need time with my baby!" Tucker declared.

Nichelle smiled and wiggled her body in his direction.

"Well, lover boy, how about we have our own, private celebration, right now in the shower. You know how wild you get in the shower."

Nichelle headed toward the bathroom and when she looked back, Tucker was chasing her in and he was as naked as she was.

She looked forward to many, many more nights of being tangled up with him in any way they see fit.

Epilogue

May - Two Months Later

"Nichelle, thanks for agreeing to do my makeup for this last-minute photoshoot. I told them I wasn't ready to do a photoshoot so soon after having Diezel, but they told me they had a mother/child shoot in mind and that I could have both babies on the set. Diezel is only a month old, but Dexter thought it was okay. He's actually going to sit in on a few photos too. I like that idea. I can get a photo of us as a family to hang someplace in the house. How are you and Tucker doing?" Alyssa asked.

Nichelle smiled like a silly school girl hearing Tucker's name.

"We're great. I'm in the middle of all of the wedding arrangements and my sister has been helping me find a house. Sienna called and said that a house in her development was for sale. I looked at the offer and there were so many zeros, I almost passed out. Tucker saw it and said if I like it, get it. He has been holding on to that money his father gifted to him and he was waiting for the right purchase to use some of it on. Looks like we're about to be homeowners. We're going to move in before the wedding and

I can't wait to decorate it."

"You will love that. My brothers are in town and I just finished decorating the lower level of our new home and both have already tried to claim a spot as their own for when they come to town."

"No more knocking anybody out in the family?" Nichelle joked.

"Oh, you mean the Dexter thing between him and my brothers from when they met in Vegas when I was pregnant? They are better now. Joey has a wrestling match tonight and should be on his way to the casino. Torrence has decide that he's going to have monthly matches, amateur and pro-wrestling and both of my brothers are now on the casino payroll. I don't want them living with us, so with them both working, I suggested they get a place together. Carlos was supposed to be here by now. He wanted to come by and check out the shoot. The match isn't until later tonight, but only Joey is wrestling."

"Tucker likes that stuff. I wince at the thought of all that hitting, even if it's staged."

"So, things with Antonia have calmed or should we all expect further drama?" Alyssa asked.

"She's been silent and that's a good thing. We have all been focused on the upcoming election in November and thoughts of Antonia are already long gone. Tucker is heading into the general election in November with a gigantic lead. We will see in a few months if the people of Chicago will still have faith in what he can do. His opponent has no chance and prayerfully, nothing else will appear out of the cracks; like his ex-wife and drama."

"What did Tucker say when you came clean about your

past with the woman you were involved with back in college?"

Nichelle exhaled and leaned back, inwardly smiling that the conversation with Tucker the night of the primary election when he'd won by a landslide, had gone well. That was the second time she'd brought up the subject. The first had been the weekend after the press conference where Reese had read Antonia the riot in the ladies room.

"He told me that being with him was a judgement-free zone. I told him that weekend after the press conference and he said it wasn't a big deal and he hoped that the time in my life before him was just as happy as the time with him. He only wants my happiness and he knows that being with him is all the happiness I need. All that matters to him is that I love him and he loves me. He is a man who believes that everyone should live their lives however they choose and with whomever they choose. They aren't hurting anyone. He couldn't believe that I was hesitant to share that part of my life with him and that Antonia thought that he'd have an issue with it. I was happy when he said that every part of my life is what made me the woman that he loves. Guess what I did find out? Sasha is engaged to marry a lawyer named Milo. She was at one of Tucker's fundraisers and we talked about where our lives are now. I guess we both went through something and finally found true love. I couldn't be happier for me and for her. Now, I have to look forward to the general election and my life with Tucker as Mayor."

Nichelle smiled when Alyssa stood and leaned over to give her a tight hug.

"I'm so happy for you and for Tucker. Every woman should have a man who loves her the way he loves you; that unconditional love. I should know because I have that type of man!" she exclaimed.

"We promised each other that we'd never have any more secrets. It wasn't as big of a deal as I thought it would be."

"Are you ready to hit the political campaign trail with him? It's a lot to take on and I know he'll want you by his side," Alyssa said as they looked through makeup colors for her lips and eye shadow.

"I am and whatever he needs, I'll be there. We've got a few months to breathe between now and November and I have enough to keep me busy. By the time six-months from now arrives, I'll be ready to be his one and only first lady of Chicago!" Nichelle said.

"Alyssa, you have a phone call. It's your brother Carlos. He said he's been calling your phone and you haven't picked up. He called the hotel here and they came by with the message. You want to use the hotel phone or yours?" Destiny, her assistant asked.

"I'll call him from my phone."

"I'll come back when you're done," Nichelle said.

"Nonsense. He's probably calling to say he's going to be late. Wait one second."

Alyssa dialed and Carlos picked up immediately.

"Hey, big brother. What's up?"

Nichelle stood up from the stool she was sitting on the minute she noticed the sound of worry in Alyssa's voice.

"Alyssa?" she asked.

"Is he hurt bad?" Alyssa said into the phone as she stood and paced back and forth.

Nichelle knew whatever was happening in the conversation wasn't good.

"Alyssa? Is everything alright?" Nichelle asked.

"Is he dead?" Alyssa screamed.

People heard Alyssa scream and came running over.

"What's going on?" the photographer asked.

"I don't know. She's talking to her brother, Carlos," Nichelle said, worried.

When Alyssa ended the call and jumped around like she didn't know what to do next, Nichelle stepped back and gave her room.

"Alyssa what's wrong?" she asked again.

"Nichelle, I need you to sit with the kids until Dexter gets here. I'm going to call him right now, though he should already be close. Joey was in a serious car accident on his way to the casino. Carlos doesn't know how bad it is. An officer called him from the number in Joey's cell phone. I need to get to the hospital," she said.

"Alyssa, you can't drive to the hospital this worked up. Let me call Dexter for you and see how close he is," Nichelle said.

"I'm here! What's going on and why are you crying?" Dexter asked walking over to Alyssa who fell into his arms crying with ear curdling screams.

"He's had an accident!" Alyssa screamed.

"What? Who? One of the boys? Where are my sons?" Dexter hollered looking around while holding Alyssa close.

"Here they are," another one of Alyssa's assistants said.

"Baby, what's going on? The boys are fine. Who had an accident?" Dexter asked.

Nichelle stood to the side and wondered how she could help.

"Joey! Joey has been in a bad accident and on the way to the hospital. I have to get there. I don't know how bad it is, but I have to get there," she cried.

"Dexter, I'm good with kids and I will look after them. I'll call Reese to come help," Nichelle said, taking out her phone.

"Call my house. I just dropped Alyssa's mother at our house from the airport. Are you sure you have the boys? I only trust them with you if Alyssa and I both go to the hospital. I don't know how bad the crash is or if others are involved. I also don't know how long we'll be, but if you get the kids to the house, her mom will call the nanny so that she can get to the hospital too. The nanny will stay with the kids until we get home. Okay?" Dexter asked her.

"I got you and I'll say a prayer for Joey. I know how car crashes can be and how the idea of it can play with your mind until you see your loved one. Go do what you need to do. I got this," Nichelle assured him.

After they left, she dialed Tucker. She knew he was at his campaign office going over some speaking points for his upcoming debate with his opponent. When he answered, she cried into the phone.

"Nichelle, what's wrong," she heard Tucker say.

"I'm at the photoshoot with Alyssa and her brother has been in a bad accident. I have their kids because she and Dexter needed to get to the hospital," she said.

"Wait – I just heard about a really bad accident and I was just about to head to the scene. I knew his name sounded familiar when I asked about the parties involved. Seems that a woman crashed into him and she wasn't hurt, but he was and it was pretty critical. What do you need, baby? You need me to come to you?" he asked.

"No. Go to the accident and see what's going on. I'm going to call Reese and get her to meet me here with the kids. Their car seats are here, but I'm too shaken up to drive."

"What about Carlos? Was he with him? I only heard about one man being injured," Tucker said.

"Carlos is who called, so I don't think they were together. Hadn't Carlos just signed up to be a part of your security detail for the last leg of the campaign leading up to the general election?" she asked.

"Yes and that's why Joey's name sounded so familiar. He also applied and I was planning on hiring them both. No one would mess with those guys. They are built like that actor, The Rock. I hope Joey's going to be okay. I'll keep you posted and you stay put until Reese gets there. Call her now. If you need me, call me and I'll be right there," Tucker said.

Nichelle nodded her head as if Tucker could see her. Disconnecting the call, she immediately called Reese and filled her in. Before she could get more than a few sentences out, Reese was already on her way to the hotel to help with the kids. She hoped Joey would be alright. Car crashes could be deadly and there was no telling what the eventual outcome would be. She would keep them all lifted up in prayer including the woman who was in the other car. She and Joey both had more of their life to live and she prayed they could get back to it soon and in great health.

The following are all books by Cheryl Barton found at
www.cherylbarton.net or
www.amazon.com/author/cherylbarton

Get the next exciting installment of "The Brothers of Chi-Town" with "Crashing into Love", available in paperback and download November 2020.

His name is Joseph Kincaid and while most call him Joey, the women of Chicago call him a variety of sexy epithets that are too salacious to utter in public. He's a professional wrestler who is unmatched in the ring, untamed in his response to confrontation and unleashed when it comes to his bedroom proclivities, bringing women pleasure beyond their amorous fantasies.

For the second time in her life, Marlow Warren was responsible for an accident that altered someone's life. The first time, she ran to avoid bringing disgrace to her family while hiding from her past, but this time, she's all about making amends to the man whose life she ruined.

Everything changed when Joey and Marlow's lives collided and it wasn't all bad. Hurt, anger and unending apologies turned into lust, desire and unbridled cravings, something neither of them could fight. When Marlow's past arrives in a threatening way, Joey knew he would risk his life to protect her because he was now fighting for more than a future back in the ring; he was ready to fight for love.

Make sure you check out book 1, of "The Brothers of Chi-Town", *I Can't Let Go* – now available for download and in paperback.

Carter Garrison vowed to love, honor and cherish his wife, Sienna, forsaking all others, something he forgot to do during a weekend of fun, bad company and poor judgement.

Sienna Garrison never dreamed her college sweetheart, Carter, whom she pledged her life to, would break her heart and when he did, she moved out and moved on - or tried to.

What better occasion is there than a friend's wedding to stir up old feelings and memories of love, intense passion and nights of sensual titillation. Gazes from across a room after almost two years apart revealed depths of love that had never died.

Seeing Sienna again reminded Carter of what he'd lost and he vowed to never let go by doing whatever he could to get his wife back even if it included begging and pleading. Is Sienna ready to forgive and take a chance on life again with the only man she'd ever really loved?

When Carter brings on the charm and turns up the heat, no woman is immune, especially Sienna.

Don't forget to snag your copy of book 2, *Swagger and Baggage*, in "The Brothers of Chi-Town" series – now available

It's not a coincidence that casino owner, Torrence Allen, ran into his college sweetheart, Reese Michaels again; it's fate. As his memories unfold, he had tried everything to keep her in his life and his bed back then and failed at both. She wasn't ready for him then, but he hopes she is ready for him now.

Reese Michaels never thought she'd see Torrence again. Their split in college was dramatic and hurtful and still, no man had been able to win her heart. She considered herself the permanent third wheel to friends who had found love and marriage.

Their whirlwind affair, quickly turned into love just as it suddenly crashed and burned when a woman shows up to claim Torrence as hers. When it's also revealed that this woman isn't the only 'other woman', Reese finds herself left with a broken heart, shattered love and dreams of forever beyond her reach. How did she not know about the other part of Torrence's active and amorous life?

Torrence isn't ready to give up on having Reese in his life after his deceit. He finds himself in the fight of his life to finally have the love and commitment he wanted only with her. His swagger had always won women over, but it's his baggage that's causing his life to spiral out of control and he could once again find himself without the woman he has always loved.

Have you checked out book 3 of, "The Brothers of Chi-Town" series, "Claiming His Child"?

Business magnate Dexter Patterson refused to let anything keep him from checking off all of the boxes equating to achievement in life to prove that though he came from a rough childhood on the south side of Chicago, he still thrived and became a success. Looking around at those closest to him, Dexter found that he was still missing something...Love.

When aspiring model, Alyssa Kincaid met Dexter, she couldn't get enough of his sexual magnetism, fiery nights of passion, and secret rendezvous. She thought they were headed toward forever when a surprising call from him ended what they had causing her to leave Chicago, taking with her a secret.

Dexter thought that no woman could ever tame him, not even Alyssa who entranced him with her sexy body, smoky, sultry voice and untamed desire. Too little, too late, he realized he'd made a mistake by walking away and then she was gone.

Time and distance didn't diminish the chemistry between them and the child Alyssa carried and never told him about had him in the fight of his life to win back her heart and the chance to have the family he'd always wanted.

Will Alyssa continue to curse kismet when Dexter suddenly reappears in her life or will she believe that his yearning for her isn't just because of their child, but because when she left Chicago, she took his heart with her?

Don't miss book 4 of, "The Brothers of Chi-Town," series, "Always Bet on Black." Now Available

Sexy, debonair, Delvin "DJ" "Black" Michaels, left Chicago as a man in search of a better life than the one he had where everyone knew him as "Black". Being fair-skinned, his nickname wasn't because of the color of his skin, but was due to his inclination to always wear the color black from head to toe.

DJ had his share of hits and misses when it came to relationships and just when he thought he'd found "the one", she turned out to be caught up and a ring of crooked cops who were all taken down in a sting and his job ended up on the casualty list. He'd been duped by a woman name Justice who batted her hazel colored eyes at him and before he knew it, he had fallen under her spell.

Deciding to leave New York for a fresh start as head of security at his future brother-in-law's casino back in his hometown of Chicago, DJ is surprised to see Justice, whose real name is Avalon Hart, sauntering through the casino like she owned it. He knew she had to be up to a new scheme and he hoped her treachery didn't include the casino.

Avalon Hart had lived her life on the edge, making due the best way she knew how even if it meant scheming men out of their hard-earned money. She learned how to survive from the streets and she was a woman who had a way with men that got her whatever she wanted, that was until she encountered DJ Michaels in Chicago, a man from her past who she had once easily swayed to her desires. She realized early that the man she encountered in New York had grown immune to her tricks, even the ones she learned how to do in bed that he loved so much.

DJ and Avalon are on a roller coaster ride to love and neither knew it. He had a lot to lose if he let Avalon get too close to him again. This time, whatever she was plotting, he was ready to take her down, even if it meant losing his heart in the process. He was betting on "Black" for the win, but so was Avalon, in her own way. There was no telling who would end up on top, but one thing was for sure – the road to getting there was going to be filled with hot, sexy fun, a pair of handcuffs and a whole lot of sensuality that neither could resist!

Available Now – *True Lies or True Love by Cheryl Barton*

FBI Agent, Quintin Bell was sent to work undercover at Tee King Investment Securities to get proof that Carlos King, owner and hedge-fund boss, was embezzling money from his own employees' retirement accounts. In a chance encounter, he noticed Carlos' daughter, Meadow and before he could keep his heart from getting lost in her beauty, he found himself at a crossroads between doing his job and following his heart.

Meadow King wasn't looking for love that day in the café, but there was no way she could resist the handsome, rugged looks of a stranger when the intoxicating vibe between them became undeniable and irresistible. Unbeknownst to Meadow, the man she's fallen in love with has a secret that could not only ruin the love that grew between them, but it could topple her entire world.

Quintin knows that love can be real and it can be true, but his lies are what create a façade of their love affair and could cause it to crash and burn just as it has begun to heat up with passion that neither of them had ever experienced before nor could they see themselves without ever again. Quintin is running out of time in trying to find a way to do his job and hold on to the woman he loves. His biggest hurdle will be if he does his job, can he convince Meadow that his lies may have been true, but his love is truer!

Now available
Book 3, "Heartbreaker" of "A Lovers" Heart Series

In book 3, of "A Lovers' Heart" steamy romance series, Cameron Lymon, the sexy, youngest brother of Hollywood heartthrob, Cade Weston and Navy SEAL, Calvin Lymon, with his Master's degree in Journalism and a minor in Communications and Sports Management in hand, landed his dream job in Denver, Colorado as the co-host for a new morning talk show. Women love to call him the "Heartbreaker" because of the bevy of beautiful ladies he's left in his wake, not interested in giving up being a bachelor for falling in love. He enjoys taking after his big brother's old lifestyle of being a playboy.

Dakota Kane sacrificed a personal life and fought hard in her career to be the lead personality on Denver's top television morning show, but she was about to risk it all for passionate, steamy encounters with her new, much younger co-host, who is ten years younger and fifty shades hotter than any man she'd ever encountered. All he had to do was smile at her and she was a goner.

Cameron didn't know what he was in for when what he thought would be casual, behind closed door romps with the ever-so-sexy Dakota began to turn into much more when his heart became as invested in her as much as his body had. As things turned serious, his heartbreaker status came back to haunt him and his relationship with Dakota was threatened by his past.

Cameron and Dakota have to decide if what they are beginning to feel for each other is worth the risk of their careers when their secret love affair becomes the topic of public opinion and ridicule.

Heartthrob, Book 1 of "A Lovers' Heart Series

Cade Weston, Hollywood's most eligible bachelor and named the world's sexiest man of the year, lives life at the top with a bevy of beauties at his beck and call, people providing his every desire and more money than any one person should have.

Callie Hurston struggles to make it as a stylist to the stars in a world where women are intimidated by her beauty and men are interested in her body and not her talent.

Cade thought he had it all until he has a chance meeting with Callie and decides to take a chance on her talent and ends up taking an even bigger chance with his heart.

Can the playboy turn in his player's card and give in to love?

Heartbeat, Book 2 of "A Lovers' Heart" Series

In book two of, "A Lovers' Heart" series, Navy SEAL, Calvin Lymon, was about his country's business when he allowed himself to cross the line and his heart got involved resulting in a love lost. Injured in the line of duty, he fights to stay alive for the sake of his newborn son, Camico.

A new city and a new outlook on life were exactly what physical therapist, Ava Cortez, needed after years of living life alone and off the grid to avoid being detected by a madman. She never allowed herself to love anyone, especially a man, afraid she would be found out. When she's asked to oversee the therapy of a sexy navy SEAL, she tries to fight the immediate and intoxicating lure to a man who exudes more sexual potency than she's ever experienced. Can she forget about business and indulge in pleasure for once?

Calvin deals with the days of therapy that drain him, but nothing compares to the salacious, steamy nights of passion with Ava that are having the biggest impact on his ability to get back to reality until an old rival resurfaces and threatens his life and his loves.

Once and for all, Calvin knows he has to deal with his past and risk losing his woman and his son, who are his heartbeats.

A Better Man

Phoenix Graham is living her best life with the best man, her fiancé, Carson Stone, heir to the Stone Tower Hotel Empire. Her perfect life is shaken up when a handsome, rugged and extremely sexy mysterious man moves in across the hall and she begins to see that the rose-colored glasses she had been seeing life through were blinders. She soon discovers that Carson was the best man for her until she takes notice of a better man and his name is Gavin Black.

What's a girl to do when the best doesn't get better and better is what she craves?

Take a Knee

Professional football player, Kenrick Wilson, never thought twice about taking a knee in solidarity with his team to show support for a cause that was near and dear to his heart. He was applauded for wearing his heart on his sleeve. His greatest love was for Justine Banks, the woman who stole his heart years ago, the mother of his children and his biggest supporter. Even though he loves Justine with everything in him, Kenrick has secrets and deep-seated hurt that has kept him from taking a knee for the most important purpose in life, making Justine his wife. Can he let go of the hurt from his past to secure his family for the future?

The Lake House

Summers together at their families' lake houses as teenagers are what Danielle Fenton and the boy next door, Gannon Wilcox, loved about being on the lake in North Carolina. They fell in love at a young age and then one day it was over after Danielle ended their relationship with no explanation. The only thing Gannon remembered was seeing the woman he loved in the arms of another man.

Years later, Danielle and Gannon find themselves back at the lake, in their families' lake houses, both divorced after unhappy marriages and trying to find their next moves. They now have a chance to get this thing called love right as long as they believe in the history and power of love found at the lake that was always meant to be everlasting.

My First Love

Ethan Bennett has what everyone wished they had, money, power and respect. When his first love, Valencia, walks back into his life, the love they shared as teenagers resurfaces and reminds him that there is no love like that first love.

Valencia Ramos never forgot the first person who loved her unconditionally. Now all grown up, Ethan is still everything she ever wanted and the love she still feels for him is a love she's never been able to forget.

Discover their path to finding out if first love is truly real love.

When I Think of You

Leo Westmoreland is an ordinary guy living in Harlem, New York, working three jobs to make ends meet the best way he can in order to take care of his mother and younger brothers years after his abusive father disappeared from their lives. He hasn't been lucky in love, finding most women want more when it comes to material things than he has available to give. He has dreams and aspirations for himself, but for now, family comes first.

Raquel Johnson was born with a silver spoon in her mouth to a father who owns one of the top money management firms in Manhattan. Though she's never wanted for anything, she's made her own achievements in life and now sits as an executive with his company. Her dating life has consisted of men who value money, power and prestige over unconditional love, the one thing she desires the most.

Leo and Raquel meet and share a connection that breathes new life into them and proves that focusing on each other and the love they can have together is more important than anything else.

Read Leo and Raquel's story and discover that love and relationships are about who you are, not what you have.

"And Then There Was You," is a steamy love story, set in Malibu, California. Diezel Wilder is a sexy corporate attorney from New York who recently moved to California after a bitter divorce from a woman he married on a whim after going through a tragedy that caused him to act out. In need of a break from the drama that surrounded him in New York, he hoped for a new start in sunny California.

Brooklyn Hunter, a sexy Armenian bombshell, is a late-night, on-air radio talk show host who woos men all over the country with her sexy, sultry, seductive voice. She's coming off of a divorce from a movie studio executive who is twenty years older. When they met, she saw him as her escape from a dismal life in Nebraska, but found herself thrust into the Hollywood spotlight, revealing a marriage clouded by adultery and out of wedlock children in a scandal that was broadcast worldwide.

Seeking a new lease on life, Diezel and Brooklyn are in search of the kind of connection with a mate that leaves them breathless. Little did they know they would find it right next door.

Bring on the ice-cold water because you're about to go on one very steamy ride to love in, "And Then There Was You."

The Bachelor Series

Book 1 - Bachelor Not for Sale – Now available

Duron Knight agreed to take part in a bachelor auction held by his sister's sorority. Little did he know that he would find the woman of his dreams in the form of sexy bombshell Taija Charles, the woman in red.

Taija, in a room full of the sexiest men in Atlanta, has eyes for one handsome bachelor that no woman in her right mind could resist.

As sparks fly between them, can Duron put his unhappy past with women behind him and give his all to Taija? He may fight love, but Taija has plans to help him mend his broken heart with real love and a whole lot of lust.

Book 2 – A Designed Affair – Now available

In this follow-up to "Bachelor Not for Sale", Loren Knight has been engaging in a secret love affair with her brother Duron's best friend and business partner, Michael Bailey. He is everything she could want and more in a man, but she believes the risk is too great for any type of relationship with him beyond their steamy encounters behind closed doors.

Michael Bailey has been fighting his attraction to Loren for years. He has stayed away from her out of respect for his best friend and business partner. Now that he and Loren have finally given into the passion they have been craving, can Michael convince Loren that what they share is worth the risk of even Duron finding out?

Book 3 – A Perfect Combination – Now available

In this second follow-up to "Bachelor Not for Sale", Tyrone Davis is the king of one-night stands. The nickname, Mr. *Love'em* and *Leave'em*, given to him in his college days, still follows him as a top executive in the corporate world. He never believed in karma until it paid him a visit in the form of a very sexy and uninhibited one-night stand.

Victoria Alston couldn't forget the incredible night she spent with Tyrone Davis, someone connected to her best friends. In just one night, he stirred feelings in her she never thought she would ever experience. The next day, she disappeared, returning to reality and the fiancé she left back in Boston.

Tyrone and Victoria both soon discover that it wasn't just a one-night stand, but a perfect combination for the kind of love most people only dream about.

Book 4 – Love at Last – Now available

They had the perfect love...That's what Brian Knight thought of his relationship with Sherry Braxton until he looked up one day and she was gone and never wanted to see him again.

Two years later, he discovered that there is the possibility that Sherry may have been pregnant with his child. Hurt and angry at her deceit, he takes a flight to Baltimore to fight for his rights as a father and realizes that the love and passion they once shared had never died.

Is it possible he could still have the kind of love he thought would last a lifetime? Can he still have his love at last?

About the Author

Cheryl Barton lives in Maryland and in her spare time she loves to read espionage, crime and romance novels, cook, watch Sci-fi movies, spend time with family and friends and enjoy Maryland steamed crabs. Cheryl is celebrating 30 years as a government employee and loves writing romance novels when she's not working. Cheryl is the author of 31 romance novels, 3 inspirational novels and is proud of 4 book compilation projects with several other incredible women called, "One Sister Away: Encouraging Words from One Sister to Another" – a series of books meant to encourage, empower and inspire other women. People often ask Cheryl which book is her favorite of all of those she's written. While she finds it hard to select one favorite, Cheryl still looks to her first novel, Bachelor Not for Sale, if she had to pick a favorite because it was her first novel and the one that inspired her to continue writing.

Cheryl was a 2019 Finalist for the Emma Award given by Romance Slam Jam and a 2018 Finalist for the Literary Trailblazer of the Year award by the Indie Author Legacy Award. Cheryl is a member of the Romance Writers of America – National Chapter, the Maryland Romance Writers and the Contemporary Romance Writers groups, the Black Writers' Guild of Maryland and the International Women Writers Guild.

Indulge in more romance and inspirational novels by visiting her website at www.cherylbarton.net and connect with Cheryl on Facebook, Twitter and Instagram.

www.ingramcontent.com/pod-product-compliance
Lightning Source LLC
Chambersburg PA
CBHW031113030726
47496CB00002BA/526